The Odyssey of Homero Garcia

Jesus Uriarte

Published by UriArte Publishing & Consulting, 2024.

COPYRIGHT

Author: Jesús Uriarte

Copy Editor: Esteban A. Valdivia

Editorial Review: Rafael M Montes

Editorial Supervision: Jesús A. Uriarte

Cover Design: Jhon Simancas

Paperback Information

ISBN: 979-8-9914427-9-4[1]

Printed in the United States of America

---

1. https://www.myidentifiers.com/title_registration?isbn=979-8-9914427-9-4&icon_type=Incomplete

Table of Contents

Are the brave born or made?

Can the vicissitudes of life turn a normal person into a brave one?

The main character of this novel: a simple, hardworking, family man undergoes a great transformation due to the malice of people who represent a tyrannical government and its political-repressive apparatus: the feared Cuban G-2.

The Castro-communist government of Cuba does whatever it wants with its people, turning its opponents into criminals, with the intention of perpetuating itself in power at all costs.

You, dear readers, will have the opportunity to reflect on this issue with this novel and, in doing so, value the opponents of that regime, who desire to live in freedom, even at the cost of their own lives.

¡Patria y Vida!

The author

INTRODUCTION

I wrote this novel thinking of the millions of Cubans who have suffered under a tyranny for over sixty years. Everything is a product of my imagination, but if we consider it well, we are faced with events that happened to different people in disparate situations, and many have lived day by day. On several occasions, I witnessed what happened to dear, friends, or simply known people.

Those of us who have had the luck to leave Cuba will have the opportunity to know this process. It is a pity that those, who for one reason or another have not been able or have not wanted to (the fewer) leave in search of new horizons, do not have the opportunity.

Very serious, very depressing, very sad things are said because it is the suffering of a people with a government imposed by force, but we have tried to give it some lightness, sometimes humor, so that the reading is not so negative.

I wish to thank all the people who have helped and inspired me in this endeavor, new to me, very especially to my brother Taty, whose boundless enthusiasm instilled in me the idea of writing and almost forced me with his good intentions. To my son Tonito, who encourages me at every moment to continue. To my nephews Diana and Adolfo Noel, who have given me extraordinary support; very especially to Diana, who did the first revision in Spanish – of my Spanish, deficient for sure, after more than twelve years speaking Portuguese; to my sister-in-law Miriam for the spiritual support; to my dear mother for giving me my entire life. To Aldito, Laura, Iván, and family, Miguel Márquez and family, because they have been silent contributors to my modest work.

I dedicate this book to all Cubans who both inside and outside the country who have ever suffered under the tyranny of Fidel Castro. To those who, not being Cubans, feel solidarity with us. My book is also dedicated to those who do not understand the cause of our grievances, who do not understand how hard exile has been for those of us who did not want to bear the Castroist tyranny on our shoulders; to those who have lost their dearest relatives, shot or vilely murdered by the Castroist hordes; to those who have suffered long, painful, and humiliating prison terms in the dungeons of the suffering island. To those who have simply been mistreated for thinking differently from those who misgovern our beloved homeland. Sometimes, confused by Castro's communist propaganda, they think that the "bad guys" are those of us who cannot stand the dictatorial regime, a product of the efficient and relentless propaganda of international communism and its acolytes.

The book is also dedicated to some Latin American brothers who have been fooled by Castroist ideology, and who sometimes verbally assault us and call us "gusanos" simply because they do not understand the reality of our country. When they visit our beautiful island, they stay in luxury hotels, are treated in hospitals where only US dollars are accepted, speak only to regime officials who repeat lies; they are guided so they do not come into contact with the ordinary Cuban, the poor, the suffering, the one who goes hungry and is in need because of the Government, the Cuban who sometimes cannot express what he feels, under penalty of suffering imprisonment or being expelled from his job, universities, and being repudiated by those who hold power and their followers.

Gusano (n.): A term used pejoratively by supporters of the Cuban regime to describe opponents or dissidents.

This work is addressed to many Europeans who still have an incorrect vision of reality and, as absurd as it may seem, to some free citizens living in the United States who do not understand that communist governments are the most repressive and undemocratic in the world.

I began writing it in Rio de Janeiro, Brazil, at the end of 1999, with the hope of seeing it published in that beautiful country, which hosted me for more than nine years, so that the dear Brazilian brothers could have a real idea of what the mismanagement of my country is, since many are confused due to the fantastic, lying, and perverse publicity of that dictatorial regime.

By the will of destiny, always uncertain, I managed to emigrate to the United States, and it is here, in the land of full democracy, that I managed to finish it.

It is for everyone that I write this book with real pleasure.

CHAPTER 1

My name is Homero García, one of the eleven million Cubans living in a country that has among its virtues being the most beautiful island in the world. At least that's what I think, because I've never visited any other place, and when you only know your own, you consider it the best.

I come from a middle-class family that was affected by the Revolution but managed to study at the University – one of the few things that Fidel's regime allows people to do – and I became a dentist.

I have a small family: my wife and my ten-year-old son named Vladimir; at that time, it was fashionable to name children after Russians, and Vladimir was the name of Lenin, the leading figure of the Bolshevik Revolution.

My life went by monotonously, without major problems. I only experienced the same situation as everyone else: lack of food, clothing, money, etc. This wasn't a big problem because we were all in the same situation; and being a simple person, I unconsciously adapted to all the hardships that daily life imposed on us. Ultimately, it was the fault of the "Yankees" who, with their brutal blockade, condemned us to unnecessary hardships; or so the government said.

I inherited during my father's lifetime, who had severe vision problems that prevented him from driving, a two-tone blue 1957 Studebaker Commander that was a beauty. Its V8 engine made the tires squeal with power when you pressed the accelerator. Not to mention the speed. Before you realized it, you were already going over 150 kilometers per hour. I felt very proud when I managed to drive it through the streets of my small town in the western part of the country. Partly because of how beautiful it was, how well-preserved I kept it, and also because it was the only one of its kind in the area, giving it an air of exclusivity that boosted my ego.

I was apparently happy because I was working in what I liked, combining the useful with the pleasant; my coworkers were excellent; my family was lovely, and I could occasionally enjoy one of the things my son and I loved most: fishing.

Who could have thought for a moment that this love for fishing would bring me so many difficulties in the future!?

The weekend was sunny, cool, and beautiful, perfect for doing what Vladimir and I loved so much: fishing.

Dolores, my wife, had to do volunteer work at the company where she worked, so without much thought, we got up very early in the morning; we prepared some pork sandwiches left over from the day before, made a drink from some tamarinds we had brought from my father's house days earlier, and with half a bottle of Caney rum I had hidden for a few weeks, we got into our magnificent and beloved Studebaker. We went to a reservoir about five kilometers from the city on the road to Viñales, armed with bamboo rods, nylon, and hooks.

On the way to the reservoir, on a straight stretch of about a kilometer, urged by Vladimir, who was eager to get there and liked it when I sped up, I accelerated the car to over 120 kilometers per hour. We had a great time watching that magnificent machine, which was the pride of both me and the whole family, move.

At kilometer five, I slowed down and turned right onto a dirt road with many potholes, so I reduced speed to a minimum to avoid suffering from the jolts. It was like my heart was being hammered every time the suspension banged. We finally reached the shore of an artificial lake about two kilometers in diameter and somewhat round.

We chose our usual spot, the concrete retaining wall, where most of the fish were concentrated. I parked the car under some lush trees to shield it from the sun, surrounded by several male mango trees offering ripe yellowish-red fruit that made our mouths water.

We set about digging on the shore for worms for bait, which was relatively easy. We placed the bait on the hooks, and by ten in the morning, we had caught three beautiful trout, validating our stay.

Around noon, we were preparing to have our snack when we spotted, about a kilometer and a half away, a medium-sized parachute with a dark-colored box, one or two meters in size. It descended in a place we couldn't identify from where we were. We were intrigued by it, but a few minutes after it fell, we saw a green olive Russian jeep, like those used by the army, heading in the direction where we assumed it had landed. I commented to my son that it was probably a military maneuver by the army or the MTT (Militia of Territorial Troops). We finished our snack and continued our fruitful fishing, after eating some sweet, ripe mangoes tasting like sugar candy.

At five in the afternoon, we happily arrived home with seven beautiful trout, seasoned them with salt and lemon, and waited for my wife to return so we could prepare a delicious meal: white rice, black bean stew from the day before, boiled potatoes, and freshly fried fish. We were going to enjoy that wonderful day that God had provided us.

That's what we thought...

CHAPTER 2

My wife was taking a bath; the table was set, and the food was ready to be served... At that moment, someone knocked brusquely on the door. I went to it and looked through the peephole to see who had the audacity to knock in such a rude and impertinent manner at my house.

I felt a certain anxiety when I saw through the peephole several people dressed in olive-green uniforms. At that moment, I thought it was a mistake, and since those who have nothing to hide have nothing to fear, I opened the door fearlessly.

One of those people, who wore the rank of captain, according to his insignia, asked me in a severe and harsh tone:

"Are you the owner of the blue Studebaker parked in front of this house?"

"It's mine," I replied innocently.

In the blink of an eye, two soldiers who accompanied him entered the living room, grabbed me firmly by both arms, and immobilized me.

"Take him," said the Captain, who seemed to be the group leader.

They lifted me up quickly and without giving me time to alert my wife and son, who were in the room. They took me to a white and beige Alfa Romeo with a circular inscription on the door that read "State Security Department" and in the center, the initials G-2.

I didn't have time to say anything. The action was so quick that I was left speechless for the moment. I wasn't used to any of that. I was a totally peaceful person who had no notion of what political life was and even less about military activities. The only thing I knew was that you had to do MTT (Militia of Territorial Troops) guards, CDR (Committee for the Defense of the Revolution) guards, volunteer work at the center and in the neighborhood, and. I did that mechanically like everyone in the neighborhood, like everyone at the workplace.

When I finally recovered my speech, the G-2 car had already left, and the only thing that came out of my throat was a stupid question:

"What's the problem with my car?"

In my innocent mind, there was only one possibility: I felt guilty for having exceeded the speed limit when I was on the road to Viñales heading to the dam.

"The problem isn't with your car, and you know it very well," replied the Captain.

"Excuse me, but I don't know what you're talking about," I said with a voice that barely came out.

"You know very well why, and don't play dumb because we're not fools." Now, it was a soldier who spoke.

"Please, if you don't explain what's happening, I'll never understand."

"You better shut your mouth, you'll have the opportunity to say everything you know when you get to the Department," said the Captain now.

They called the Department the offices that State Security had on the road to Havana.

"But I..."

"Shut your mouth, it'll be better for you," one of the soldiers now said in a threatening tone.

Suddenly, I saw the entrance of the feared G-2 house, a modern residential construction that once belonged to a wealthy owner imprisoned at that time for counter-revolutionary activities.

After the car was checked by the guard at the entrance, it slid through a corridor that once seemed to have been a garage and reached an interior parking lot, which would be the courtyard of the house.

When the car stopped, I was practically dragged out by the soldiers and taken to a room protected by iron balustrades; they resembled those of a jail.

Seated on a stool, they indicated to me, and escorted by the two agents, I waited about five minutes without speaking until an agent appeared in a new uniform seemingly freshly cleaned and ironed, wearing shiny black military boots.

He looked about forty years old, had a commander's insignia on his epaulette, and his face was that of someone who had suffered a lot in life, although his facial features were not unpleasant.

"What's your name and what's your profession?" he asked abruptly.

"Homero García, and I'm a dentist," I responded automatically.

"Are you the owner of a 1957 blue Studebaker?" he asked next.

"It's the car my father gave me as a gift two years ago," I answered with a touch of pride.

"This morning around noon, what were you doing in your car by the shore of the reservoir at kilometer five in Viñales?" he asked in a grave voice.

I averted my gaze to a point on the wall to focus on what I thought was a stupid question from that man.

"Look me in the eyes when you answer," he said energetically.

I looked into his eyes with a kind of fear and disbelief and stuttered:

"Fishing in the reservoir," I said, without mentioning that I was with my son, because something inside me urged me to keep it to myself.

"What did you do with the contents of the box?" he said, spacing out each word.

"What box?" I responded innocently.

"If you're trying to mock us, I'll tell you it can cost you dearly," he spoke with a conscious air of superiority.

"I don't know what box you're talking about," I said sincerely.

"We have methods to make even a mute speak, so please don't waste our time and tell us where you hid the weapons."

When I heard him talk about "boxes and weapons," a chill ran down my spine, leaving me covered in goosebumps. What was this? It didn't make sense to me.

My tormented mind couldn't make sense of those words; they just didn't fit.

"Kid, you're not a fool. You're a university professional and from what we see, you speak and understand Spanish well," said the interrogator agent.

I wanted to have a slightly dignified posture and refuted that I wasn't a fool.

The agent, seeing that I was trying to confront him, stood up abruptly and slapped me across the face; I can still feel the shudder it caused.

A huge rage shook me. What was happening? I was arbitrarily taken from my home, brought to a place without understanding why, asked questions I didn't know, and finally mistreated.

I wasn't a criminal. I hadn't done anything illegal or unusual. I had only peacefully gone fishing with my son to a reservoir, something that was usual for me.

What was happening in my life?

Was this a dream or reality? It wasn't a dream, because dreams don't hurt, and my face was burning with pain. Moreover, the people around me were real; and if it were a dream, it must be one of the most unpleasant nightmares of my life.

In an act that seemed to flatter his boss, the soldier next to my right grabbed me by the shirt and practically lifted me from the chair. Pressing my face to his, he said:

"If you want trouble, you'll get it, faggot!"

I was never brave, not even in school, but at that moment, a burning sensation rose to my face, and instinctively, I pushed the soldier, who lost his balance and fell on his butt on the floor.

The other soldier, realizing my action, wrapped his arm around my neck tightly and squeezed until I almost lost my breath. It seemed like I was going to die from lack of air, and when I was about to faint, the Commander ordered him to let go.

I took several breaths until my lungs filled with oxygen. They pushed me back onto the stool and put a pair of handcuffs on my wrists after tying my arms behind my back.

What was this, my God? I thought with a dull mind and blurry vision.

It couldn't be speeding, because they were talking about a box and weapons. Fishing wasn't a crime, and I hadn't fished weapons or boxes, only trout. So, something I didn't know was causing all this confusion.

The Commander sat down again and focused his gaze on mine.

"Please forgive me if I did something wrong, but I don't understand what's happening to me," I said in a pitiful tone.

The officer kept his gaze as if scrutinizing my brain and said in a way that showed he was containing his irritation:

"Let's see if we understand each other. I'm going to ask you the question once more, but I'm going to warn you that I won't tolerate any more nonsense," he paused, placed his hands in an inverted V shape on his lips, and began to ask as if speaking to a five-year-old.

"Where the hell did you take the weapons that arrived by parachute?"

The word parachute had the effect of a detonator. Suddenly, I remembered clearly that while we were fishing, Vladimir and I saw a parachute fall about a kilometer from where we were. I began to realize that there might be a mistake with these State Security officers. It was just explaining what I had seen, and surely, they would release me immediately because I had nothing to do with that.

"Now that you mention a parachute. While we were at the reservoir, I saw one fall about a kilometer away," I said, almost with a smile on my lips.

"Stop the hypocritical smiles and tell the truth because if you don't, we're going to mess you up," the officer insulted me.

My face petrified, and I could only stammer a few loose words, "I'm not laughing at you, believe me, please."

"The next time you want to fool us, you'll regret it," he raised his fist in a threatening gesture.

There, with broken words and unable to form a coherent idea, I explained what I had seen: I thought it was a military maneuver... then I saw a Russian jeep that seemed to be from the army going in the direction of the parachute.

The officer observed me attentively while I explained. I thought I was being convincing since it was the pure truth.

"What was the license plate of the jeep?" he asked again. "Was it civilian or military?" he continued.

"Honestly, I can't tell you because it passed far from me, and since it wasn't important to me at that moment, I didn't notice," I said, conscious that I was being honest.

"So, the CIA sends a shipment of weapons, and you're going to make us believe that an army jeep picked them up," he added. "Do you think that because you're a university-educated doctor, you're going to fool us?"

He leaned back against the wall with the chair he was sitting on. "We didn't study like you; we had to scrape by in the mountains to get here, but we're not fools, you know?"

"I'm telling the truth, believe me," I said desperately, seeing that they didn't believe a single word I was saying.

"Take him away," he told the soldiers. "I don't have the patience to listen to more nonsense today," and with a gesture of his right hand, he ordered them to remove me from that room.

Almost pushing me, they took me to a cell at the end of a narrow and dark corridor. The place was two square meters in size, with moisture seeping through the walls and floor, surely due to the lack of windows; neither sunlight nor clarity entered. Besides being damp, the cell was dirty and had a penetrating smell of rotting flesh.

When they closed the cell gate and removed the handcuffs, I sat on a sort of iron cot covered with hard, cold vinyl, and my mind began to spin like it was on a carousel. I remembered when my son Vladimir was two or three years old, he liked me to take him to the "little horses" and hold him; I got a bit dizzy to the point of fearing my son would fall off the wooden horse. That's how I felt at that moment.

It was an inexplicable situation.

CHAPTER 3

Dolores stepped out of the room and called for Vladimir to hurry to dinner. She was exhausted from the day's labor. They had spent the day picking tobacco, a grueling task, especially for someone like her who wasn't accustomed to such work. She had been up since five in the morning to make sure she was ready for the six-thirty departure.

Realizing I wasn't there, she asked Vladimir, "Where did your father go at this hour with the hunger and tiredness I have?"

"I don't know, mom," my son replied.

"He must have gone to Chucho's house to have a little drink of rum, as usual." She then asked Vladimir to look for me urgently.

Vladimir returned and informed her that I had left with some men. Dolores, a bit annoyed by what she thought was inconsiderate of me to leave at that very hour to eat, began to curse and went to the porch of the house to see if she could find out who I had gone with and where.

As she stepped onto the porch, she saw our neighbor, who approached with a very worried face and informed her that I had been taken away by some members of State Security.

"The G-2 people took Homero," said Dolores with a mix of anxiety and fear. "But why did they do that?" She asked now, with words choked by anguish.

"I can't tell you; the only thing I saw was that they practically forced him into an *"alfita"* (an Alfa Romeo used by State Security at that time) and took him away —our troubled neighbor replied.

Dolores, now in a state of panic, went to my friend Chucho's house to ask him to please take her to the State Security offices since she didn't drive well and didn't have a driver's license.

Despite the great friendship we felt for each other, my friend Chucho hesitated a bit but finally agreed to help, not without first asking Dolores not to involve him in trouble with the frightening G-2 people.

They arrived at the Security offices (the place where I was detained) and asked the soldier at the guardhouse if I had been brought there after giving my name and personal details.

"I'm sorry, but the person you're looking for isn't here," he said somewhat sarcastically.

"But... where else could they have taken him?" Dolores asked.

"I'm sorry, but I can't give you any more information," indicating that the conversation was over.

At that moment, an officer from the house-office came out and, hearing the conversation, asked Chucho if the car was his.

"It's our neighbor's husband's," Chucho said timidly, pointing to Dolores.

"Then give me the keys; that car is under investigation," taking the keys and handing them to another soldier next to him, ordering him to take it into the courtyard.

"Comrade, I don't understand what's happening; why are you taking our car?" Dolores said, a bit agitated.

"We're not taking anything, comrade; the car will stay here for a few days for investigation, and don't ask me more because I can't answer." He ordered the soldier at the entrance not to answer any more questions and to dismiss my friend and my wife. "Comrades, for your own good, I ask you to leave; otherwise, I'll have to take measures," he said in a harsh tone.

Chucho advised Dolores to leave and not insist because "something strange is happening," he said with a visible tremor in his voice.

The soldier driving the car into the G-2 courtyard apparently didn't know how to drive and, while maneuvering, hit a concrete post, denting the front right fender and destroying the headlight on that side. From afar, Dolores and Chucho witnessed the barbarity and saw the soldier draw a mocking smile. The officer who ordered it to be brought in made no comments and turned his back, entering the main building.

Since the Security house was a few kilometers away from our neighborhood, they had to "ask for a ride" —Cuban slang for hitchhike— which they managed to do after several attempts.

Dolores was crying uncontrollably because of what had happened and the inhumane way she had been treated. She knew I was there, but the G-2 soldiers wouldn't admit it. She couldn't even guess why. Everything was very strange, and after drinking a cup of linden tea to calm her nerves, she asked Vladimir what we had done during the day.

"Mom, Dad and I only fished all day," my son said naively.

"Tell me the truth, my son. Didn't you enter anywhere, meet anyone on the way, or anything?" Dolores continued interrogating Vladimir.

"I swear, Mom, we only fished at the reservoir." Vladimir replied with the innocence of a child.

Despite her exhaustion, Dolores decided to go talk to my childhood friend Perucho, who was a member of the G-2, hoping to get his help in clarifying this mysterious episode.

She reached Perucho's house with considerable effort since transportation was even worse on Sundays. She was received by his wife, Marta, a wonderful, polite, and decent person.

"Dolores, what are you doing here today? How can I help you?" Marta asked with her usual politeness.

"I came to see if Perucho could help me because I'm desperate." Dolores explained what was happening to our friend.

Marta explained that Perucho had left early and hasn't returned, not even for lunch. "You know how his job is!" She spoke compassionately, seeing my wife's state.

She regretfully told Dolores that it wasn't advisable to wait for Perucho because she herself didn't know when he would return; but she promised that as soon as he arrived, she would ask him to investigate my case. She would call our neighbor, a police officer, who had the only phone on our block, no matter the hour. She tried to comfort Dolores with encouraging words and bade her farewell with true affection.

Dolores trusted me; she knew I wasn't one to get into difficulties or problems, much less with politics. Knowing the friendship that had always existed between Perucho and me, she believed he would do something to solve or at least investigate what was happening.

She couldn't sleep all night. Her anxiety and fear prevented it. In the morning, she called her workplace, explained the situation, and apologized for not attending. She also called my parents and told them what had happened, causing great despair, especially in my mother, who is very emotional.

At eleven in the morning, she received a call from Marta, explaining that Perucho didn't know what had happened to me but that as soon as he found out anything, she would call again.

It wasn't possible for a high-ranking G-2 officer not to know what was happening in his department; it was unheard of, and this reasoning gave Dolores a very bad feeling. Something terrible was happening, and she didn't know what it was. Her nerves were becoming more strained with each passing minute.

After lunch, around three in the afternoon, she received a visit from her boss, who was a member of the Communist Party but seemed like a decent and trustworthy person. He asked what had happened and promised to take an interest in the matter with his colleagues in the Inner Party.

"Don't worry; everyone knows that Homero is a wonderful person, incapable of doing anything wrong, so I assume it's some misunderstanding." José María, Dolores's boss, said in a reassuring tone.

By now, Dolores was indignant and simultaneously fearful that something was wrong. Her intuition told her that the matter wasn't as simple as the "comrades" wanted her to believe.

Days passed, one after another, and despite not stopping for a moment to search everywhere, ask for help from friends with government influence, and repeatedly visit the Security offices where they always told her the same thing: "Comrade, we don't know anything about your husband; please don't come here again."

"I feel like you're not telling me the truth, and until my husband appears, I will come as many times as I want," she told an officer who attended to her insistence.

The days passed, the anguish increased, and the nerves became more intense. She requested unpaid leave from work, because, as things were, it was impossible to focus on anything other than finding out what was happening to me.

It was worse than death because one can come to terms with death. What made no sense was the absurd situation my family was in because of this circumstance It was barbaric!

CHAPTER 4

Several hours had passed since I had been in that cell, thinking about the situation destiny had led me to. More accustomed to the prevailing darkness and the strange noises I heard, I felt a voice coming from a room or cell next to mine. I strained my ears because it sounded distant, like a whisper, and I could understand what they were communicating to me.

An unusual and absurd dialogue ensued, which I recount with reasonable accuracy if my memory does not fail me.

"Pirate, pirate, a friend is speaking to you," were the words that reached me in a distant way, so to speak. Possibly it was due to the fact that the cell walls were very thick and did not allow sound to pass through well.

It shouldn't be directed at me because I wasn't called that, so I didn't respond immediately. Again, the same voice and the same phrase were repeated twice.

"Pirate, don't be afraid, I'm a friend," it insisted repeatedly.

In my mind, still confused by the recent events, that nickname began to make some sense. During my university days, some of my friends affectionately called me "the Pirate" due to my habit of getting books from the Faculty library that were not allowed to be borrowed, thanks to a "deep friendship" with Teresita, the beautiful librarian, who was the most sought-after woman at the university.

Noticing the persistence of that person and thinking, absurdly, that it might be someone I knew—absurd because I couldn't see anyone, only hear that voice—I responded somewhat irritated:

"Buddy, I don't know who you are or why you call me Pirate, which was my nickname at the university, but what do you want?"

"My brother, tell me if they received the 'package,'" the voice asked.

"What package are you talking about? I don't know of any package," I replied sincerely and with some annoyance at the absurd things happening to me lately.

"Alright, I like that you don't trust anyone, but the only thing I'd like to know is if it's in a safe place," continued that ghostly dialogue.

"Whoever you are, I ask you to leave me alone because I'm not feeling well and I might be rude, ~~which I don't like,~~"-I said, trying to end the conversation.

That night, I couldn't sleep because, on one hand, my thoughts tormented me, and on the other, it was impossible to sleep in that cell on that cold, hard, and narrow bed.

Time passed, and I never knew if it was hours, years, or centuries. After that interval, since my arrival in the cell, they slid a plastic tray with a plastic pitcher of coffee with milk or something similar and a piece of hard, half-stale bread through a small slot at the bottom of the cell door. I don't drink milk because I'm lactose intolerant, and that bread was inedible. Besides, I had no appetite whatsoever. I left the tray untouched.

After some time, I heard the cell door open, and a soldier with no rank insignia (he must have been a private) said dryly,"Get out and follow me."

I had to make an effort to walk straight; the discomfort of that place and the humidity had caused joint pain that made it difficult for me to move.

We arrived at the same office where I had been interrogated before; they put handcuffs on me, which were attached to a metal chair bolted to the floor with cement.

A few minutes later, an officer with the rank of captain, bearded and wearing dark glasses that obscured his eyes, entered and ordered the soldier who had brought me to leave the room.

"I have all the time in the world to talk," he emphasized the phrase, "so I hope you'll be cooperative," he said with an air of sufficiency.

Something inside me told me not to speak and just wait for the bearded officer to do so.

"I have a recording I want you to listen to carefully because it might make things easier," he said, pressing a button on a large tape recorder on a table next to his chair. I heard a conversation that I didn't understand well at first, but then I realized it was my voice.

I thought these things only happened in science fiction books, not in real life, but now I saw my mistake.

I heard the brief and confused conversation I had with "the voice" in the cell.

"I already heard it; I admit that someone I don't know asked me some questions I didn't understand. What do I have to do with that?" I said in a tired, impersonal voice.

"That's exactly what I'm asking you: what do you have to do with the package?"

"I tell you the same thing I answered to the person who spoke to me in the cell: I don't know what you're talking about," I said a bit irritated but cautiously, fearing they might mistreat me again.

"We're both speaking the same language. Spanish. We both heard the recording where you were recognized as the Pirate, so what more do you have to deny?"

"That Pirate nickname was given to me at the university. That's what I clarified to the voice that wanted to talk to me," I emphasized.

"You know very well that the person in charge of receiving the weapons was the Pirate, and you are that person. Why insist that you know nothing?" he added. "You are an intelligent person with a university education, and although you see me bearded and in uniform, I am also a university graduate, so let's not fool each other anymore."

"I'm not fooling anyone; I'm simply telling the truth. I don't know why they brought me here; I don't know anything about any 'package,' and I don't know who the person who wanted to communicate with me in the cell is or their intentions." I said this in a way I hoped was convincing. First because it was the pure truth, and second because I wanted to end that nightmare once and for all.

The bearded officer slowly got up from his chair, walked around the desk, passed behind me with calculated steps as if thinking. When he reached the wall, he turned around like military personnel do, passed behind me again, stood in front of the desk, bent over so his face was almost level with mine, fixed his gaze hidden behind his glasses, and after what seemed like studied moments, spoke to me again.

"You should know that it's not difficult for us to make someone talk," he paused and continued, "we have our methods, and we could well use them on you. Why not? You're no better than anyone else. But since the matter at hand is delicate, we won't use them. You're lucky after all."

Those words hammered at my senses because I felt unwell, perhaps due to high blood pressure or fatigue or the impotence I felt and couldn't control. The fact is that it was turning into a martyrdom, an agony difficult to endure for long.

As if it were a horror ~~and mystery~~ movie, countless situations from my uneventful life ~~filled with unimportant routine things to the most absurd thoughts~~ flashed through my mind.

Finally, the bearded officer called out loudly to the soldier who was surely behind the door and ordered:

"Take him to solitary."

CHAPTER 5

The solitary cell was an even darker, damper, and smaller room than the previous one, and additionally, it had no furniture. No bed, no chair, nothing except a hole in one corner about six to eight centimeters wide, which I later confirmed was for attending to my most basic needs.

In that place, no noise could be heard for at least some time, which I couldn't estimate, but suddenly, a "plink, plink, plink" began, sounding like a drop of water falling into a pot or pan. It was spaced, continuous, constant, and seemingly infinite...

Initially, it wasn't so unpleasant, but after a certain amount of time, maybe hours, days, or months, I couldn't say, I began to go mad. What initially seemed like drops of water turned into hammer blows, then into sledgehammer strikes, and finally into constant atomic bombs, one after another...

I was desperate, insane, and weakened because the food they served me through the slot in the door was inedible. There was no way I could eat with that torment. I thought I wouldn't be able to endure it any longer and that I would die. I wished for a rope to hang myself, a revolver to shoot myself in the temple, or a deadly poison to finally rest, but I had no rope, nor could I make one because they had left me only in my underwear. Additionally, there was no place where I could hang myself.

Time passed, and I couldn't keep track of it. It could have been hours, days, or weeks—it was all the same to me. I was on the verge of total madness, unable to think about anything, concentrate on a fixed idea. The only thing my brain repeated was, "Make the dripping stop, make the dripping stop, make the dripping stop..." which unconsciously coincided with the cursed "plink."

First, I sat with my back against the wall and my hands on my head, trying to cover my ears. Then I lay on the cold, wet floor, rolling from side to side to stop it, which I logically couldn't achieve. Thus, I spent all my time; my sense of smell vanished as if by magic. I couldn't perceive the fetid odors emanating from the hole in the floor or the food left for me to eat, which rotted over time. I vaguely remember trying to eat something due to hunger, but I had neither the strength nor the will left. Besides, I wanted to die.

That malevolent sound suddenly ceased. A deadly silence invaded the space. In my mind, if I still had a brain, it felt like I had died. Thank God, it had stopped.

A metallic noise like the opening of a lock began to be heard, a creaking of metal grinding, and suddenly, a light like a lightning bolt in the dark night invaded the room. It was like being stabbed in both eyes. I closed my eyelids with the strength I had left, and shortly after, I opened them upon hearing a voice that seemed to come from beyond the grave, saying something I couldn't understand.

With great effort, I managed to glimpse a silhouette that seemed human standing in front of me. It seemed to be sideways due to my position. Finally, I understood the order being given to me: "Get up; we're going for a walk." After saying this, I felt pressure on my right arm, what seemed like a claw instead of a hand, pulling me up, causing excruciating pain. Seeing that I couldn't get up alone, the soldier called another one, who grabbed my other arm, and between the two of them, they lifted me. I couldn't stand on my feet. I had no strength. Additionally, all my bones, joints, muscles, and even my skin hurt.

They dragged me to the usual room, half-conscious with a foggy, muddled mind. They sat me in the same metal chair, handcuffed me, and shortly after, I heard footsteps approaching. It was the same bearded man, now without dark glasses. With difficulty, I managed to lift my face and open my eyes, meeting his eyes—black as night, half-closed with upper eyelids almost touching the lower ones ~~(like people with myasthenia gravis)~~, sunken in deep sockets, explaining why he invariably wore dark glasses, which, for some unknown reason, he wasn't wearing this time.

"You're weak," he said, pausing before continuing, "You prefer to die than to talk, right?" He paused longer this time. "Or you're a coward, which is most likely, or you have extraordinary resistance."

I didn't respond, not because I didn't want to, but because I couldn't even move a facial muscle. Such was my weakness...

"I'll ask you the question again. Where did you hide the box with the weapons? This is the last time I'll ask, I swear on my mother."

No idea formed in my obstructed mind. It seemed like I had become completely idiotic. Finally, a phrase reached my mind, and after making an almost superhuman effort, I articulated with a tongue tied as if I were utterly drunk. It came out as things must come from the depths of the soul:

"Fuck your mother, you son of a bitch."

Total silence. Not even the rustling of a fly's wings could be heard, drowned by the stench emanating from my body.

Suddenly, I heard a phone being picked up and the bearded man's voice speaking to someone who seemed to be his immediate superior, judging by the submissive tone.

"The results are negative. What should I do?" After a pause, presumably receiving instructions, he hung up the receiver and called the soldiers who had brought me.

"Take him to the suite. Special treatment, okay?"

The soldiers took me to a spacious, bright room, furnished normally; a bed with a mattress and white sheets, a two-door wardrobe, and a bathroom with a white bathtub. They put me in the bathtub, turned on a warm shower, gave me a Nácar-scented soap, and left me under that blessed stream, where, with extraordinary effort, I managed to soap myself. They later gave me a clean towel, with which I barely dried myself.

They helped me put on pants that seemed to be the ones I wore when I arrived and a white cotton pullover, then led me to the bed, where I lay down, feeling like I was on a cloud, and instantly fell asleep.

I don't know how long I slept; I only remember a persistent voice waking me from that wonderful sleep:

"Get up to eat; the table is set," said a soldier who was a new face to me.

A bit more recovered but still dizzy and struggling to move, the soldier helped me to the table, where I sat in a wicker chair. In front of me was an aluminum tray with several compartments containing white rice, red beans, minced beef, fried potatoes, and bread with guava paste. It was hard to believe! My hunger returned with astonishing intensity, and I eagerly devoured the incredibly tasty meal. Afterward, with a satisfied stomach, I staggered back to the bed and fell asleep.

It was night or early morning, and I woke up needing to urinate. I got up, went to the bathroom, relieved myself, and returned to the bed, now with thoughts; my thoughts had returned! My mind was functioning again. I began to reflect, and suddenly, a joy filled my soul. Surely, they had realized I was innocent of what they accused me. They were finally convinced I had nothing to do with weapons, parachutes, or anything like that. Oh no. They would hear from me. They needed to learn it was not right to make unjust accusations against a decent person.

I fell asleep again, now with the feeling that it had been a nightmare.

Three days passed, and I stayed in that room, being treated the same way, but without anyone telling me anything. I kept asking the soldier who seemed to have been assigned to "look after" me, but my efforts were in vain. I couldn't extract a single word from his mouth. He seemed mute.

It was early morning, as the sun had just risen, when the soldier, who hadn't talked to me in three days, brought me breakfast and said: "Get ready; we're leaving."

I felt a mix of joy and anger—joy because it seemed I was finally leaving and would reunite with my dear family, and anger because I had unjustly suffered the whole time I had been there. Both feelings filled my being.

I washed my face and shaved because, surprisingly, they had provided me with a razor. I brushed my teeth for the first time since leaving my house and left the "suite" room, now fifty percent recovered and with the hope of finding my wife Dolores and my beloved son Vladimir either waiting for me or at home. God tightens, but doesn't strangle. That was the thought I had at that moment.

CHAPTER 6

It was impossible to guess that the special treatment I had received was to lead me to a trial like those typically conducted in Cuba. I don't want to go into details because those farces would make any civilized person living in a democratic country sick. They appointed me a lawyer, someone I actually knew well because he had once belonged to the Ministry of the Interior; in other words, if he defended anyone, it was the State.

They leveled numerous accusations against me for activities against the revolutionary laws, obviously without evidence, and the defense presented by my appointed lawyer was:

—Given that the citizen is a professional and has not previously committed any crimes against State Security, the defense requests that this conduct be considered a mitigating factor in the sentence —in short, my defense lawyer was my enemy.

I was sentenced to four years of detention at a rehabilitation farm with the right to practice my profession. How kind of them! The most ironic moment came when the defense lawyer told me he was pleased because they had been lenient with me. I had to restrain myself from telling him to go to hell.

Needless to say, they did not let me speak with my family, who were the only ones present that day at the trial.

The farm where I was imprisoned was vast, housing thousands of prisoners from various categories; fortunately, none were petty criminals. I was assigned to a dormitory where each inmate had an independent cell. The daily routine was strict: wake-up at 6:00 a.m., breakfast at 6:30 a.m., followed by work at the clinic starting at 8:00 a.m. Lunch was at noon, and a second work session ran from 1:30 p.m. to 5:30 p.m. Personal hygiene was at 6:00 p.m., dinner at 7:00 p.m., and by 8:00 p.m., we were back in our cells. Visits were allowed every other Sunday, and visitors could bring lunch.

Dolores and Vladimir always came to visit, and my parents came whenever they could, though their advanced age made it difficult for them to handle the hassle. I asked them not to talk about unpleasant things and not to mention the causes of that mess anymore—it filled me with immense rage and affected my health.

During the first visit when Dolores and I were able to talk privately, I told her everything exactly as it had happened, explaining that the only reason for my existence was my parents, my son, and her. I told her I was not willing to accept such an injustice and that I had no intention of spending four years paying for a debt that did not belong to me. She begged me not to do anything foolish, fearing that I might get killed. That time I told her:

—My love, the only thing I ask of you is that you behave with serenity and naturalness. Don't do anything that could harm you or our son, and if by any chance you get the opportunity to go to the United States with him, don't think twice —and I asked her to solemnly swear it to me.

She reluctantly agreed, knowing that I am as stubborn as a mule... and that I would not forgive her if she broke her promise.

I became taciturn, and never spoke to anyone. At the clinic, I behaved with a coldness and lack of enthusiasm that were not typical of my character. I had always been a cheerful, communicative, and cooperative person. The trauma I had suffered and carried with me had changed me radically. Sometimes, I hated myself for some of the behaviors I exhibited, which were often unjustified. In this way, two months passed.

One day, before I began attending to the first patient at the clinic, an officer in charge of the medical post came and ordered me to go with him. There was a situation at the Luis Lazo Penitentiary, and they needed a dentist that day. Although it was not to my liking, I accepted without saying anything since I had made a firm decision upon entering the farm to not speak. I was not going to let the slightest emotion slip. They would never know what my true thoughts were, and my reactions would always be silent and deeply thought out. I spent the nights cultivating this kind of character and thinking about all the possibilities for a possible escape.

They put me in a four-door Russian jeep. My companions, in addition to the driver, were a plainclothes soldier in the front seat and a fat sergeant who almost left me no space in the back seat next to him. They placed handcuffs on me, which they secured to the back of the front seat, and we left the farm. For me, it was just another ride, but distrustful as they had forced me to become, I was on high alert. It could be another interrogation session like those before my sentencing. If that was the case, I wasn't going to allow it. I had to do something to stop it.

We started moving along the Luis Lazo road, which is very winding with many sharp curves and deep ravines. In a perhaps demented impulse, when I saw that the driver was somewhat distracted, discussing a play from the previous day's Vegueros baseball game, and since we were very close to the edge of the ravine, I gave a powerful kick that made the jeep plunge off the road in a matter of seconds. After bouncing over a rock, it flipped over several times, causing the plainclothes soldier in the front seat to be thrown out forcefully. After the jeep rolled from side to side, crashing into a tree with the left fender and ending up overturned on that side, I found myself on top of the fat soldier.

Everything happened so quickly that I barely realized anything, and when the jeep finally stopped, my head was still spinning. A warm liquid covered my right eye—blood oozing from the soldier's skull—and I felt intense pain in my chest and right arm, as well as in my wrists, which were cut and skinned from the handcuffs. It was a miracle that I was alive after so many tumbles.

I was in a daze, unable to define the time that passed. When I started to analyze what had happened, I realized the magnitude of the accident I had caused. The driver was practically decapitated by the windshield glass—dead. The fat soldier, who had served as a cushion during the tumbles, was also unconscious, and, as I later confirmed, dead as well. My mind quickly cleared; I had to do something, and the priority was to free myself from the handcuffs. I struggled to remove my shoes and socks because my whole body hurt, especially my chest. With my right foot's toes, I fumbled in the fat soldier's pocket and, after several attempts, managed to grab the handcuff keys, which I used to free myself.

But where was the plainclothes soldier who had been in the front seat? I painstakingly crawled out of the jeep and scanned the area. About ten meters away, I spotted his body and cautiously approached him, still in great pain. He was dead, apparently because his bloodied head had struck a rock when he was thrown out.

I didn't think twice; I stripped him of his civilian clothes, which were a bit too big for me—he was much larger than I—and put on his prisoner uniform. I dragged him to the jeep, placed the handcuffs on him as if he were me, gathered all the weapons and ammunition they had: an AK-47, two Makarov pistols, and a .38 revolver, and with deep sorrow but knowing it was necessary, I opened the gas tank cap. With a hose I found, I siphoned several liters of fuel, doused the jeep, including the bodies of the deceased, with the flammable liquid, and, using a piece of rag soaked in gasoline and some matches I took from one of them, set the jeep on fire. I ran to hide behind a large rock. The jeep began to burn like a torch and soon exploded with a great roar, scattering flames all around. I had to quickly move away to avoid getting burned as well.

I started to move away from the road as quickly as my legs and body would allow, carrying the heavy weapons that made it difficult for me to move easily. From a distance, I could see the flames of the fire I had caused, which seemed to be growing as the column of smoke rose hundreds of meters into the air. I had to take advantage of the confusion and get as far away from that place as possible. I couldn't predict if they would realize my ruse. At least between one thing and another, I would have plenty of time. Whenever I saw an open field or a peasant's house, I moved away to avoid being noticed, although in that irregular terrain, I spotted few houses.

I walked, and when I got tired, I stopped for a few minutes to rest before starting again, thinking that this was my path to salvation. As night fell, I had no more strength left. I spotted a small light in the distance, seemingly from a peasant's house. After resting for two or three hours, I walked cautiously in that direction. I could see that it was a small hut made of wooden planks and yagua, with a guano roof—very rustic. Next to it was a small granary where peasants usually stored their harvested crops.

With extreme caution, I approached the granary and was pleased to find freshly harvested corn cobs that were still tender. I took several and stored them in a sack I found, along with the weapons, except for the .38 revolver, which I kept at my waist as a precaution. I moved back to a safe spot away from the house and found a hiding place to rest for a few hours. Beneath a rock, there was a hollow about a meter high and two meters wide. It seemed safe because several branches almost covered it. I lay down on my back; that was the position I used when I wanted to have a light sleep, and I fell asleep in an instant.

Fortunately, the first rays of the sun hit me directly in the face, and the sound of birds chirping woke me up. I quickly grabbed the sack, slung it over my shoulder, and despite the pain in my body, especially in my chest, I started walking, trying to get closer to the city. My first thought was to go to my house, but I soon dismissed that idea completely. It was a stupid idea, and if I wanted to get out of that risky situation successfully, I needed to think more intelligently.

I headed toward the junction of Las Ovas, perhaps instinctively. As I walked, I remained vigilant, never allowing myself to be distracted, ensuring no one noticed my presence. Lost in thought, I remembered an old friend of my father's who lived on a small farm a few kilometers off the main road, just before the junction. I recalled visiting him once with my father, who was buying pigs for fattening at the time. Like my father, this friend had been affected by government interventions and had been forced to retreat to the only possession he had left: a tiny farm, where he now raised pigs to make a living.

I spent the whole day walking and feeding on the corn cobs I had taken and some wild fruits. Almost at sunset, I entered the path, which was really a trail, leading to Torcuato's house—the name of my father's friend. By nightfall, I had reached the vicinity of the house, which I remembered well. It was a tiny building, about four by five meters, with wooden walls and a thatched roof, a typical country construction. But since I didn't see any lights, I decided to go to a nearby thicket of marabou bushes. Using a yagua sheath as a shield, I entered that tangled mess of thorns and prepared to rest until morning when I could decide what to do next.

I had to be cautious, and before doing anything that could jeopardize my life, I needed to devise a plan and think it through many times. I was overcome by sleep, exhaustion, hunger, and thirst. Before closing my eyes, I saw the Big Dipper drawn in a clear, starry sky. I thought of what I had told Dolores many times: "When you're thinking of me and feel sad, if the sky is starry, look at the Big Dipper and remember all the sweet and passionate moments we've shared together." The Big Dipper was designated to be the spiritual link between Dolores and me.

Despite the fatigue, the unpleasant events of the accident I had caused, which filled me with much remorse for the lost human lives, after asking God for forgiveness for my actions, I felt a moment of fullness in my heart as I gazed at the constellation and saw reflected in it the sweet, beautiful, loving, and honest face of my beloved wife. I suppose a joyful expression, resembling a smile, appeared on my face, and at that moment, I fell asleep as easily as one does in a comfortable five-star hotel.

CHAPTER 7

Entering the first street to the left at the Las Ovas junction, a small town a few kilometers from the city of Pinar del Río, was the store owned by Torcuato Pérez, a descendant of a Spaniard who had arrived in Cuba along with my paternal grandfather. Both were close friends throughout their lives. Torcuato and my father, who were both in their sixties in those early years of the Revolution, shared the same dream: to become store owners and each have their own wholesale store. Torcuato had among his employees a young man who was not very hardworking but very ambitious. When my father and Torcuato talked, they referred to him with a certain disdain; they were hardworking and tireless men and looked down on those young people who had no love for the noble sentiment of industriousness. Since they had been lifelong friends, they used to visit each other—or rather, my father frequently visited him because poor Torcuato was very overweight and suffered from emphysema due to having abused the habit of smoking cigars throughout his life.

When Fidel's government began to intervene in all Cuban properties, my father and Torcuato did not escape its clutches. Ironically, that young employee of Torcuato, who was the most despicable and cynical being on the face of the earth, became the store's intervener, immediately firing the owner and taking possession with the arrogance and ferocity typical of souls possessed by the devil. So the poor man had no choice but to sell his house—the only property he had left—and move to the small farm where he raised pigs and a few dairy cows, cared for by a caretaker who had been his employee for many years but could no longer perform well at the store due to his advanced age. Torcuato had become a widower, and his only son, who was married with two grandchildren, had fled to the United States when they saw the situation that was looming.

From one of the trips my father made to visit his friend at his small farm to buy pigs, I learned the road. We spent hours and hours talking about how unfair life had been to them, especially in their later years when they thought they would enjoy some of what they had achieved with so much sweat and sacrifice day after day, without rest.

Poor Torcuato suffered greatly whenever he spoke of his son and grandchildren, the only family he had left. He deeply regretted having only that one son who, despite having a heart of gold, was not as blind as his father in failing to see what was coming with that madman who wanted to take everything for himself—"for the people," as he said in his speeches—all that people had built with effort and sacrifice, some through malice, others through hard work. We knew that some people had grown rich through force and ill will, sometimes at the cost of suffering and death. But they were the minority, not the majority.

The dictator wanted—and achieved—total control of all the country's wealth, from the most modest property to the grandest factory. It didn't matter if it belonged to a national or a foreigner—he wanted it all. Absolute control to govern with an iron fist. He was building socialism, which he said was not as "just" as communism. My goodness! If that madness, which was less severe than communism, was already unbearable, what awaited us in the future? At that time, I wasn't particularly passionate about one cause or another. I felt sorry for those hardworking people suffering so much, especially my father, but sometimes I was confused by Fidel's propaganda and his cohorts, who were the best in the world at propaganda, capable of making people commit atrocities like betraying their own parents and siblings who didn't agree with the ideas of the Revolution.

To achieve its goals, the Revolution was fueled by low and dishonest people like that employee Mario, who intervened in Torcuato's store with cruelty and despotism in the name of the Government. These were the champions of the Revolution, those who executed, killed, and imprisoned so many dignified men and women simply for refusing to let their properties be stolen and not allowing those vile ideas to be imposed on them.

There were also those who, though honest, were confused by the subtle and seemingly correct propaganda of the Government. Together, they contributed to destroying the national identity, the ethical and moral values passed down by our ancestors, the aspirations and desires of many, many thousands of just and hardworking men who forged the foundations of a country with sweat and tears. A Cuba that, while it didn't have a correct and much less perfect government, at least respected private property.

CHAPTER 8

The heat inside that thicket of marabou bushes and the mosquito bites woke me up before sunrise. This was fortunate because it was very dangerous for me to be discovered there in those circumstances.

With great care, I stealthily approached the house and pressed my ear against the walls, trying to hear something. On one of the walls, I heard a strong, persistent cough that I assumed belonged to Torcuato or the caretaker.

I went to the place that seemed safest to me: the latrine in the yard, just a few meters from the house, and I waited for someone to show signs of life. Some time after sunrise, as the sun was becoming stronger, I heard the clatter of pots or jars coming from the back, which surely belonged to the kitchen. A few minutes later, I saw a window open, and through it, a person appeared who I didn't recognize at first, but then I realized it was Torcuato. However, it was not the Torcuato I had in mind—the fat one—but a thin, pale, emaciated version, clearly announcing an advanced illness. I spent several long minutes waiting to see if anyone else was with him, and seeing that no one seemed to be, I decided to approach him without startling him.

I knocked gently on the front door but got no response. I knocked again, this time with a bit more force, making sure the knocks wouldn't sound alarming, and I heard a tired, old voice respond to my call:

"Who is it?"

I responded with the most normal voice I could muster:

"It's me, Don Torcuato, the son of Rodolfo García."

"The son of who?" he asked again. At that moment, I realized he might have difficulty hearing due to his advanced age, so I answered more loudly:

"The son of your lifelong friend, Rodolfo García."

I heard a bar being removed from behind the door, and the old man appeared, almost unrecognizable compared to the Torcuato of years past. He squinted his eyes, almost closing them because the morning sun was shining in his face; when he recognized me, he gave what seemed to be a smile:

"Come in, my son. What a pleasant surprise!" he said as he stepped aside to let me in and invited me to sit, offering me a jícara of freshly brewed coffee.

"But what are you doing here at this hour of the morning and looking so downcast?" he asked after noticing my dismal state.

"My friend, I come in the name of my father, whom I know you hold in great esteem, to ask for a favor. But if you can't do it, don't worry, I won't be offended."

"A request from the son of my dear friend Rodolfo is an order for me," he said, raising his voice for emphasis.

"I trust in the Lord, as my father always did. I'm going to tell you everything, and then you can decide if you can help me or not."

Then, with the greatest detail, I told him everything that had happened to me, and I watched his face closely to see how my words affected him.

"This humble house is at your complete disposal. It's a shame that my age and illness prevent me from helping you as I would like," Torcuato said with a voice trembling with emotion as I finished my story.

Together, we began to plan what we could do, first to help me recover and also to avoid being seen, much less caught by someone who might betray me.

He suggested that I rest during the day when he could keep watch, and if I needed to do something, to wait until night. I agreed with him on that point. He also told me that for added security, I could sleep in the shed he had by the stream, about sixty meters from the house. I completely agreed with him on that as well.

He gave me some spare clothes, a towel, washing soap (he didn't have any bath soap), a blanket because sometimes it got a bit cold at night, especially when it rained, and even a pillow that had belonged to the caretaker, who had passed away a few years ago.

Torcuato shrugged. "I don't have much in the way of good food to offer you, but what I eat, I'll share with you, and you'll never go to bed with an empty stomach ."

I spent several days on the farm, recovering from my wounds, the exhaustion, the remorse for the actions I had been the main actor in. Due to my Christian faith and fear of God, I thought I would never obtain divine forgiveness.

In my prayers, I asked God to forgive me. The weighty reasons that led me, in a completely instinctive and self-preserving manner, to do what I was so ashamed to remember haunted me. My friend Torcuato, older and wiser than I, told me not to torment myself with those thoughts, as God would forgive someone who had not done those things out of malice or driven by evil instincts, but as an irrational reaction to an excessive and unjust aggression committed by my enemies. Those wise words of comfort and encouragement helped me a little, but I really didn't believe, nor do I believe, that I was ever capable of such an atrocity.

Days passed, my strength began to return, my wounds healed, and my mind was a bit calmer, so I began to draw up a plan for my future.

What was to become of my life? In Cuba, it's impossible to be on the run for long. I didn't know if they had discovered my trick of swapping my body to appear dead in the eyes of everyone. Besides, if they believed it, how would I circulate on the streets without identification documents? Everyone knows that, in my country, walking around without identification is synonymous with jail.

I remembered that one of the books that had most impressed me years ago was *The Discourse on Method* by René Descartes. Once or twice during my student life, I had used Descartes' method to organize my studies with very good results. So I grabbed a pencil and an old notebook that Don Torcuato had, and I made an analysis of what I could and should do.

The first thing I remembered were his principles:

Start from scratch.

Put everything in doubt.

I think, therefore I am.

Descartes said:

First: We should not admit anything that is not very evident.

Second: Each problem must be divided into as many particular problems as necessary to solve it.

Third: Order thoughts from the simple to the complex.

Fourth: Enumerate all the data of the problem and verify that each element of the solution is correct to ensure the exact answer has been obtained.

So I must not admit that:

They consider me dead.

I am foolish enough to walk freely on the street.

I will fall into the foolishness of going to my parents' house or my own house, as well as any close relatives or intimate friend's house.

If they considered me alive, I would not surrender meekly.

Now let's divide the problems: It may be that they consider me dead or not. a) If they believed that I was the charred body, my danger perspectives would decrease. b) If they discovered my trick, the danger was total because they would realize I am no fool.

Analyzing the second hypothesis, that is, walking freely on the street, I would break it down like this: a) To walk freely on the street, I have to be either disguised or unrecognizable. b) I need to have an identification card, which obviously should not be mine. c) I need to always be in places with a lot of people, avoiding being alone. d) I have to distrust everyone.

Third hypothesis: This hypothesis is completely discarded due to the risks it entails, even if they believe I am dead.

Fourth hypothesis: Here I have no choice but to admit that there is only one option, and that option is not to let myself be caught alive under any circumstances.

This plan needs to be reviewed a bit later because it may be subject to variations depending on future events.

Now, after having rested a bit and with my wounds almost healed, my three-week beard growing, and having been subjected to so much suffering and deprivation as well as the stress that came with it, I noticed that my hair had turned gray. It seemed that I had aged twenty years. "This could be of great help," I thought at that moment, to go unnoticed even if I happened to run into someone I knew.

One fine day, after getting tired of so much inactivity and unable to sleep during the day as I had agreed with Torcuato, I decided to go to the house, taking the necessary precautions. To my surprise, it was closed. That didn't bode well, so I took extra measures. Something was happening that wasn't normal—my intuition told me so.

I peeked through the only window that was open and heard a faint groan coming from Torcuato's room. I didn't think twice, carefully entered through the window, revolver in hand, and began to crawl like a reptile across the floor of the house, which was damp and cold despite the time. I peeked through the door, which was ajar, and saw poor Torcuato lying halfway on the bed, dressed, with a face that showed he was in great pain.

I quickly went to him and asked:

"Torcuato, Torcuato, what's happening? Please answer me!", he began to mumble some nearly unintelligible words and, making an effort, told me that he was in great pain in his chest and felt like he was dying.

"No, please. Don't leave me now when I need you so much". I said, unable to hide my anguish.

"My son, I am one step away from the beyond, but before I go, I want to tell you that under the bed, there is a loose floorboard. Lift it, and inside a can, there is some money. You will need it more than I will", saying this, he suffered a spasm of pain, clutched his chest, and his head fell to the side. His gaze became fixed and glassy. I tried to revive him with chest compressions, but it was in vain. My friend had passed away to join the Lord. I said a prayer, closed his eyes, and gently laid him face up on the bed.

I had to sit down afterward to avoid falling to the floor because my legs were giving way. It was a harsh blow at that moment. I had lost my only friend and confidant in those difficult times.

I spent over an hour in that situation, praying and looking at that lifeless body of a dear friend who had entered my life in a very special way. After some time, I realized that I was in danger of being discovered there and that I had let my guard down. That couldn't happen again—one of the rules I had set for myself was to never let my guard down if I wanted to preserve my life.

I asked God for permission to do what I was thinking. My friend had no family and practically lived alone in those remote areas. It would have been right to give him a Christian burial, but if I took him to the town, I would expose myself. Besides, I am sure that he would agree with me in doing one last favor: using his identity. From then on, I would become Torcuato Pérez.

I didn't think twice and wrapped him in a blanket and a sheet, carried him as far as possible into the woods, far from the stream that, with its floods, would overflow several meters and could uncover the body. On a small mound, I dug a grave and, with love and devotion befitting a great friend, I buried him. I prayed and asked the Lord to forgive him if that good man had committed any sins in his life. I placed no cross above the grave to avoid exposing myself and returned to the house to search it.

Remembering what he had told me about the can under the bed, I removed a loose floorboard, and just as he had explained, I found over three thousand pesos, certainly all the poor man had saved with great sacrifice. I took it, knowing I would need money, and besides, he had offered it to me in his last wish.

I searched the closets, and in a cigar box, I found his identification card, birth certificate, and marriage certificate, as well as his wife's and son's death certificates, the ration book, some documents he still kept from the store that had been confiscated, and family photos.

I looked at his identification card and realized that the age difference was too great, which would be an obstacle. I had to carefully remove the plastic, placing it over the steam from an old typewriter I found, changed the birth year to make it more compatible with the age I appeared to be at the moment—about fifty. One essential thing was missing. A photo of myself. How was I going to get that? I had to take a risk and get ID photos taken.

Going to Pinar del Río was impossible. The Las Ovas junction didn't seem advisable either, so I decided to go to Viñales. It was a town with many national and foreign tourists, so it could seem more normal.

I dressed in clean but not too flashy clothes, put on a straw hat that my friend Torcuato had given me, and with the look of a peasant, I went out for my first contact with the everyday world since I was first imprisoned. I had to act as naturally as possible to avoid arousing suspicion, but it was also necessary to take extreme precautions not to fall victim to naivety.

I reached the highway and hitched a ride from several passing vehicles until a trucker picked me up. Upon reaching the entrance to Pinar del Río, just beyond the Provincial Hospital, I asked the driver to drop me off, thanking him for his help.

I positioned myself at a bus stop across from the Rumayor Club and waited for over an hour until a bus on the Viñales route passed by. I boarded naturally, paid the fare, and without lowering my guard, I pretended to be disinterested, looking out the window, avoiding conversation with the woman sitting next to me. I didn't want to make contact with anyone. That's how Cubans are, especially those from Pinar del Río—communicative, talkative, and gregarious.

Upon arriving in town, I went to a photo studio and had several ID photos taken. I asked the young woman at the reception desk to have them ready as quickly as possible, slipping her a two-peso tip, which she gratefully accepted, and two hours later, I had my photos. I went into a print shop and bought glue, an eraser, a blue pen (for which I had to pay extra because they weren't for sale), two school notebooks, and several letter envelopes. I thought I might need these at some point.

I convinced a shopkeeper who was alone at the moment in a small store, paying twenty times more than they were worth, to let me make a small purchase of food and a set of khaki clothes, as well as a brand new pair of rustic boots in my size, because up until then, one of my biggest sufferings had been wearing shoes that didn't fit. My feet were enormously grateful.

I was constantly remembering my friend Torcuato. Even in his death, he had been an angel to me. In one of the many bars for tourists, I got a bottle of Guayabita del Pinar. I needed something to lift my spirits in moments of nostalgia.

I didn't want to take excessive risks, so I took the regular buses back. By late afternoon, I returned to Torcuato's house, which would now be my new home, at least until something happened that could change the course of my life. I had no idea what my future would hold.

Carefully, I swapped the photo on the ID card, placed my own photo on it, and resealed the plastic with a hot knife around the edges, being very cautious. I sat down at the table to eat the dinner I had prepared. After satisfying my appetite, I began to review the recent events.

Then I decided that for that night, I would sleep in the usual place and see what to do in the future. "Tomorrow is another day," I thought. There's nothing better than one day after another. It was important to remain calm. I remembered an old peasant saying: "Those who rush eat raw meat." I slept, and in my dreams, I saw my friend Torcuato ascending to heaven and sitting beside a throne where a man with a white beard placed his hand on his shoulder.

CHAPTER 9

T he clock I inherited from my friend showed seven in the evening when I arrived at the highway. I had devised a method to communicate with Dolores; after much thought, I realized that I had to trust someone and that someone was my beloved.

How would I do it? Let's see later. I arrived in Pinar del Río and went to the Vélez neighborhood because on one of its streets lived a young man named Papito who made some very good kites to sell. I didn't want to risk going directly to him, so I asked a boy, about nine or ten years old, who seemed suitable because of his somewhat naive appearance, to go to Papito's house and buy me a kite, but it had to be gray, black, or dark blue with a tail made from used typewriter ribbon and a big spool of thread. I told him I would give him two pesos if he got it quickly. He rushed off, and a few minutes later, he told me everything was arranged, and that the kite would cost forty pesos with the tail and thread, which was an exaggeration, but I didn't mind. I gave him the money, and shortly after, he came back with a *barrilete* (kite) with black and dark blue horizontal stripes that seemed perfect for my plans.

I gave him five pesos instead of two and explained that my grandson was crazy about a kite and that it had left me without a cent in my pocket. I said this because it seemed I had misjudged the boy—he wasn't as naive as I had thought at first.

At ten o'clock at night, always walking through the darkest places, I arrived at an empty lot near the back of my house. That lot was full of tall grass. I went in as far as I could to see the back of my house without being seen.

My heart tightened when I looked at what had been my home. Millions of sweet memories with my family flooded my mind. Sometimes I imagined myself in the living room in my favorite chair with Vladimir on my lap, asking me the classic questions of that age, and me trying to give answers that matched his knowledge. Other times, I imagined myself in bed with Dolores in my arms, discussing the plans we made for the future, how we were going to face the reality that Vladimir would have to go to boarding school and be far from us, our vows of eternal love, and all the beautiful things we shared during all those years of togetherness. Tears streamed down my face, and my chest tightened to the point of squeezing my heart.

I spent more than two hours there, contemplating my house and hoping that Dolores would come out to the yard, but nothing happened. I decided to go back and return the next night. Maybe I would have better luck.

The next night, always with my eyes and ears alert, I returned. Nothing. She didn't appear in the yard. Not even the kitchen window opened. Could it be that they weren't eating? I thought. I didn't see any movement in the kitchen.

My tension grew by the moment, despite my firm resolve not to let my nerves get the better of me—it was impossible. I needed to see them, even from afar. I needed to at least communicate to her that I was alive. I had written a letter explaining more or less what had happened, without many details to avoid distressing her, and without mentioning anything about where I was living. That was enough to give her some encouragement, which I supposed was greatly needed, given her likely deteriorating mental state.

I looked up at the sky and saw the Big Dipper. A soft but constant breeze caressed my face. Suddenly, I looked towards the house and saw the back door opening. My heart began to pound, and with my own eyes, I saw, as if the earth would swallow me up, the magnificent, beautiful, precious silhouette of my dear Dolores. Without wasting any time, taking advantage of the gentle breeze, I quickly tried to fly the kite. On the first attempts, it got caught in the surrounding bushes and weeds, but finally, I managed to fly it, and with a skill I never knew I had, I directed it towards the yard of the house where my beloved wife was "contemplating the Big Dipper." It was magnetic, telepathic, spiritual communication—I don't know; all I know is that there was a strong connection between our minds. At the tip of the kite's tail, I had tied the letter I had written, and I maneuvered it until the tail was almost in front of her face. At first, she was startled and thought it might be some kind of flying bug or something, but then she realized—she was very perceptive—and grabbed the kite's tail, perhaps following some instinct, and seeing that it had a note with large letters: "FOR DOLORES" and beneath that: "go inside quickly, read it, and let go of the kite."

She looked around, trying to see who it was, but realized it was essential to do what the note said quickly. She let go of the kite, went inside the house, and I saw her from afar reading my message.

I quickly retrieved the kite and, without thinking much, swiftly left the area, returning to my house, which I reached in the early morning, not without difficulty due to transportation issues.

I had achieved one of my objectives. So far, things were going well, thanks to God's guidance.

CHAPTER 10

D olores entered the house and began reading my message in the kitchen. It said:

"My love, first of all, a big kiss for you and our dear Vladimir. Second, I am alive. Third, lock yourself in the bedroom and, above all, don't tell anyone, not even Vladimir, about any of this. OK?

As you can see, I'm alive and well. I won't explain some things to you to avoid tormenting you—you must have already suffered a lot. You are the only person who knows about me, so for the love of God, don't mention anything to anyone, not even my parents. After reading this letter, burn it. Please don't disobey me, as it could put me in danger, and you too. I know you are intelligent and will understand.

I want you to know that I love you very much, and I carry you and our son in my heart. But as you know, either I am presumed dead, or I am a fugitive hunted by all the repressive organizations in the country. Either of these scenarios is fine with me because I will not allow myself to be captured. You can be sure of that.

I want you to fulfill your promise—let them say whatever they want. Try by all means to leave the country. Contact my uncle and godfather to see if he can help you. My greatest ambition right now is to know that you are safe in a free and democratic country. Only when you are safe will I be happy.

I will try to get out too, but it will be much more difficult for me. But I will succeed, first because I have God's help, second because I am determined to do it, and when a person sets a goal, they achieve it—sometimes with more difficulty, sometimes less, depending on luck and destiny.

I love you, and I dream of you every day. I love Vladimir, but I know I can't let him know. Someday, when the three of us are safe, I will be able to show him. Keep acting naturally—if they consider you a widow, play the part (you are the prettiest pretend widow in the world). Don't despair; everything will turn out fine. Trust in God, who can do everything. He will help us. I love you very much. A kiss for you and Vladimir. Homero.

P.S. Burn the letter now!"

Dolores was trembling with emotion. She wanted to keep the only link she had between us, but as I had asked—and not just asked, but ordered—she burned that letter with a sadness that was heart-wrenching. A mixture of sorrow and joy filled her soul. I was alive—what a miracle! But I was also a fugitive, exposed to being killed. These were conflicting yet congruent feelings. Hope began to manifest in her heart. She had lost the will to live since she was informed of my death... Yes, because even if they had doubts, they weren't going to admit that someone had mocked the "efficiency" of the repressive system that the Revolution's leaders so boasted about.

I was alive; she was not a widow; her son was not an orphan. So many things at once, so many thoughts, so much confusion. How did everything happen? What was I going through? What was I thinking? These and many other questions crossed her mind. "The important thing," she thought, "is that he is alive. I have to do everything possible to fulfill the promise I made to leave here. From now on, my efforts must focus on completing this task." She was a determined woman, and if I was giving her an example of tenacity and courage, she would at least imitate me—and why not, surpass me. She knew that it was another way of helping me.

She went out to the yard again, hoping to see me, even if only from a distance, but when she saw neither the kite nor any sign of me, she looked once more at the Big Dipper, the symbol of our love and the transmitter of it. She thanked God that I was alive and had communicated with her, and she closed the door, now aware that it wasn't wise to stay in that place for too long at such a late hour.

She happily went to bed, but not before giving Vladimir two kisses on the forehead—one from me and one from her. She undressed completely, covered herself with a sheet, and began to imagine me beside her, making those physical, loving contacts that always filled us with pleasure and left us exhausted.

CHAPTER 11

I slept on the floor and woke up past nine in the morning. What carelessness! This could never happen again. I had to be careful if I wanted to achieve my goals. I promised myself to be more cautious.

I went to the house, always attentive to the road, and prepared a hearty breakfast since I needed to eat well because although my muscle mass, previously deteriorated and damaged, had somewhat recovered, I was still not in top shape. I needed to eat as much as possible, exercise, and go on long walks whenever I went out, while also thinking about how to accomplish the plan of activities that needed to be modified as new tasks were on the horizon.

The objective of my life couldn't be solely to take care of myself. I had to do something against that cruel and inhuman system. I would start with the simplest things.

I dressed modestly, like any peasant. This time, I went out during the day, although taking the utmost precautions.

I headed to the town of Consolación del Sur and, before reaching its outskirts, crossed a barbed wire fence. Upon seeing a rather old and battered horse grazing alone, I lassoed it with a rope I had brought from home, led it to a gate, and carefully tied a couple of signs to its mane on both sides of its neck that read: "I AM A HORSE, BUT I AM NOT A SON OF A MARE." I let it go and gave it a few pats so it would run toward the town. Since it seemed to be a cart horse, I assumed it knew the way and soon lost sight of it as it disappeared into the town.

I quickly headed in the opposite direction, walking along the roadside until I reached a bus stop, intending to hitch a ride, which I managed to do after more than an hour in one of the few remaining private trucks, until I reached the Las Ovas junction. I got off there, walked along the road to my house, and arrived with great satisfaction. I hadn't performed a heroic act, but if my plan worked, by that time, many people would be laughing in the streets of Consolación, and many policemen and government agents would be "cursing their mothers" for being the laughingstock of everyone as they tried to remove the signs.

I was beginning to be the Homero of old. Risking my life for a joke like that was a step forward. It was the only cheerful thing I had done since the fateful day I went fishing with my son.

I rested for two days, and on Saturday evening, I set out with a small package in my hand containing some very old red paint I had found in the house and a worn-out brush.

I arrived in Pinar del Río, got off at the stop behind the Hospital just after eleven at night, and waited hidden in some bushes until two in the morning.

With great care, trying not to be seen by the few vehicles that passed by at that hour, I used the brush and the red paint to write on the bus stop at the Hospital, where I knew many people gathered: "DOWN WITH FIDEL! NO TO SOCIALISM, YES TO DEMOCRACY!"

Then I crossed the street and did the same on the back wall of the Hospital.

Once finished, I left with my little bundle in hand, walked until I was almost in front of the Minint (Ministry of the Interior), and in a trash barrel, I deposited it among the garbage that had accumulated there for at least two days. Right in front of the Minint—what a daring move!

That night had been enough. I walked more than five kilometers out of the city and waited inside a small grove at the foot of a thick-trunked tree for sunrise, without even closing my eyes, attentive to everything happening around me.

With the first rays of the sun, I boarded the first bus heading to Consolación del Sur. At the Terminal, I got on another bus bound for Las Ovas, which passed by the junction. I got off at the junction itself, walking back to the path leading to the house. Arriving with my feet sore from the nocturnal walk, but happy, I had successfully completed another mission. I needed to be careful, though—I was getting too bold and needed to think more about future actions and space them out because, by now, they must be going crazy searching for the author or authors of those acts.

I say that anything we can do to demonstrate that the desire for freedom and democracy is alive in the minds of most Cubans is good. It's healthy. It helps in the mission to destroy the seven-headed monster that misgoverns our homeland.

I didn't have the resources to do something more concrete and dynamic, like setting off a bomb in a place that wouldn't endanger people. Killing people, even the most hated and perverse regime members, was not my goal. Taking the lives of fellow human beings—only God should do that; I ruled out the possibility of personal attacks.

But there are many ways to fight, and one of them was to propose democratic propaganda to battle their efficient communist propaganda. I didn't have sufficient means, but I would do something. Meanwhile, I was thinking about how to flee the country. I couldn't rely on luck because one day, it might fail me.

I spent several days on the farm, first with the goal of avoiding being found if they were searching for the subversive, and second, because I was trying to devise a plan to carry out some more effective or subtle demonstration of repudiation against the regime.

One Monday morning, a regular day with a lot of activity, I went to the road with a paper bag containing a two-liter plastic container filled with paint. In my pocket, I had a fine brush and a paintbrush.

I arrived in Pinar del Río, and at the Terminal, among the crowd waiting for the buses, I paid for a ride to San Juan y Martínez.

San Juan was a tobacco-growing municipality. It wasn't just famous—it was home to the best tobacco in the world.

I got off at Vivero, where the best covered tobacco plantations in the country are located. I entered the path leading to the station, and near the farm of Fidel Castro (not the dictator, but a man with the same name). I went into the woods and sat in a place I considered safe, because from there, I could see who was approaching. I couldn't be seen by anyone. I waited until the shadows of the night covered the entire tobacco plantation with their cloak.

It was almost eleven at night and dark as a wolf's mouth. I headed to the road leading to San Juan and chose a huge tobacco barn—a place that, as everyone knows, is used to "cure" tobacco and is filled with the aromatic leaves. We were in the middle of the harvest season. I was very careful of the night watchmen, the militiamen who, like me and many other citizens, were forced to stand guard to protect the "people's property."

I spent two hours observing, trying to locate the watchman on duty, until I finally realized it was just one man. With a rifle slung over his shoulder and showing signs of enormous fatigue based on his way of walking, the man was in charge of the entire area where several tobacco barns were located, some near each other. Among the barns was a larger one, the *escogida* of the area. The *escogida* is a warehouse where hundreds of workers, mostly women, gather to select tobacco leaves, which are then distributed according to their quality to different factories and separated for export. Fortunately, the entrance door of the *escogida* wasn't very strong, and I was able to enter without much difficulty.

There was a platform where the "readers," people who read aloud while the workers worked, usually sat. With the brush and black paint, I wrote a sign on the wall of the *escogida* that, luckily, was painted white, so the message stood out well. It said:

"TOBACCO WORKERS. YOU WHO HAVE ALWAYS LOVED DEMOCRACY AND FREEDOM, THIS IS THE TIME TO DEMAND IT FROM THE GOVERNMENT. WE DEMAND FREEDOM FOR THE UNJUSTLY DETAINED AND DEMOCRACY FOR THE CUBAN PEOPLE."

My mission was complete. The important thing now was to leave as discreetly as possible.

I walked out carefully and took the path leading to the train station. After walking about two kilometers, I arrived near it.

I waited until morning because the train from Guane passed by at five-thirty. It arrived with some delay, but at five-fifty, I was on my way to Pinar del Río. I continued walking until I reached the Bus Terminal, where I took a taxi to the Las Ovas junction, getting off before reaching the town, and from there, I walked back to the house.

It was another mission successfully completed. I thanked God for His help and went to rest—the day had been exhausting. My feet were in a deplorable state, and I was extremely nervous about what I had just done.

I had placed a small stone—a modest one, to be sure—in the construction of a more just society, a democratic and free society.

CHAPTER 12

In the central offices of the Minint (Ministry of the Interior), a meeting was held with the Provincial Delegate, the Director of Prisons, and Gilberto (the bearded officer who had been directly involved in Homero's case). It was eight in the morning, and due to the urgency of the summons, the "bearded one" assumed that it was something important.

"We have little time, and at nine, I have a meeting with the Deputy Minister, so let's be objective and dynamic," said the Provincial Delegate of the Minint, raising his chin to signal the Director of Prisons to speak.

"The situation is as follows: A few weeks ago, the jeep transporting a prisoner had an accident, as we all know, but what intrigues us the most is that when the forensic examination was conducted on the bodies, the one who appeared to be the prisoner was not. It is evident that they tried to deceive us. Additionally, only three bodies were found, yet four people were traveling in the jeep. If you wish, I can provide you with the file containing all the details later."

"That will be sufficient for now," said the Delegate, continuing, "Gilberto, since we know that you were directly involved in the investigations with the detainee, this Homero García, we have called you to this meeting so that you can exclusively dedicate yourself to unraveling this mystery. I have already contacted your superiors in the Department, and you have carte blanche to pursue this."

"Comrade Director, give me all the data you have at hand, and I will begin my work right away," Gilberto responded, making a gesture to stand up, considering the meeting over.

"Wait," ordered the Delegate. "I want to make it clear that we all know that this gentleman who was unjustly sentenced to four years in prison—" and he emphasized the phrase— "earned that sentence due to the 'brilliant' conclusions of your investigations. And this is not the first time. You know that. Therefore, if he is alive, see what you can do to 'clean up' your mess," he said, standing up to conclude the meeting.

The Director of Prisons stood up without looking at Gilberto, avoiding the gaze that was always hidden behind dark glasses, while the Captain remained petrified in his seat.

"I said the meeting was over. Please leave, as I have many pending matters," ordered the Provincial Director.

Gilberto stood up like a spring and left with his head down, not deviating his gaze. As he was leaving the central Minint building, he was approached by an assistant to the Director of Prisons, who handed him a file full of documents labeled "SECRET."

Gilberto got into the jeep he had parked in front of the offices because he always wanted everyone to know that "he was very important." His arrogance led him to have a superiority complex, which truly revealed his underlying feeling of inferiority due to a physical defect he was born with on his face. His friends mockingly called him "hawk-eyes." This nickname irritated him intensely, to the point where he sometimes felt like drawing his pistol and shooting whoever called him that. On the other hand, he had been a very dedicated university student, having abandoned his studies to join the Escambray Mountains (perhaps for a short time, as he did so when it became clear that the "dictator" Batista was about to be defeated). He wanted to earn ranks in the new government. Later, since he was a close friend of Commander Efigenio Ameijeiras, he followed him and practically begged him to release him (with a salary and retaining the military rank of captain, which he had almost imposed on himself) so he could pursue his university degree in Legal Sciences.

He was aware—because he was a very shrewd person—that most of those Sierra fighters, even those who held the rank of commander, were mostly semi-illiterate, uneducated people. He had been educated in the best private schools in Havana and would be superior to all of them with his university degree. He could become a Minister or "something more"—why not?

He was furious about what the Provincial Director had said to him—who was he to criticize him like that! It wasn't a criticism; it was a real insult. That idiot was just one of those who had higher positions because they had joined the Sierra earlier than him, but he was simply an ignorant man who had barely finished primary school. He couldn't even write well because every time he saw him "scribbling," he felt like laughing.

Moreover, he was a "brute from the East" and not a well-educated Havana native like him. It was humiliating to take orders from such a person. This wasn't what he had planned for his life.

But something within him betrayed him—he indeed had let that case slip out of his hands a bit. He felt it was his duty to do everything possible to condemn that man who, with his stupid face, had insulted him in the most sensitive way. "That scoundrel insulted my mother," he remembered.

"If he had been a little less arrogant despite his university education," he continued thinking, "maybe since I am also a civilized person, I would have 'put in a good word' with the boss. I could have waited a little until it was discovered who was responsible for the weapons cache. They would have released him, and it would have been just a misunderstanding. The only thing he would have had to complain about was the terrible conditions of his cell, which were the fault of the imperialist Yankee blockade, and perhaps a few slaps—infinitely less than what Batista's people did before."

Now he was going on a more than special, honorable mission. He had to resolve it elegantly and efficiently to prove that he was superior, that he was the best, and that they were all ants compared to his mastodon-like figure.

In short, he calculated that this Homero wasn't much. He had simply been lucky to survive that accident and perhaps had a bit of cleverness to swap the bodies. "But he doesn't realize that we are not fools, and we have some Soviet specialists who are experts in the field. It was just luck, and luck doesn't last forever. It's going to run out because I am much smarter. He's just lucky for a day," he thought.

He went to his house, a small apartment located near his office. He lived alone—he hadn't found the woman of his dreams: beautiful, intelligent, and with a close family connection to an important figure who could give him a "push." That was what he needed to succeed in life—just a push.

That woman hadn't appeared, nor had others. He simply assumed that his difficulty in finding a companion was due to his lack of free time. He practically worked from Sunday to Sunday, didn't have a nightlife because it was dangerous given his position as a G-2 officer, and didn't have friends who genuinely appreciated him enough to invite him to their homes. How he got angry when one of his colleagues boasted about the "little party we had at home" and how delicious the roast pig was, and how well Otero danced casino...!

After all, they didn't invite him, but they could all go to hell, those "guajimenes" (a derogatory term for peasants) with their casino dances, which didn't interest him because he didn't even know how to dance. Besides, he couldn't eat those greasy and overly seasoned foods because his liver hadn't been functioning well for some time. But he was irritated by the comments they made around him; he was sure they were meant to annoy him. He didn't know why, but he noticed that he wasn't very popular within the group.

CHAPTER 13

One of the mistakes I made, and I admit I'm not very experienced, was the sign I placed at the corner of the main street and the Central Highway at the Las Ovas junction due. It said, "DOWN WITH INJUSTICES. LONG LIVE DEMOCRACY." First, because it was in my usual route, since I lived nearby and almost always had to pass through there. Second, because an injustice had been done to me, and I was projecting my own feelings.

This would draw the attention of State Security and make my movements more difficult. Later, I would realize and regret my stupidity.

My most important plan was to escape to the United States, so I dedicated several days to devising a plan that would be as effective as possible. It wasn't going to be easy; I didn't know any fisherman well enough to ask for help. I also wasn't an expert in navigation and didn't even know what the ideal place would be to attempt a successful departure.

I had heard stories of people leaving Cuba and, after sailing for several days, returning to our shores thinking they had reached the United States. There were also tales of fishermen offering to help people leave the country and, after everything was prepared, reporting them to Security, often to earn merit within the fishermen's cooperatives or secure positions.

It had to be a well-thought-out plan, calculated down to the smallest details.

The end of 1979 was approaching, and I thought it was an opportunity to take advantage of the New Year's celebrations.

One morning, I woke up early as usual, went to the house, and lit the stove to prepare breakfast. After making coffee, I heard a noise that sounded like a car coming down the road. I quickly looked out the window and confirmed that it was indeed a car approaching. I left everything as it was and, in a flash, closed the door and window, and headed out to hide in the nearby woods. On my way past the clearing, I hid my belongings as best as I could, scattering some corn husks I kept there as a mattress and to cover the spot where I had buried the weapons.

I heard the car arrive and the doors open and close. Although I couldn't see what was happening, I managed to listen.

"Don Torcuato, Don Torcuato, are you there?" I heard a voice that sounded like a farmer's. The call was repeated two more times.

Another person said:

"Someone must be inside or very close because there's the smell of freshly brewed coffee."

"Maybe he's milking the cows," said the voice that sounded like a farmer.

"Where is that?" asked another voice.

"Close by, just within a rooster's crow," replied the farmer.

"The old man lives alone, right?"

"He lives alone, my friend, and he's getting a bit feeble these days."

"Let's head back to town, and I'll leave you in charge of contacting us when you see him. We want to know if anyone is with him these days."

"Don't worry, my friend; I'll pass by later."

When I was sure the vehicle had left, I exited through the other side of the woods leading to the road and saw the dust rising in the distance. There was no doubt—I had made a colossal mistake, and it was going to cost me dearly. From now on, I would tread carefully and keep my eyes as wide open as an owl's.

I needed to change my route and find another place because when they realized that Don Torcuato wasn't around, investigations would begin, and everything would get complicated.

I was racing against time, and decisions had to be made quickly. I returned to the clearing, took the weapons from their hiding place, gathered the remaining money, and dug up some yuca from the field. In a sack, I placed the weapons, keeping only the .38 with me, and covered my rifle with the yuca. In a bag, I packed the militiaman's uniform, which could be useful in the future. I dressed in my dirtiest and simplest clothes, along with a pair of well-worn boots. I had to look like a true peasant.

I followed the path to the stream where the cows were and found Don Torcuato's horse, which was so fat from grazing that it looked like a pregnant mare.

I left the sack in a safe place, returned to saddle the animal, and although I wasn't a skilled rider, that horse was gentler than a cat. I went back to where

I had left the sack, placed it behind the saddle like the guajiros do, and took off on the other side to avoid using the main road. I had to avoid any possible encounters with people, including that farmer I didn't know.

I had to take a big detour because the barbed wire fence wouldn't let me get onto the road until I finally found a gate, which I crossed, and as soon as I started moving in the opposite direction of the junction, I heard the noise of a vehicle approaching from behind.

I didn't want to look back—I had to act completely natural. I lowered the brim of my straw hat to cover almost my entire forehead and continued as if nothing was behind me.

A four-door military jeep passed slowly by my side. In the front seat, next to the driver, was an officer with a thick black beard and dark glasses who made a slight movement as if to look out of the corner of his eye. I recognized that figure instantly. My nerves tensed, and my hands began to tremble uncontrollably. Despite this, I kept my gaze fixed on the ground and continued at the same pace as the horse, which was moving slowly.

As soon as the jeep disappeared around a bend, I took the first trail I found and headed into the woods. I knew that man wasn't ordinary—he was a bloodhound worse than the Hound of the Baskervilles.

I entered the woods and waited for a while. Circling back in the opposite direction I had been going, and keeping far from the road, I crossed a pasture and sat for about an hour in the shade of a fig tree to think about what to do next.

I found my way back to the road and decided to head toward the junction. It might have been dangerous, but my intuition told me it was the best option. I reached the junction, turned onto the road leading to Las Ovas, and followed it for quite some time until I reached the outskirts of the town.

It had been many years since I had visited those areas. I only remembered going there as a young man with my mother to visit relatives who had a farm and grew rice, which was very common in that area. I tried to locate the house out of pure curiosity, and I finally got close to it. It was unlikely they would recognize me after so much time (I had only seen them once or twice in my life, and back then, I was quite young), and considering that they knew I was a dentist. How could they recognize me when I looked like a real *guajiro*, now with my gray beard making me look much older than I actually was?

I took the risk of entering, perhaps driven by that sense of familiarity and also as a test to see if they could recognize me.

I dismounted, leaving the sack tied to the saddle. I greeted them with "Good afternoon" since it was already almost two o'clock, and in the usual manner of Pinar del Río peasants, they invited me in and offered me a seat in the kitchen, where they served me a meal. I tried to apologize for the unusual hour of my visit, but when they insisted after asking my name, where I was from, and what I was doing in those parts—which is customary for any peasant—I couldn't resist the temptation and sat down at the table to enjoy a plate of rice and beans with fried pork chunks and yuca. A real delight.

I explained that I was looking to buy pigs and that I lived near Consolación. They offered me a thirty-pound piglet at a reasonable price, and not wanting to contradict the story I had told, I tied the piglet, placed it on the saddle, and after savoring a delicious freshly brewed coffee, I bid them farewell.

CHAPTER 14

Gilberto, the bearded hawk-eyed officer, sat in his office reviewing the reports from the past few days. There had been several counter-revolutionary demonstrations happening lately, which were causing significant concern among the G-2 agents. The higher-ups were demanding some response to these disturbances, and everyone was utterly disoriented.

One report, however, caught Gilberto's attention. It was about a sign that had appeared at the Las Ovas junction, talking about justice and democracy. These were phrases that didn't belong to just any ordinary *gusano*. His instincts told him that this wasn't the work of just anyone.

That *Homero* running loose, and these things happening... even though they were in different towns... and that talk of justice and democracy... there were too many indications for him to not suspect that it had something to do with that *Homero*.

Could that fool, whom he had underestimated, have suddenly become a skilled and active subversive? He didn't want to believe it, but something inside him told him not to dismiss the connection. He decided he would personally take charge of the situation at the junction.

He left with a small squad composed of three vehicles and ten men. When they arrived at the junction, he contacted the local police and asked for information about the residents.

The local Police Chief considered that the act must have been committed by someone passing through, as there were no people in that area who were brave or reckless enough. Still, Gilberto insisted on getting a list of all the disaffected individuals, including those who had been harmed by the Revolution. The policeman typed up a list of about thirty people and warned him that several were so advanced in age that they could hardly do anything on their own. The list included Don Torcuato, who, although he lived far from the town, had been one of the most affected.

Gilberto distributed the list among the three vehicles, while he stayed behind to analyze the people from the center of the small town. He asked the Police Chief to get him some guides who knew the area well to assist with the investigations. One of them went to Don Torcuato's farm but returned without finding him.

They spent the entire morning on these activities, and by noon, Gilberto decided to leave the town and take a drive around the surrounding areas. As they were driving along the highway, they encountered a peasant riding a horse. As they passed by him, a sensation like the hairs on the back of his neck standing up shook Gilberto. He made a slight movement with his face and glanced at the peasant out of the corner of his eye. Something had bothered him at that moment, but they continued on. After advancing about a kilometer around a curve, an impulse made him order the driver to turn around immediately. Something was telling him that he had to go back, and that something had to do with that peasant.

When they returned, they couldn't spot him again. Gilberto ordered the driver to stop several times to look on both sides of the road, but it was in vain. The earth seemed to have swallowed him up.

They returned to the junction, where Gilberto once again spoke with the Police Chief. He vaguely described the peasant, but the response was not positive:

"We have so many peasants that fit that description, comrade, that not even a fortune-teller could give you an answer," said the Police Chief.

Gilberto was certain that something strange was going on with that man and decided to explore the area a bit more. He would go to Las Ovas; perhaps he would find some useful information there.

He arrived around noon and went to the Police Headquarters, looking for the Chief.

"He's not here," he was informed. "He went home for lunch," said the orderly.

Gilberto decided to find a place to grab a snack because the men with him were hungry. They stopped at the only bar in town that sold anything, particularly "surprise croquettes" (so-called because no one really knew what they were made of) and a somewhat bitter guava soda due to the llack of sugar.

It was around two in the afternoon, and while they were returning along Central Street to the Police Headquarters nearby, the peasant Gilberto was looking for was walking down another street, searching for a relative's house.

After speaking with the acting head of that post and obtaining little information—since the man was somewhat slow-witted—Gilberto and his entourage decided to return to the junction and later head back to Pinar del Río.

A sense of anxiety weighed heavily on Gilberto's chest, and something inside him kept insisting that he should continue investigating that area.

He was highly intuitive—a trait he inherited from his mother, which gave him a mix of pride and resentment.

That night, in his apartment, unable to sleep, he began to reflect on his childhood, his youth, the life he had led...

Images of moments that had marked him flashed through his mind like episodes. He remembered his late father, who owned a bar-restaurant on Águila Street, frequented by many middle-class people and a few politicians. His mother, in addition to being the cashier, also handled all the accounting. She was very well-educated, having trained as a professional accountant, and although she didn't practice professionally, she was highly valuable in the business she shared with her husband. His father was somewhat slow but very hardworking and skilled in business, but it was his mother who ran the operation with an iron fist.

She was a fierce woman, so cunning that she even outsmarted her own husband by secretly stashing away part of the profits in a private bank account without him noticing.

Once, out of resentment, Gilberto asked his mother why he had a facial deformity that caused all his classmates and neighborhood friends to mock him.

She explained that the doctor attributed it to an accident she had while pregnant, which caused some minor but painful injuries throughout her body. His father, who had always been arrogant and had drunk too much that day, demanded X-rays from head to toe when they arrived at the private clinic. Since it was a private clinic and the radiologist was one of the partners, they took advantage of his father's arrogance and told him it would be expensive. As usual, his father pulled out a wad of bills and said disdainfully, "Do all the X-rays you need and more because I have enough money to buy this miserable clinic."

Due to his arrogance, they took twenty-two X-rays, only to confirm that he had no bone injuries. According to the pediatrician who treated him as a child, this excessive exposure to X-rays was likely the cause of the deformity.

When his father died of a heart attack, his mother took over the business alone, using it for many supply tasks, which irritated Gilberto because he sometimes had to miss school. When the Revolution triumphed, he had finished high school, and his mother, who was a fierce woman, quickly got involved with a Captain from the Sierra who was very close to Fidel. She seduced him so that she could remain the administrator of her own business when it was nationalized. Thus, from owner, she became the administrator, which was practically the same or even better because she didn't have to invest anything, and she pocketed most of the profits.

Gilberto had inherited his mother's skills as well. The only friend he had in school, if he could call him that, was very poor and sometimes didn't have money to eat. Gilberto would tell him to come after three in the afternoon when everyone had finished lunch at his mother's restaurant, and he would offer him the leftovers—larger pieces of steak, a few pieces of chicken, leftover minced beef with rice, and so on—placing them in a container and offering them as if it were a regular meal.

This friend had connections with the members of the 13th of March Movement, especially with Faure Chomón and Cubelas, and Gilberto asked him to help him join the Sierra del Escambray, where the members of the Movement were rising up.

It was mid-1958, and the fall of the Batista regime seemed imminent. It was necessary to seize the opportunity, join the movement, and later take advantage of the Revolution to secure important positions in the new government.

Gilberto presented himself as a university student, which was a lie, and almost self-appointed himself the rank of captain without participating in a single skirmish since he avoided them due to his immense fear of bullets.

As soon as Batista's escape was known, he quickly descended and arrived in Santa Clara, skillfully managing to join Che Guevara's forces, who was the most prestigious and important commander at that time.

Upon arriving in Havana, Gilberto maneuvered his way into an officer position at La Cabaña and later joined the fledgling State Security

Department. Through his distant friendship with Efigenio Almeijeiras, who was then Chief of Police, he was allowed to pursue a career in Legal Sciences while receiving a salary (though he didn't finish the degree, as with everything he started). This was going to bring him many benefits, the first of which was being appointed one of the chiefs of the G-2 in the province of Pinar del Río, along with the rank of first captain.

It was one of the solid steps toward achieving his goal: holding a high position in the government. He felt destined for it.

When he was a child, perhaps seven or eight years old, he used to visit the home of a neighbor—a man in his fifties with blond-gray hair, a firm face, and piercing eyes, with ruddy skin and a voice that had a foreign accent, somewhat garbled like Americans or Germans. For some unknown reason, the man was paralyzed from the waist down and had to move around in a wheelchair or sometimes with crutches and metal braces that secured his knees, which made it difficult for him to move.

The neighbor spent most of his time reading books, which he stored haphazardly on shelves that covered all the walls of the living room. He didn't seem to have many friends—perhaps none, except for Gilberto, who, not having any playmates himself, enjoyed going to Hans's house, which was the man's name.

The boy had become friends with him and spent hours and hours listening to Hans talk about his "adventures" from his youth when he could walk and run like everyone else.

Gilberto delighted in Hans's tales of when he was a soldier and fought in the "Second War" under Marshal Rommel, the most daring, brave, and intelligent man in the world.

Gilberto didn't know much about that marshal, or the other names Hans mentioned, but in his childish mind, he began to create a character that resembled the descriptions Hans gave of the military man.

"You should have seen that man," Hans would say. "He was a personality like no other. With his impeccable uniform, commanding soldiers with iron discipline. He wouldn't let anyone contradict him, nor would he accept opinions from uneducated fools."

Then Hans would tell him stories of when he was an investigator in the secret police of his country—his great country, as he always called it.

"To be an effective investigator, the first thing you need is a cold-blooded nature," he explained in a proud and captivating voice. "No compassion for anyone. Always think of the person you're after as your enemy and give them no quarter. I had to unmask an enemy of my government. I followed him day and night until I detected that he was doing things that didn't please my superiors. Then I caught him, and he was easy to bring in. I personally made him talk because all men have a limit in life, and you have to push them to that limit by any means necessary."

At that young age, Gilberto couldn't fully understand what he was hearing from Hans, but his mind absorbed every word and phrase as if they were lessons from a teacher—perhaps better, because he had never had a teacher in school who captivated him like his friend Hans.

He didn't understand much, didn't know which country Hans was talking about, but what was clear to him was that everything he heard was impressive, and those words were etched into his young mind.

Day by day, he would go to Hans's house, delighting in the fabulous stories from his friend, with the intrigues becoming more and more interesting each day. Gilberto enjoyed it immensely when Hans's face would come close to his, and almost in a whisper, Hans would tell him things that would imprint on his spirit, such as how he intimidated his prisoners, the methods he used to achieve his goals, and those endless and engaging conversations continued for many years. By the time Gilberto was a young man of twelve, he still delighted in Hans's wild stories.

One day, Gilberto went to Hans's house and found the door closed. When he knocked persistently, the neighbor told him that Hans had died the night before and that his body was being mourned at the funeral home.

With a deep sadness he had never known before, Gilberto went to the funeral home to pay his last respects to the man who had fulfilled his deepest desires with his stories. Hans had been the person who had the greatest influence on his life, more than his own parents, who were too busy with their business to care for him.

There was no doubt—when he grew up, he would emulate the character his friend had instilled in him. He felt it—he would be just like him.

CHAPTER 15

I crossed the plain that separated the town of Las Ovas from the port of La Coloma on horseback. I had to use unexplored shortcuts, but after an exhausting journey, I saw the masts of the boats usually anchored in the port and its surroundings.

I wasn't entirely sure why I had used that route to flee from the possible pursuit by that bloodhound. I suspected that for this creature, it had become a matter of honor. I wondered why, out of all the Security officers, I had to encounter this one on my path. It just wasn't normal.

I didn't know anyone in that area, and I wandered without direction or destination. I stopped at a small store on the outskirts of the city on a side street, aiming to get something refreshing because the heat was intense, and I had swallowed a lot of dust on the way. The fields were dry due to the lack of rain, and the paths were scorched by the sun. A man who happened to be looking around asked if I wanted to sell the piglet. I had bought it to have an excuse, but I wasn't going to be able to keep it. Seeing that he offered me more than what I had paid, I decided to sell it. That lightened the load on the horse, which was tired and sweaty since it had spent many days grazing without any effort and had gained a lot of weight, making the journey difficult; aware of this, I walked at a slow pace. I wasn't in a hurry, and walking slowly allowed me to think more clearly. I had to find a safe place to leave the weapons I was carrying so dangerously.

I mounted again, always using side streets around the town, and as I turned a corner, I almost fell off the beast because I came face-to-face with a car I instantly recognized—my beloved Studebaker. Stunned, I noticed the miserable condition it was in. It couldn't be that carefully maintained, clean, "pristine" car as people used to describe those that were in good condition despite their age. It's true that what's easily obtained is not cherished. That's why the regime that wanted to impose collective ownership didn't advance. It wasn't collective ownership; it was simply taking something from one person to give it to another who, since they had acquired it "for free," didn't value it and used it until it gave out. It must have belonged to some official or a member of Security.

It was past five in the afternoon, and in a few hours, it would be night. I directed my horse to a grove about two blocks away, from where I could clearly see my car. Fortunately, the person using it now didn't move it from there. When night fell, I hid my horse in a well-concealed spot and, taking advantage of the shadows, reached the car. I was going to see if that small defect I hadn't fixed still persisted. I pressed the rear left door inward and operated the lock, managing to open it without difficulty. I opened the driver's door, entered carefully to avoid unnecessary noise, and hotwired the ignition wires.

I started it and smoothly drove off, turning at the first corner. Seeing that the gas tank was half full. I parked it about five blocks from where I had left the horse, retrieved the sack with the weapons, released the poor animal that had served me so well so it could graze, and returned. This time, I drove at a speed that wouldn't attract attention but allowed me to urgently distance myself from that town. It was a huge risk, but I couldn't resist the temptation to see my beloved car and not do something. I considered that God had placed it in my path, and I took advantage of that divine gift.

I arrived in Pinar del Río and entered through a side street, heading toward the Viñales exit because my next stop would be Puerto Esperanza. I needed to explore that area to see if I could achieve my ultimate goal—leaving Cuba.

I saw a sign on the road indicating that the city was two kilometers away. I left the main road and used a side road among some mangroves until I reached a deserted spot on the coast. To my left was a hill that allowed me, with some difficulty, to drive up with the car. I reached the top and found a cliff about twenty meters high, with the calm, serene sea below. It seemed deep. I positioned my once-wonderful car facing the cliff about five meters away, placed a heavy stone on the clutch pedal, shifted the gear to first, and put another stone on the accelerator. I started the engine, left the door open, and removed the stone from the clutch, jumping aside as the car sped forward. It leaped into the void, taking a curve several meters out, and plunged into the sea, sinking slowly in those deep waters.

I felt an indescribable anguish as I watched my beautiful Studebaker, the car my father had lovingly given me; I still remember his words: "Son, I can't drive anymore because of my eyesight; besides, you're a professional who needs it more than I do. Take the car." I knew he was parting with the last property he had left. I promised him and myself that I would always take good care of it with great affection. But to let a degenerate enjoy it after it was brazenly and impudently taken from me by a rogue government. No. I wouldn't allow that. It was better to see it at the bottom of the sea; at least the fish could use it for shelter.

I returned along the path to the road. Among the mangroves, I spotted a large ceiba tree and went to it. It seemed like an ideal place to leave the weapons. It was too risky to keep carrying them around. Between two of its powerful roots that protruded nearly half a meter, I placed the sack, covering it with a bit of dirt, leaves, and dry branches. I returned to the road, always with my .38 at my waist because I wasn't going to let myself be caught easily. I marked the spot to avoid getting lost if I returned and walked several kilometers until I reached the town.

It was almost ten at night, and there were few people on the streets. I spotted a small restaurant where I took the risk of asking for something to eat despite the late hour. Fortunately, they offered some fried sardines and a bit of flavorless pea soup, but as the saying goes, "beggars can't be choosers," so I was satisfied and, in passing, struck up a conversation with the employee who served me—a man about my age who, according to him, was born and raised there.

Speaking with a peasant's accent, I let him know that I was looking for some relatives, whose whereabouts I wasn't sure of, with the last name Pérez (Pérez is the most common surname in Cuba), and the employee laughed and told me:

"Compay, there are more Perezes in Puerto Esperanza than crabs," he said with a smile.

"But if you tell me the first name, I might be able to guide you. I know almost everyone around here."

"Inocencio, Inocencio Pérez," I made up, not knowing where I was going with this.

"There's an Inocencio Pérez here, but he's a very old man who hasn't been seen on the streets for a long time—at least five years," he lowered his voice, seemingly out of pity, "since his son was caught trying to take a boat to the Yuma. They gave him ten years."

"What a shame! I didn't know his son was a *gusano*," I said, using the derogatory term as an excuse.

"They were revolutionaries, and Daniel was the boat's captain, but some people from Havana gave him a bunch of fulas(dollars), and when he was almost at the maritime limit, he was caught by a coast guard boat," he continued. "I don't know what got into Danielito because he, better than anyone, knew how tightly this place is watched."

"Where did you say Inocencio lives, comrade?" I asked.

"Keep going until you reach the beach, turn right, and in a little green house with white doors that has a boat named Dany on the porch, you'll find Inocencio, although I don't know if he'll be awake at this hour."

"Thank you, comrade. I think it's better to visit tomorrow," ending the conversation, I paid my bill and headed toward the beach.

I turned right, and after walking about fifty meters, I found the green house. The boat was one of those used by fishermen, and the name Dany made me think it was short for Daniel. There was an open window, and a yellowish light indicated someone was still up.

I began to think and rethink. Should I take the risk? Lately, I had been doing some crazy things... it made my hair stand on end. I couldn't always rely on luck. I shouldn't push it. But an instinct I didn't know I had, one that wasn't usual in me—a person who had always been methodical and fearful—had shaken my being. I decided to see what would happen and let fate take its course.

I knocked on the door and a voice worn by years and perhaps by suffering answered:

"Who is it?"

"It's a friend of Daniel's, Don Inocencio. I'd like to have a word with you," I said in an apparently familiar tone.

The door opened, and a man of about seventy years appeared, with a white beard, dry and wrinkled skin from the sun, typical of fishermen, noble eyes, medium height, slender, and with tired eyes, not so much from age but from suffering. He looked at me for a few seconds, seemingly trying to recognize me, and said:

"You're not from around here. What's your name? How do you know Daniel?"

The questions poured in, and I was taken aback. They were asked with suspicion and hostility.

I had to take the risk—that old man with a white beard and a face full of suffering didn't deserve lies.

"My name is Homero. I was imprisoned at Farm No. 2, and to be honest, and to avoid lying to a decent and honest person like you seem to be, sir, I don't know your son," I said with all the courage I could muster.

Don Inocencio scrutinized me deeply. I held his gaze for a few seconds that felt like centuries. Finally, he said:

"Come in and tell me your story."

Without thinking about the consequences, I told that man I told that man—I had just met—everything about my life, point by point. He listened without saying a word.

When I finished my story, he stroked his beard, leaned back in his seat, staring at some random spot on the ceiling, and after a long pause, he said:

"Many years ago—I think Fidel wasn't even in the Sierra yet—I heard a radio soap opera that closely resembles what you just told me," he was now addressing me formally.

"I wish my story were a soap opera and not the harsh reality I'm living," I said with a sadness that left no doubt it was sincere. "No one better than you knows what it's like to lose your loved ones. I have my parents, my wife, and my son, who, though they are alive, thank God, are suffering, and I can't even get close to them," I continued, "and you, with your son in prison, serving ten years for doing something the government doesn't like but isn't a crime anywhere in the world, much less deserving of such a severe sentence."

The words flowed from within me with deep and sad emotion.

Inocencio's eyes welled up, and he asked:

"Do you have a place to sleep tonight?" I answered no, and he offered me his home.

"We'll talk more tomorrow. Sleep in my son's bed," he said as a parting gesture and pointed to a room. I entered, fully dressed, always ready for any eventuality, and lay down on the bed. Something told me I had done the right thing. I fell into a deep sleep without even realizing it.

CHAPTER 16

"Captain, last night they stole Lieutenant Roque's car," was the first news he received upon arriving at his office.

"What do you mean, they stole the car?" he said, irritated. "Who did it, and how?"

"I don't know, comrade Captain. The Lieutenant is preparing a report to submit to the police."

"Call Roque immediately," he ordered furiously.

An officer with the rank of lieutenant entered his office and saluted him ~~militarily~~.

"What's this story about your car being stolen?" he spoke loudly and very angrily. The lieutenant, visibly apprehensive, explained that he had been at home resting after the previous day's guard duty, as it was his normal rest period. The car, which he had personally left for him to use to go to La Coloma, where he lived, was parked outside. When he woke up, he realized it wasn't there. He never thought someone would dare to do something like that. He reported it to the Police Chief, and they searched the entire town without finding it.

"It's very strange," he said regretfully.

"When the report is finished, give it to me personally. I'll handle everything."

Idiots. They were all incompetent—the only one with a bit of gray matter in their brain was him. The others must have sawdust.

This was Homero's doing, but how could that man be in so many places at once? How could he dare so much? Was it possible that the same person was committing so many crimes?

These questions kept spinning in his head over and over. This guy was going to drive him crazy, ruin his reputation in front of everyone. He couldn't believe it. Deep down he was sure. It was him. There was no doubt about it. Was he going to suffer this humiliation because of that damn Homero García?

He called all the police stations in the province, all the regional CDR committees, all the Security units. He had to find that car because, with it, he would find that son of a bitch.

He started pacing back and forth in his office, almost losing his mind, with one name hammering in his brain—HOMERO GARCÍA.

Was this mentally weak person going to stand in the way of his victorious climb to the top of the world?

He had to do something concrete. Think calmly, devise an effective plan, and capture that filthy *gusano*.

But how? He didn't even know where to start. He wouldn't go to La Coloma; he realized that Homero wasn't stupid enough to stay there. Now he couldn't underestimate his intelligence as he had done before. He had to face a different being from the one he had interrogated and sent to prison months earlier.

How is it possible for a person to change so much in such a short time? he thought aloud.

He had to accept that he had made a grave mistake in blaming that innocent man. He didn't know why, but from the first moment he spoke with that wretch, something had instinctively bothered him. Maybe that's why he emphasized the negative report on the subject. Or perhaps, in his eagerness to climb the ranks, he had lost his good judgment.

For him, it was essential to ascend. He had to reach the top in life. He wanted to live in one of those mansions in Miramar, with many rooms, the luxury befitting his class, several cars in the garage at his disposal, a beautiful and influential woman who would help him get ahead, and children whom he would ensure were perfect, without physical defects. He wanted to see them happy, playing with their bicycles, swimming in the pool, envied by everyone. He wasn't going to be as stingy and backward as those deputy ministers and his own Minister of the Interior, who spent every weekend throwing parties with those television actresses who weren't actresses—they were a bunch of whores rising professionally because they were protected by the "*mayimbes*" (as they called the top government leaders), and everyone knew that getting into trouble with people of that level wasn't "good for one's health."

No, he wanted a decent family. He wanted to travel with them to Paris, London, Madrid, Berlin, Rome, Egypt, Moscow, and so many other beautiful places in this world. Traveling was one of his obsessions. In those moments of solitude, he had two main pleasures. Seeing tourism magazines where he could enjoy those beautiful landscapes, those gorgeous places—Rio de Janeiro, so beautiful... And the other pleasure was repeatedly looking at the pornographic magazines that he had discreetly placed in his coat when they detained that pimp-faced guy trying to enter the country with those obscene, prohibited magazines. He delighted in the poses of those beautiful naked women and those engaging in sex, masturbating over and over until he was exhausted.

He had never had sexual contact with women. He wanted to remain intact until he married. The only time he attempted something was with a prostitute who, when undressing, told him:

"Take off those dark glasses; we're not at the beach." Hearing that half-mocking phrase filled him with such arrogance that it prevented an erection. Slapping her, he dressed, threw five pesos on the floor, and left with a slam that must still be echoing throughout ~~the~~ Colón ~~neighborhood~~.

What the hell was happening to him? Instead of focusing on his work and this Homero, he was distracted by such nonsense.

He asked the orderly to bring his jeep and ordered the driver to head to the city.

"Where are we going, Captain?" the driver asked. "Just drive, and don't ask questions. I'll tell you when it's necessary."

He didn't have a predetermined route, but he needed to get out on the street because Homero was somewhere out there, and he had to find him.

A message came through the radio saying that the car in question had been seen near Rumayor.

"To Rumayor, quickly," he ordered the driver.

He took the road leading to the Rumayor cabaret. He had visited that place only a few times and always on official missions like now. The driver parked the car, and he headed for the main door that led to the restaurant, where the administrator's offices were located.

Rumayor is a rustic cabaret. It was mostly built with logs simulating indigenous huts, with thatched roofs, very well designed, spacious, with stepped paths surrounded by vegetation connecting the different structures. There were dance floors, spots among the trees and reeds that gave the place an exotic tone, dressing rooms where the artists got ready... It covered an area of about five hundred meters in diameter, and the food in its restaurant was genuinely delicious, especially the Rumayor-style chicken and its tasty *congrí*.

He entered the administrator's office without knocking on the door. At that time, the deputy administrator was there because the other had gone out to run some "errands."

Gilberto was known by everyone in the city. It was well known that he was a tough and uncompromising officer. Everyone feared him, even his colleagues.

"They told me a blue 1957 Studebaker was here last night. I want information about it," he said without even greeting.

"No one saw that car as far as I know," the deputy administrator stammered.

"Any information regarding it, I want it immediately," he said in a threatening tone. "You know how to do it."

He left the place, and upon reaching the road, he curtly ordered the driver:

"Viñales."

CHAPTER 17

"Did you hear, Dolores? Fidel is going to open the Mariel port so that anyone who wants to leave for the North can do so," a coworker said. "Now, whoever has a relative in the North who comes to pick them up on a boat is saved."

That day, Dolores went to my parents' house and told them what everyone already knew. She always visited them on weekends because Vladimir loved playing in the yard, climbing the guava and mango trees, and enjoying the affection both his grandmother and grandfather gave him. She had always told them she was convinced I wasn't dead. They thought it was just the love she had always felt for her son, but it gave them hope.

She called them aside, and while Vladimir played with the neighbor across the street, she told them what had happened that wonderful night when she found out I was alive. She asked for forgiveness, but they understood it was an order from me, and she asked for their consent to leave with Vladimir if she could use that opportunity.

My father said he would contact my uncle, who was well-off in Miami, to ask him to come and get them. He tried to convince them to go with her and their grandson, but they refused, saying they couldn't leave behind the only things they had in life—the house and their memories—and that they were too old for such adventures.

That night, she returned home, and her thoughts tormented her. She wanted to fulfill the promise she had made to her beloved, but at the same time, she felt guilty about leaving the place where I was, especially since I was in danger.

An internal struggle ensued between her heart and her reason. Her heart, as a wife, told her she should stay and face the same dangers I was facing, and perhaps even help me in a risky situation. But reason dictated that she should leave, as it would fulfill the promise she had made and would be one less burden for me. That would make it easier for me to try to leave the country and meet her in the United States, where we could start a new life full of love and hope.

She spent several days in that internal struggle. She couldn't work or do house chores. Vladimir saw her in that state and asked:

"Mamita, what's wrong with you?"

And she would reply:

"It's nothing, my little one, just memories of your daddy."

Two weeks later, the exodus began. Boats and ships of all sizes started arriving at the Mariel port to pick up their relatives. At first, Fidel thought it was a small thing, but when he realized he was going to be left practically alone, with those malevolent instincts that always characterized him, he released every common criminal, murderer, rapist, and pedophile from prison. He also released the mentally ill from psychiatric hospitals and mixed them with the healthy people. Additionally, he gave carte blanche for all homosexuals who wanted to leave to use that route.

Dolores received a message from my parents and went to visit them. They had contacted my uncle, and he had promised to come and get them on a boat, as well as several other relatives who had asked him. They just needed to confirm the day they would arrive. She thought that news would bring her some joy, but instead, she felt immense anguish knowing she was leaving her beloved husband behind. What would become of him? Would they ever meet again? These and many other questions kept running through her mind. She couldn't find the answers because they were in the hands of fate and the powerful hand of God.

With the savings she had, and summoning all her courage, she decided to go quickly to the Cobre sanctuary. She went to ask the Virgin of Charity for protection for them, and especially for me. She left Vladimir with my parents and made that journey, which was a torment given the transportation conditions. She was a very determined person with a lot of character.

When she returned to Pinar del Río, they told her that in a week, they would be expecting her at Mariel, so she set aside the things she was going to take and waited for that day, always thinking about the love of her life.

The day came when they informed her she had to go to Mariel. For several hours, a small group of people had gathered in front of her house, shouting insults, throwing eggs, mud, and even stones at her. Those were desperate hours until she managed to leave with Vladimir and get into the car that would take them to the Mariel port. She felt immense contempt for those people who stooped to such humiliations, even seeing some coworkers among them who had always treated her with kindness.

They arrived at Mariel, and she almost lost her mind. It was chaos! People were trying to leave without having been invited, lists upon lists where neither she nor Vladimir appeared. She showed her Immigration permit to several people until, finally, they directed her to the location of the yacht that had come to pick her up.

She spotted the yacht and approached the officer who was helping people board. She didn't see her uncle anywhere, but a young man, just over twenty, told her he was there on his behalf and was the nephew of his wife.

She boarded the yacht with tears in her eyes. She saw Vladimir tense because she was sad, and he couldn't understand what was happening due to his young age.

It was four in the afternoon when the small, old yacht, which had a capacity for about fifteen people but was carrying over twenty, slowly left the port. With every meter it moved away from the coast, the pain in her temples, which had been there since she left her home, intensified.

She spent the entire journey to Miami with Vladimir on her lap, holding him tightly, crying, and praying to the Virgin of Charity of Cobre to protect me and let me escape and reunite with her.

After a long journey, fortunately without any incidents, they spotted what they were told was one of the ports in Florida. They had made it to freedom!

CHAPTER 18

In the search conducted in La Coloma to find the stolen car, the only thing that stood out was the discovery of the head and legs of a horse along with a saddle. That was the only strange thing they found.

Upon being informed, Lieutenant Gilberto requested that the saddle be brought to him for analysis. When they brought it, he began inspecting it inch by inch. In one corner, it bore the initials "TP" and the logo "Serafín y hno" encircled. This clue would later lead him, after investigations, to discover that the saddle had been made at the Las Ovas junction. Without wasting any time, he went to the junction to find out where that saddle-making shop was. It wasn't a factory but two brothers who had been making saddles for a long time but had stopped due to a lack of materials. During the investigation, Serafín, an elderly man over seventy, told him that he had made the saddle for Mr. Torcuato Pérez, the former owner of the "Bodegón" (as they called the store that Don Torcuato owned).

He returned to speak with the Police Chief, who informed him where Torcuato lived and also that one of the units that had been with him had been to his house without finding him.

He took a guide and went straight to the farm where Homero had spent some time. His instincts told him that this was the right path to catch the wretch.

They searched the place thoroughly, and he had no doubt that Homero had been there. He didn't have to think much to realize that the fugitive had left the place in a hurry. Nevertheless, he ordered the place to be watched closely, giving a description of how Homero looked when he was detained and how he should look now, thinking of the fleeting image of the bearded peasant on horseback. He knew it was like a beacon guiding all criminals. He was a true investigator, a born detective who intuited everything. Why hadn't he stopped at that moment to get a better look at the man on horseback who had disturbed him so briefly? He would never know.

He ordered the surveillance on Homero's house and his parents' house to be intensified. Homero had to appear one day, and that's where he would catch him, never to leave prison again. He would do everything possible to ensure he was executed. Yes, that was the best way to get rid of that vile creature who had challenged him. There was also the possibility of faking a heart attack, which wasn't difficult for the Russian specialist they had; he performed "miracles."

He was informed that Dolores had requested to leave with her son through Mariel. Initially, when he heard this, he thought of intervening with Immigration to deny her departure, but then he reconsidered. It was a real opportunity to catch him. Homero might try to leave with her or at least want to say goodbye to them, he thought.

The aim had to be precise; the prey was about to appear. He laughed to himself, congratulating himself—he was a genius. Now he was going to catch him easily.

He called all his subordinates and explained his plan. They were going to tighten the net and have a small unit at Mariel with all the details about Dolores, Vladimir, and Homero.

Two plainclothes officers would be stationed in front of her house, and another two at his parents' house.

The day of departure arrived, and Gilberto was at maximum tension. He knew he would have to confront Homero, and from what he had seen, he would need to be more cunning than him. It was a great opportunity, and he couldn't miss it.

He moved to Mariel with over twenty men, all trained directly by him.

Over the radio, he was informed that they had left the house and that the protest they had organized had been a success. "They were pelted with eggs," they said.

He saw her arrive with her son. At that moment, he felt tremendous envy for Homero because he knew step by step what that woman was doing. She hadn't left the house and had dressed in half-mourning since they had declared her husband dead; he knew who she talked to, and once in a while, some security informants, posing as friends, had suggested that she remarry, saying she was too young to remain in mourning. She insisted that her late husband had been and would always be the love of her life. Who could find a woman like that?

Most of the women the Captain knew were frivolous, only thinking about how to get some "imported clothes," going to fancy restaurants where only tourists and those with dollars could go, and other such trivialities. True love was what she had. Damn, even in that, that son of a bitch was better than him!

He did everything possible to hinder her departure, sending her from one place to another to see if he could spot Homero. He had to be there. He sensed it, and when he had a hunch, it was as good as confirmed.

Hours passed, and they couldn't find the fugitive. He was there somewhere. He ordered that Dolores be allowed to board the yacht that had come to pick her up. He had several agents who would alert him to any irregularities, but Homero didn't show up. The yacht departed, and Gilberto watched as it slowly drifted away, even boarding a patrol boat and following it until it reached Cuba's maritime boundary. He returned empty-handed.

Once again, he had been defeated.

CHAPTER 19

Inocencio had changed since I arrived at his house. His demeanor had gained a freshness that signaled renewed life. Since the conversation we had the day after my arrival, he had committed to helping me.

"It's difficult to leave without being noticed," he reminded me, recalling what had happened to his son. "He was a true master of navigation, yet he failed. Imagine you, who have never even been on a boat, not even twenty meters out to sea."

"With your help, your instruction, and some luck, I'm going to try. If I don't succeed, bad luck," I said with a look that left no doubt about my decision.

From that day on, he began giving me lessons that not even the most skilled of my teachers could have done better. He patiently taught me the art of navigation—how to handle a compass, how to orient myself by day and by night, and the art of fishing, which I would need during the journey. On some dark nights, we would go out in his boat, and discreetly, I would board it. He would then teach me how to fish, how to find where the fish were, how to row against the current, and how to make use of the tide, the winds, and the Gulf Stream, which could be treacherous or friendly, depending on how it was used. I spent several weeks hiding at Inocencio's house, and I began to feel like he was part of my family.

One fine day, Inocencio brought the news that the Mariel port had been opened for anyone who wanted to go to the United States.

I couldn't use that route without taking a huge risk, but I didn't rule out the possibility of taking advantage of it if it was feasible.

I asked Inocencio to buy some hair dye for me and explained my plan.

He brought the dye and peroxide; I shaved and cut my hair in a German style, dyeing it blonde—my hair, my eyebrows, and the mustache I had grown. I even dyed the hair on my arms and chest. I looked like I stepped right out of a campy movie.

My idea was to pretend to be gay and leave through Mariel, as they were letting homosexuals leave with much ease.

Before heading to Mariel, I wanted to see my house from afar and, if possible, my wife and beloved son.

I put on some clothes belonging to Inocencio's son that were a bit tight on me, which accentuated my apparent homosexuality. I transformed my identity card again, this time inventing a name: Justo López, and I placed a new photo on it. I left for Pinar del Río during the day, and upon reaching the vicinity of my house, I noticed some strange activity. I went to the porch of a house a block away from mine, where I saw a "colleague" sitting, who, judging by his appearance, was a homosexual. I asked him how things were in the neighborhood, saying I wanted to go to Mariel to see if I could leave from there. He, being in solidarity with me because we were on the same side, told me he was also planning to use that route. He mentioned all the people around who were thinking of leaving through Mariel and pointed to my house:

"A widow and her son are leaving tomorrow. They've already sent the Committee people to organize a repudiation rally."

He invited me to his house, subtly suggesting that he lived alone. To avoid drawing any negative attention to myself, I told him I would return the next day because I had many things to do.

I began to wander around, always cautiously. My disguise could be discovered. I didn't have the soul of a homosexual, much less that of an actor.

I went to a seedy hotel in the city center and asked for a room. The receptionist told me bluntly:

"We don't allow any "queer stuff" here, you hear me, sweetheart? If anything happens, I'll call the police."

I lay down on a damp bed with sheets that hadn't been changed for at least a month and started thinking about what I would do. After several hours of meditation, I made up my mind. I would go to Mariel to see what I could accomplish and wait for Dolores and Vladimir to leave before trying myself.

I went to the Interprovincial Terminal, which was packed with people. I bribed a driver with fifty pesos and got on a Pinar-Havana bus. I got off at Guanajay and took another bus to the port. Everyone looked at me with mocking expressions, thinking I was surely going to Mariel to take advantage of the situation and get out.

It was morning when I arrived at the port. It looked like a boiling cauldron with so many people. The confusion was overwhelming. On the street, I met two homosexuals—real ones—who told me:

"Our time has come, girls; let's take advantage of it."

I laughed at the joke, but I didn't join them; I couldn't adapt to the idea of hanging out with that kind of people.

I was circling the area very carefully, and suddenly, I felt a chill down my spine. I was covered in goosebumps because, as I looked at a group of soldiers, I recognized a figure, almost with his back to me, unmistakably, as the "Hound of the Baskervilles." He was unmistakable with his beard and dark glasses. It gave me a bad feeling, and I began to back away when I saw a bus arrive, and Dolores and Vladimir got off. My heart raced. They were there, less than fifteen meters away, and I couldn't get close to them. I observed Gilberto, who made some gestures, giving orders not to lose sight of them. I felt powerless and defenseless. They were right there, and I couldn't do anything... I would wait for them to leave and then think about what to do next.

From a distance, I watched all of Dolores's movements, her comings and goings, and finally, her departure with Vladimir to the pier, where she boarded a white yacht. I waited with true impatience until they set sail. I saw Gilberto's maneuver, using a patrol boat to follow the yacht. There was no longer any doubt—he was after me. I needed to get out of there urgently, and so I did.

I made my way back and arrived at Puerto Esperanza just before dawn. I called on Inocencio, told him everything that had happened, with tears in my eyes and sobs I couldn't control. He listened in silence, respecting my sadness, and then said some words that partially comforted me:

"Homero, you must learn from the unpleasant experiences and focus on the good things. Thank God your family is safe right now in a free country."

That gave me some encouragement, and I went to bed, although I couldn't sleep because the image of Dolores and Vladimir on that boat, possibly leaving me forever, wouldn't leave my mind.

The next day, I asked Inocencio again to buy me hair dye, this time brown, and I dyed my hair to a color similar to my natural one. I applied Vaseline to my hair and slicked it back. I shaved off my mustache.

I was a new person, and now I had to devise new plans.

CHAPTER 20

Gilberto spent the entire day in a state of high alert. It was in vain; no one resembling Homero appeared along the way. He had reviewed the list of people one by one and even scanned the faces of all the men from a distance, regardless of age, including some *pájaros* (homosexuals) who were making a big fuss to get out. He couldn't trust anyone. The next day, he left instructions with several of his agents and headed to Pinar del Río, where he had been urgently summoned by his immediate superior.

When he arrived at the State Security Department, he was ordered to go to the Commander's office. He identified himself to the secretary, and shortly after, he was told to enter.

"Captain Gilberto, do you think this is a circus and I'm a clown?" the Commander said with a scowl, his voice raised, without even asking him to sit down.

"I... I don't know, Commander. I was carrying out a mission," Gilberto stammered, feeling as if his anal sphincter might relax from fear.

"I give the orders for missions here, you *comemierda* (idiot). Don't mess with me, or I'll make your life miserable, just so you know," the Commander said, his eyes nearly bulging out of their sockets.

"Forgive me, Commander. I know perfectly well who's in charge here, but the mission..." Gilberto began, but the Commander cut him off.

"If you know I'm in charge, then how the hell do you take most of my men to Mariel and leave me almost without officers, without even informing me?"

"Comrade Commander, I left a note explaining everything with your secretary and mentioned that I was at your service by radio," Gilberto said, almost on the verge of tears.

"What you did will cost you dearly. I swear I won't forgive you for this. Get out of here immediately before I put a bullet in your head."

Gilberto left as quickly as he could, almost running. He was so terrified of his boss that he could hardly breathe just seeing him from a distance.

He went to his office and felt that everyone turned their faces away as he passed by, with a few even wearing mocking smiles.

He collapsed into his chair, feeling utterly defeated. What was happening to him? How had he lost the credibility and trust of his superiors recently? And all because of that damned Homero García. How much he hated him! He, and only he, was the cause of all his misfortunes. If things continued like this, he would be demoted, or worse, expelled from the Ministry.

His head throbbed with an excruciating pain. It felt as if a vein was about to burst in his brain. He was lost. He was nobody. His boss hadn't even had the decency to close the door when he hurled all those insults at him.

Tears of rage, humiliation, hatred, and fear began to flow from his sunken, half-closed eyes. What was going to become of his life?

After a few hours of being in a state of despondency, unable to think about anything other than Homero, he heard a knock at the door.

It was an orderly with a letter. He opened it with trembling fingers and read:

Memorandum;

To 1st Captain Gilberto Duarte Fernández Subject: Transfer of Duties

The General Staff of the State Security Department of Pinar del Río Province orders your transfer to the municipality of La Palma, where you will report tomorrow to Lieutenant Jorge Salcedo, Head of that Unit. We hope that your services will be efficient this time and useful to the tasks assigned to us by the Socialist Homeland.

Signed: [...] Provincial Commander of the State Security Department, Ministry of the Interior Approved: [...] Provincial Delegate of the Ministry of the Interior

Gilberto read the letter several times, unable to internalize it. Was this real? A dream? A nightmare? He was being transferred to some random municipality, reporting to a mere lieutenant; he, who was a First Captain and a genius within the organization, was being humiliated simply because he had taken some initiative.

He decided to go to the Commander's office to explain things better; surely, the Commander would revoke this order. However, the secretary stopped him cold:

"Captain, I have express orders from the Commander not to let you in. Besides, I advise you not to speak with him, as he's in a rage," the secretary said in an authoritative tone.

What was happening? Even the secretaries were treating him like a subordinate.

He went to retrieve his jeep, but the driver said apologetically:

"Captain, you've been assigned another vehicle, so you'll need to go to the Head of Transportation to get it."

"Another car!" What was happening? Was this a complete downfall?

He went to the Head of Transportation's office, and without much explanation, he was given the keys to a rundown Chevrolet parked at the back of the building.

He looked at the wreck and, unable to believe what was happening to him, got in, turned the key, and after a sputtering noise, the engine started with a sound that resembled a ship. "Must have a bad spark plug," he managed to think.

He bumped along out of the building where he had once been treated almost like a prince—Prince Machiavelli.

He arrived at his apartment and began packing his few belongings. He only had a few field uniforms, one ceremonial uniform, and two or three changes of civilian clothes that he rarely used because, since working in the Department, he had only worn military attire.

His mind was flooded with memories of his childhood, of his friend Hans, who, through his tales, had instilled in him a passion for intelligence and counterintelligence work, perhaps unintentionally or perhaps preparing him for the future.

How was it possible that such things were happening to him, someone who had known from the time he was old enough to reason that he would be the best investigator in the world? He was going to embody all the characters Hans had described to him over the years in their long conversations.

He couldn't believe he had made these mistakes in his life. He was the most important person to walk these grounds and had to rub shoulders with inferior minds and tolerate them.

What was happening? How was it possible that because of an insignificant dentist, who had nothing special except some intelligence, this was happening to him—him, a genius of security, a master in the arts of military intelligence who, on his own and without anyone knowing, had read some of Hitler's works, especially *Mein Kampf*, of which he was proud because none of those dimwits even knew of that superior being's masterpiece?

He clearly remembered the classes he had taken in the course that KGB officers had taught years earlier, ~~to which he had been honored to attend.~~ It was true that the methods were unorthodox and even far exceeded those used by Batista's thugs, who were amateurs compared to those Soviet officers.

He had always done what he was taught. He had put all the theoretical lessons into practice with his enemies. Why were they now punishing him? Why were they humiliating him in such an unfair way?

Ah, but one day, those bureaucrats would bow at his feet. He would have them on their knees, begging for forgiveness for doubting his limitless capabilities. How absurd everything was! His own teachers in the art of defending the values of socialism, those who had taught him to act against the enemies, were now turning against him.

The tactics he used were those his "teachers" had taught him. And now he was the bad guy?! What was happening? He didn't understand anything!

He went to the kitchen, grabbed a bottle of Santiago rum, and began drinking large gulps. A few hours later, he finished that one and opened another, but after only a couple of sips, he collapsed to the floor as if struck by lightning. He was nearly comatose.

CHAPTER 21

Several days passed during which my mind devised various plans. Each time I thought of one and discussed it with Inocencio, he, with great goodwill, pointed out the negative aspects. I would then begin to think of another plan, and so on, until one fine day, we both agreed on one that had potential. We then dedicated ourselves to perfecting it. There could be no mistakes, as they would be costly—possibly with our lives.

I needed, among other things, to memorize everything that this good man, with so much patience, told me about the art of navigation and fishing. We also set up his rowboat in my room and built a mast that wasn't too large but strong enough to withstand the strong winds that sometimes battered the Florida Straits. We made sails out of bedsheets, one main sail and another secondary one, and added everything needed to maneuver them. Inocencio caulked the entire boat; we secured several medium-sized inner tubes around the boat, leaving three inside to serve as life preservers and spares. I obtained a tire pump, several plastic containers to store water, and three empty cans with lids to carry biscuits, bread, and other food items.

And so, the days passed. I stayed indoors during the day, and when Inocencio went fishing at dawn and there was no danger, I would go out with him to practice the art of navigation and fishing using an old friend's boat, claiming that his own boat was under repair because it was rotting.

During those days, I felt content; I assumed my family was safe in Miami. On the other hand, I was sad because my parents hadn't gone, so I hadn't seen them with Dolores. Did my wife tell my parents that I was alive? I reasoned it was very likely because Dolores was a very sensitive woman and probably didn't want to torment my parents with the thought that I was dead. Even the Security personnel had informed them that I had disappeared after a traffic accident, but they wouldn't consider me dead until my body was found.

I felt a strong need to see my parents, who were poor, old, and suffering. But reason told me that it wasn't possible without taking an enormous risk. With Dolores and Vladimir out of Cuba, only my parents remained, and the Security forces knew that. They must have had the CDR members, the police, the MTT, and all the informants in the area watching the house. My parents weren't as clever as Dolores, so I didn't take the risk, more for their safety than mine, as they could be accused of harboring a fugitive and imprisoned, or at the very least, mistreated.

Another thing I wanted to do was communicate with Dolores in Miami to ensure they were safe. That was also too dangerous, but I could do it indirectly.

To that end, I instructed Inocencio to call Dolores's parents and, without giving his real name, ask about her and Vladimir. Inocencio called and said he was a friend of hers who used to sell her chickens, eggs, and other products, and wanted to know where she was because her house was empty, and he had heard she had left the country. Her parents confirmed that she had indeed left, that she was in Miami with her son at the home of her "late husband's" uncle, and that they had recently spoken with her.

A sense of calm settled in my heart upon hearing that. From then on, I only had to worry about my own situation. Thank God, my family was safe and sound.

As the days passed, however, Inocencio grew increasingly concerned. It was mid-1980, and hurricane season had begun. From June to October, tropical hurricanes frequently hit the island, and a storm had been announced that, despite forecasts predicting it would pass through the eastern provinces, could always change course. These storms often veered north-northeast, complicating navigation through the Florida Straits. The weather needed to be extremely favorable for a successful crossing, and experienced fishermen never got that wrong. It was impressive how they could detect, by smell and hearing, when bad weather was approaching, when it would rain, and when the sea would calm down.

Everything was properly prepared, and in the days following the hurricane that passed far from the eastern shores and didn't enter the Florida Straits, the sea was as calm as a plate every night. I thought it was the ideal time, but Inocencio, with his experience, told me, "After the calm comes the storm." And sure enough, after a few days, bad weather began, bringing rain across the entire national territory. Torrential downpours caused floods in various parts of the country, especially along the southern coast.

It lasted over two weeks, and I was starting to lose patience. My nerves were getting worse by the day. Inocencio, with the wise calm of a fisherman, kept telling me, "Patience, Homero, your day will come."

Finally, the weather cleared up completely, the sun appeared, and the sea, once raging like a mythological monster, slowly released its fury and fell into a tranquil slumber. A gentle breeze drifted among the stars that shone infinitely above. Could this be the time to set off?

Inocencio listened to the weather report and confirmed that it was. Days of fair weather were coming, and the waves during those days wouldn't be a concern for small craft navigation, so my departure was imminent.

I started trembling with emotion, and Inocencio quickly prepared all the provisions: enough water for more than six days, food adequate for seven days... I went to retrieve the weapons I had hidden, and fortunately, I hadn't lost them. Though the storm had uncovered them, and they were rusty, I set about drying and cleaning them. Fortunately, the mandatory military training I received during university came in handy for these tasks.

The departure was set for that night; I prepared myself for the most extraordinary adventure of my life. I trusted God to guide me. Despite my desperation to reunite with my family and flee from that cursed place (my beloved homeland), I confess I was dying of fear. I really have to admit it—I was terrified, and even though I didn't want to show it to my friend Inocencio, it was difficult to hide it.

These comforting words relieved my tension:

"Don't be ashamed; we all feel fear of the future in life. We are human beings, and that's one of the things that makes us think carefully before doing something foolish."

"I know it's normal to be afraid, Don Inocencio, but mine seems too much. I don't know if I'll be able to control it."

"You will, my son, because you're determined, and you have a goal to achieve. That will make you strong," he said with certainty.

The shadows of the night fell upon the beach. The zero hour was approaching. After midnight, my first experience as a sailor would begin. "God will guide me," I thought, fixing that thought in my mind.

CHAPTER 22

The sun's heat streaming through the living room window woke Gilberto as it hit him squarely in the face. He was lying on the floor, fully clothed, with a bitter taste in his mouth and the stench of alcohol on his breath. His head throbbed as if it might burst, and when he tried to stand and walk, dizziness and cold sweats took over. He stumbled to the bathroom and began vomiting yellow, bitter bile. He knelt by the toilet for several minutes before dragging himself to the shower. He turned on the cold water and let it wash over him for more than fifteen minutes until he shivered like a leaf in the wind. He dried off with a towel, rubbing his skin hard to bring back some warmth, and feeling slightly better, he dressed in civilian clothes.

In the kitchen, he forced himself to prepare a hearty breakfast. An empty stomach wasn't good, he knew that. Though he had no appetite, he drank strong coffee with little sugar, orange juice, and ate a ham and cheese sandwich. Being a *"seguroso"* (a pejorative term for State Security agents) had its perks, like access to a well-stocked military market. Occasionally, a "guataca"—an ass-kisser—would give him something extra for free, thinking it might save them trouble if they ever needed his help. They were wrong. He despised those people even more and treated them worse than anyone else.

He collapsed onto the bed and slept for two hours. When he woke, the aspirin he had taken with breakfast had dulled the pain. He dressed in his military uniform, packed his few personal belongings (everything else belonged to the Ministry of the Interior), got into the decrepit Chevrolet they had assigned him, and set off for La Palma, where he had been "assigned"—or rather "punished"—for doing his duty too zealously.

His boss must have been glad to get rid of him. Gilberto overshadowed him, and his subordinates couldn't stand him, probably out of envy. He hated them all—his boss, his subordinates—and above all, he hated Homero García, the cause of all his problems. "I won't rest until I see him at least imprisoned, or better yet, executed," he thought relentlessly.

The gas tank was full, at least something worked well in that wreck of a car. He took the central road and turned left when he saw a sign for La Palma. Upon reaching the town center, he went to the State Security municipal offices. Despite being a small town, they had very good equipment and a strong presence. He knew why—one of the thirty-two guesthouses for the *Comandante en Jefe* was nearby. Although it was vacant most of the year, only Fidel's personal security staff and anyone he personally authorized could enter. It was a mansion fit for a magnate like Aristotle Onassis, where the *Jefe Máximo* could relax from the intense responsibilities of leading the Homeland.

He presented himself to Lieutenant Salcedo, trying to give an explanation that wouldn't seem dishonorable. But Salcedo cut him off bluntly:

"I know why you're here. I've been ordered to take you under my command, but I'm warning you, if you do anything I haven't ordered, you'll regret it. Remember, a warned soldier doesn't die."

Gilberto froze with embarrassment. Being spoken to like that, despite being an officer of higher rank, stung. But he bit back the retort that came to mind. Now wasn't the time.

Salcedo handed him the key to a room at the end of a corridor in the same building. Gilberto took the keys and brought his belongings to the room. It was basic: a single bed, a medium wardrobe, and a small, dirty bathroom. He dropped off his things and returned to his new boss.

Salcedo didn't wait for him to ask about his mission. "You'll patrol Puerto Esperanza with a soldier I'm assigning as your partner. Focus on any attempts to leave the country illegally. After the Mariel exodus, we need to stop this."

Gilberto complained about the car they had given him, saying it had mechanical problems. They gave him a two-door jeep with G-2 insignia. The soldier assigned to him was both his driver and his shadow. Gilberto knew that the soldier's real mission was to watch him and report back to Salcedo.

The road between La Palma and Puerto Esperanza had many curves, but it was short, and they arrived quickly. At the Security office, Gilberto introduced himself to the officer in charge and gathered the information he needed. He knew he had to redeem himself with his superiors, and the only way to do that was through efficient work.

He received a list of people suspected of not supporting the regime, as well as the addresses of those arrested for counter-revolutionary activities. He planned to visit each house personally.

After several days of investigation, he came across the family of a fisherman named Inocencio, whose son had been imprisoned for trying to take a fishing boat to the North with a group of *gusanos* from Havana. Like the other cases, he went to the CDR to gather information about Inocencio and his son, Daniel. They told him that Inocencio was over seventy years old and had almost given up fishing after his son was imprisoned. But in recent weeks, he had been seen going out to fish at night with a borrowed boat, as his own was under repair.

Gilberto's instincts told him something unusual was going on, and he dug deeper into this case that caught his attention. Trusting his intuition, he passed by Inocencio's house several times and gave his phone number to the CDR and the State Security personnel, instructing them to inform him immediately if they noticed anything unusual.

He continued updating his knowledge of the area. After several days, he received a call about something suspicious related to Inocencio. A fisherman who had worked with Inocencio's son didn't have a favorable opinion of him due to the "mess" he had caused.

Gilberto went to the CDR and spoke with the fisherman.

"What did you see that seemed unusual?" he asked.

"Comrade Captain, what seems strange to me is that old Inocencio, who didn't want anything to do with fishing and hardly left his house, is now fishing a lot at night. And I think someone was with him, hiding in the boat," the fisherman replied.

"Have you noticed anything else unusual?" Gilberto continued.

"He's been seen buying food for what looks like a several-day trip, which seems unlikely at his age. And it sounds like he's been hammering or repairing something on his boat, which he keeps in a shed."

"That's very strange and important. I'll personally take care of the case," said Gilberto. "Pay close attention and inform me of even the slightest detail."

Gilberto sensed something unusual. He went to the office and requested a secure house near Inocencio's where someone could be stationed to keep watch. He assigned a soldier to monitor Inocencio's movements day and night.

Despite his surveillance, Gilberto hadn't seen Inocencio but had a photo to identify him. He returned to La Palma and reported his findings to Lieutenant Salcedo. He requested permission to investigate further, which was granted.

That night, around eleven, a call came in reporting unusual activity. Gilberto and his driver sped to the area near the fisherman's house. After contacting the informant, they proceeded to the house where the lookout was stationed. From their vantage point, Inocencio could be seen maneuvering to take the boat from his shed, mounted on a kind of cart with plow wheels. The two men waited to see what would unfold as the boat was brought to the shoreline and left afloat. Afterward, Inocencio returned to his house, and they continued watching, expecting further movement. When a long period passed without any sign of his return, Gilberto decided to investigate the house himself. Something didn't feel right; once again, he was gripped by that eerie sensation of danger approaching.

He reached the door, which was slightly ajar, and knocked, shouting:

"State Security! Everyone come out with your hands up!" His Makarov pistol was cocked, as was his assistant's. "You have five seconds to come out, or we'll come in by force, and I won't show mercy to anyone," he commanded in a loud and imperious voice.

CHAPTER 23

Comandante Pineda, then the Provincial Director of the Ministry of the Interior (Minint) in Pinar del Río, was on his way to Havana. He was in his four-door jeep, which people jokingly called "Boniato" because it was round like that tuber and as clumsy as all the things produced by the Soviet Union. He had been summoned by the National Chief to discuss a very important, last-minute matter. While on the road, he was reading the folder that detailed the events leading to this visit.

The report covered the counterrevolutionary demonstrations that had recently taken place in the province, alarming everyone in the government. It also mentioned a Captain Gilberto, whom Pineda knew well and for whom he felt no sympathy, but at least he recognized the man had a commendable sense of duty in carrying out the missions assigned to him. At least that's what he believed.

Pineda was also thinking about the surprise he would give his wife, because he hadn't told her about this trip as he usually did. His stay would be very short, and he didn't want her to get her hopes up, thinking he would stay home longer than necessary. He dozed off for the rest of the journey, and when they neared the Minint offices, his driver woke him.

The meeting with the Director was unpleasant. He was harshly criticized for the work being done in his province, which many considered a cornerstone of the counterrevolution. He was reprimanded and told to improve his performance or risk losing the prestige he had earned through his dedicated service to the Revolution.

Pineda left the offices furious, both with his subordinates and with himself. It was true; he had relaxed a bit in his work over time, but he couldn't admit that to the Minint Chief.

He arrived at his house and called out for his wife, as he always did, but there was no answer. He went from the living room to the kitchen, thinking she might be doing something and had gotten distracted, but she wasn't there. He climbed the stairs to the bedrooms, opened the door, and—

Dammit! What the hell is this?" was all he could say because there in his own bed was his wife, naked with a young man.

The shock and fear were evident on the faces of both his unfaithful wife and the young man, who was quite handsome and athletic. Instinctively, they covered their naked bodies with the sheet.

Without thinking, Pineda pulled his pistol from its holster, cocked it, and squeezed the trigger, ready to kill them both on the spot. The pistol, which he rarely used and neglected to clean out of carelessness, jammed and didn't fire. Enraged, he charged at the bed and began punching both his wife and the adulterer with all his might. Instead of defending himself, the young man bolted from the room, completely naked, and fled down the stairs.

Bleeding from her nose and mouth, his wife, sobbing uncontrollably, begged for forgiveness, pleading with him not to hurt her anymore, asking for mercy. He stopped hitting her but grabbed her by the throat, nearly choking her as he dragged her off the bed and out into the hallway.

"Look at yourself, you degenerate! Look at the life I've given you! Don't you remember the misery you lived in when I met you? Don't you remember the hunger you endured with your family? I pulled you out of that hell, made you 'somebody,' and this is how you repay me, you whore," he raged, his voice shaking with anger.

"Forgive me... please... don't hurt me anymore," she replied, overwhelmed with regret.

He glared at her with a look of pure contempt, as one might look at a repulsive insect. He released her, and she crumpled to the floor, a sobbing, pitiful heap. With barely contained rage, he said:

"Pack your things and get the hell out of here. I never want to see you in my house again."

"And my children... I mean, our children. What's going to happen to them? What will they say? How will they suffer because of my actions? I understand your anger, but please, forgive me... do it for them. They're innocent in all this," she cried, desperate.

He stared at her with a rage he had never felt before. He wanted to say many things but held back. Finally, he said:

"You'll stay in the house with my children, but forget I exist. If I ever hear that you're back to your whoring ways, believe me, I'll kill you and your damned lover."

With that, he stormed out of the house and got into his jeep. The driver, who had heard almost everything and had seen the naked young man flee, didn't utter a word. He knew that saying anything at that moment could result in Pineda's wrath being redirected at him, despite being innocent in the matter.

All he heard from his boss was:

"Let's go, dammit. Get us the hell out of here."

CHAPTER 24

Darli, the name she had given herself after moving to Havana with Pineda, was sitting on the hallway floor, too drained to move. Her face, chest, and arms ached; she was still bleeding from her nose, and clotted blood covered her lips and gums. One of her teeth throbbed painfully, loosened by the brutal blows. Immobilized by the pain, she could only think. Memories of her childhood, when she was called Sinforosa—her birth name, which she hated—came flooding back. She remembered the palm-board shack with a guano roof where she lived with her parents, twelve siblings, and grandmother. The images of that miserable, precarious life that God had offered her entire family remained vivid in her mind.

She recalled with precision the day she was digging up sweet potatoes from the small plot where her father and brothers also grew yucca, plantains, and beans—their basic diet—along with corn, which they used to make "funche," a coarse cornmeal ground at home... And when she looked toward the forest at her side, she saw men dressed in green, bearded, hairy, filthy, and smelling like a sow in heat, armed with rifles and pistols, approaching her.

At first, she felt fear—she remembered it clearly now—but then something inside her told her there was nothing to be afraid of. They looked like rebel soldiers, the kind she had heard were fighting in the Sierra Maestra mountains in the eastern part of the country where they lived.

One of them, a young man not yet twenty who seemed to be the leader of the six others with him, said:

"Don't be afraid; we didn't come to harm you. We just need some food, but we'll pay for it."

"We don't even have enough for ourselves," she managed to say, "so how could we sell you anything? If my father finds out I sold you a sweet potato, he'll tear the skin off my back," the girl said.

The men began laughing at how she said this, but the one who seemed to be the leader spoke with a serious expression:

"Don't worry; if you don't want to, we'll leave."

"I feel sorry for you because you look hungry. I'll see what I can do," she said sympathetically toward the young man.

With that, she dug up a few more sweet potatoes, then went to the yuccas and pulled out a few of those too. She gave them two bunches of ripe plantains and asked them to leave quickly, because if her father caught her giving them this, he would kill her.

"We'll protect you if it comes to that," the young man said, ordering his men to carry the produce. "We'll be nearby," he added before heading back to the forest from which they had come.

Darli then remembered what her father did when he noticed the missing produce. With a thick belt, he lashed her repeatedly across the back and buttocks, insisting that if she gave away their food again, he would kill her.

The next day, she was sitting under the shade of a *guácima* tree, covered in bruises from the beating, her entire body aching, when they came again. The young man looked at her with such tenderness and pity that it moved her deeply, and he said:

"Do you want us to kill him?"

"No... Nooo..." was all she could say. "He's my father; he's brutish, but he's my father. He could do it."

"Then what will you do?" he asked gently.

"I don't know," she replied.

"Why don't you come with us to the mountains?"

"With you? To the mountains?" she asked, scared.

"Yes, that way you can escape your father's beatings and start a new life. I promise no one will harm you as long as I'm alive."

Many questions without answers raced through her mind. Her feelings were jumbled, but the possibility he offered didn't seem unpleasant. She imagined leaving that shack, escaping the daily hardships. No more enduring her brothers' constant whining about unwashed clothes, dirty dishes, or the cornmeal being a little burnt. There was so much to gain by leaving. At thirteen, she was already a woman in every sense, and she had always been very decisive.

"I'll go!" she said in response and left with those men to experience life as a guerrilla, the wild life in the mountains. She didn't know what she was getting into or why she was willing to go with those total strangers, but something deep inside told her she could trust that young man because the life she was about to have couldn't be worse than the one she suffered through rather than lived.

She recalled the months of fear, the battles she witnessed but wasn't allowed to participate in, the relentless marches when they were being pursued, but also the sweetness with which that young man, so determined, honorable, and passionate, treated her. One day, she gave herself to him completely, body and soul, and became a woman. And she was happy.

When the Revolution triumphed, she went with her husband to Havana in the caravan with Fidel. Upon arriving in the capital, they were given an apartment to live in. Despite his youth, her husband was already a captain, and later he was promoted by Camilo himself to commander.

From that point on, her life changed. Her husband climbed the ranks within the military, then the national police, and later the Ministry of the Interior, where he held very important positions.

Her life changed, and she changed her name. She no longer liked being called Sinforosa. She would be Darli, like how Americans called their girlfriends in the movies.

Over time, they had three children and moved to a two-story house in Miramar with a pool and everything, and she became the wife of Commander Pineda.

But one day, he was assigned to the province of Pinar del Río. He said it would be for a short time and that it wasn't worth moving the children out of their good schools, that he would come to Havana frequently since it wasn't far, and time passed, years went by, and his work intensified. Her husband's visits became less frequent and shorter. She lived alone with her children, who spent most of their time in school. In that big house, she was as lonely as a dog. It was almost worse than when she lived in the shack in the Sierra where she was born.

First, she asked her husband to station a guard at the house because she was afraid of being robbed. Then she asked for a car to do the shopping and take the children to school and for him to buy her more clothes since the ones she had were old and worn out. He always complied but with difficulty. Sometimes he would say with a scowl, "Remember who you were, where you came from. I won't allow you to get airs. You're still the same *guajira* who joined us in the Sierra." That bothered her, but since it was true, she kept quiet.

She began to feel anger at first, then contempt because she felt misunderstood. Alone, almost without a husband, without family, visits weren't allowed, and she spent her days and nights with that feeling of emptiness.

Until one day, she noticed the new recruit assigned to guard the house. Sometimes he would abandon his post, strip down to his military underwear, and dive into the pool without asking permission or anything. What audacity!

When she saw him do it a second time, she called him over and said it was disrespectful to use the pool without permission, that it wasn't his job to do so.

"Sorry, Mrs. Darli, I thought it wasn't a big deal to use the pool," he said with a smile as fresh as a lettuce. "You know, we have a pool at home too; my father is a vice minister, and I'm used to taking a dip every day, so I thought it was no big deal. But if the lady decides I shouldn't do it anymore, your orders will be obeyed," he said boldly.

Instead of getting angry, she found it amusing. She looked him in the eyes and apologized for the harsh way she had reprimanded him, then gave him permission to swim every day whenever he wanted, as long as he didn't neglect his duties. He responded:

"You are a goddess of love."

That was how their relationship began, first as friends, then as lovers. The young, bold, athletic man stole her heart and breathed new life into her. Happiness had arrived until that fateful day when her husband caught them. She didn't feel shame, but she did feel fear. Fear of losing everything—the house, the children, her car, her good life. She was terrified at the thought of being thrown out and having to return to the misery she had escaped.

Another thing that tormented her was that, living in a world so far removed from her family's, she hardly had any contact with them. She didn't want them to visit; she was embarrassed by their poverty and ignorance in front of her neighbors and acquaintances. As a result, she and her family were estranged. She would rather die than return to the misery and brutality she had once left behind, never intending to return.

She had to win her husband back, bring him back to her side, regain his trust. Of course, that was what she had to do instead of writhing on the floor in pain. She had to think about getting him back. She would go to Pinar del Río, pamper him, beg for forgiveness on her knees, do anything to be forgiven. She still had enough charm to do it. "This is my last move, and I have to win," she told herself.

CHAPTER 25

Pineda left Havana in a rage. He was completely demoralized. In just one day, his boss had reprimanded him, primarily because of Gilberto's incompetence— that little captain who had been driving him crazy—and then because of the scene with his wife in bed with another man. Damn her! She was nothing but a whore! A *comemierda guajira* he had pulled out of misery, and now she repaid him like this! And that shameless bastard, placed there as a favor to his father, a vice minister, so that the little "bourgeois" wouldn't have to go to the mountains and dig trenches like everyone else in the SMO (Compulsory Military Service)! He was just a few blocks from his home with all the privileges in the world, and on top of that, he was sleeping with his wife!

Suddenly, it occurred to him that he couldn't let this slide. He had to get revenge. He gave a brusque and rude order to the driver to turn back to Havana, and they went to the General Staff of the FAR (Revolutionary Armed Forces), where his friend and fellow comrade from the Sierra, Bartolo Rojas, worked as Chief of the Coast Guard.

He found Bartolo in his office and asked him to join him for lunch at a discreet restaurant nearby. He needed to discuss something very personal.

At the restaurant, they sat apart from everyone else. The place, reserved for foreigners and those with foreign currency, was half-empty. They could enter any place they desired; after all, they were *mayimbes*, as the high-ranking leaders of the Revolution were called.

Pineda recounted everything in great detail. Bartolo was his soul mate, his comrade from the Sierra and the plains, and he knew Darli (formerly Sinforosa). The worst part was that Bartolo himself had assigned the young man to guard the house at the request of his mother, who was his lover.

"Help me get rid of this son of a bitch," Pineda pleaded earnestly.

"I'll send him to a torpedo boat, and he and his dear father will regret it. That way, I can fulfill my duty to you, my brother," Bartolo replied.

"That's not enough," Pineda protested. "He needs to suffer something worse."

"Leave that to me. You go back to Pinar del Río and continue with your work. I'll take care of screwing over this little punk."

"But how will you do it? Give me a hint," Pineda said, anxious.

"The boat's chief is a brother to me, just like you, and I trust him completely. I'll order him to break that little pimp's ass," Bartolo ~~said, then~~ added that Pineda shouldn't ask any more questions because that was all he could say. "You'll hear news about that little pimp soon," he said in parting after downing an espresso and lighting a special *Cohiba* cigar, one of the "Comandante's specials," as they used to jokingly say.

CHAPTER 26

Wearing the olive-green shorts he had grabbed in his hasty exit from Darli's house, Yaser, the soldier who had made the grave mistake of sleeping with Commander Pineda's wife, returned to his home.

When he entered, he found his mother, who questioned him about why he was dressed like that at such an hour on the street. Since he had no secrets from her—because he hardly ever saw his father due to his many obligations as a vice minister—he told her a modified version of what had happened.

His mother, horrified, immediately realized the magnitude of the danger her son was in. If Commander Pineda saw him again, he would kill him with his bare hands. She was certain of it.

She quickly called her friend, Commander Bartolo Rojas, who had helped get her son that position by violating all the Military Service norms. She begged him to send her son somewhere else.

"Bartolo, please, send my son somewhere far away from Havana," she pleaded with such vehemence that her lover replied:

"You're causing me a lot of trouble with your son lately. This is the last time I'll do something for him."

"I'll be eternally grateful to you, in every way," Lucia, Yaser's mother, shamelessly added.

"I'll place him on a coast guard boat so Pineda won't see him for a long time," he said, laughing over the phone.

"I think that's the best place for my boy," she thanked him for his interest in solving the problem.

The next day, Yaser left for his new post. He was going to serve as a coast guard soldier on a patrol boat with two other men.

He reported to Lieutenant Melchor, a mulatto with a killer's face who commanded the boat, and Salas, a soldier who had previously been a sailor. Just by looking at these two characters, Yaser had a bad feeling. "Well," he thought, "it's better to be with these unpleasant people than to run into Commander Pineda."

He boarded the boat, they cast off, and Salas skillfully steered the 32-foot, armed boat through the calm waters of Mariel Harbor until the coast disappeared from view.

In the middle of the sea, surrounded by a deathly silence, Melchor, with his massive frame, which clearly possessed brutal strength, moved to the bow of the boat. Without saying a word, without any expression on his face, he grabbed Yaser by the belt at the back and lifted him off the deck. Then, with brutal force, he pushed him overboard. Yaser, an experienced swimmer, despite his shock, started swimming away from the boat. Then Salas turned the boat's bow toward him at high speed, and without hesitation, rammed into him, delivering a severe trauma to his skull with the keel. Unsatisfied with the first strike, Salas circled around and rammed the lifeless body of the poor boy again.

The two crew members hauled the corpse onto the boat and brought it back to the marina. They reported to their immediate superior and gave the following report:

"While patrolling the northern coast of Havana Province, I—Lieutenant Antonio Melchor—along with the helmsman Julio Salas and the soldier Yaser Meléndez, experienced an incident in which the latter fell from the boat during a turning maneuver, suffering trauma to the cranial region caused by the head striking the keel of the vessel. It appears that Soldier Yaser, who was not accustomed to being on fast boats, became seasick and fell into the sea, where he succumbed to the trauma and lost his life."

The report was sent by radio to the Chief of Coast Guard Services, who, upon receiving it, picked up the phone and called his brotherly comrade Pineda and said:

"Brother, the mission has been efficiently completed. I'm informing you so you don't have to worry about anything anymore. Relax and continue with your work," he said, hanging up with a satisfied smile on his face.

CHAPTER 27

Commander Rojas entered the building and approached the desk of the officer in charge of receiving visitors.

"Comrade, I have an appointment with Commander Chávez. I am Commander Rojas, Chief of the Coast Guard of the General Staff in Pinar del Río Province," he said with a martial air.

"Please have a seat, Commander. I'll inform the Chief," the officer on duty replied.

Rojas sat down with a concerned expression in one of the many chairs in the waiting room. What could be going on? It was very unusual for him to be summoned there because everyone knew that the military intelligence and counterintelligence service didn't summon anyone without good reason. Despite his rank of commander, despite being a veteran of the Sierra Maestra, despite being a member of the Provincial Party Committee in Pinar del Río... Despite all that, in that place, no one was summoned to be awarded a medal or anything of the sort.

After an interminable twenty minutes, the officer on duty called him and led him down a hallway to an office that was quite ordinary. There was a varnished wooden desk, a swivel chair, a single vinyl-covered armchair, and a portrait of Fidel on the wall.

As soon as Rojas sat down, at the request of the officer on duty, Lieutenant Colonel Arismendi, an old acquaintance from the insurrectionary struggle, entered through a side door. Rojas knew his comrade was the National Chief of Military Intelligence, a person who was ruthless, incorruptible, and trusted by the highest levels of the Government.

Lieutenant Colonel Arismendi extended his hand in greeting and invited Rojas to sit again. From Arismendi's expression, Rojas sensed that something was wrong, and he could only manage to say:

"Comrade, it's good to see you. What's this meeting about?"

"I'll be brief and as objective as possible. I'm very busy and don't have time for pleasantries. I'll get straight to the point," Arismendi said with marked seriousness.

"Things have happened of which we have certainty down to the smallest detail. There's no need to list them because there are matters better left unsaid. What I will tell you is that I'm not speaking as a comrade from the Sierra or as a party friend. I didn't summon you to a restaurant for a private conversation. I've summoned you officially as the Chief of Military Intelligence to tell you that you're crossing the line." Rojas tried to stammer something, but Arismendi cut him off abruptly. "Shut your mouth. I already told you I have little time. Listen and keep quiet.

"Several mistakes have been made, and you are one of the main actors. The names don't matter—whether it's Pineda, Darli, Yaser, Melchor, or any other name. The names are irrelevant. The motives behind the actions—friendship, comradeship, loyalty, etc.—don't matter either. In our homeland, there is only one loyalty, and that loyalty is to Fidel Castro Ruz, our Comandante en Jefe. You know this better than I do. When secret measures are taken without approval from superiors and personal actions are carried out to satisfy the demands of friends, it's concerning. Doing something irregular out of friendship can also betray the homeland. We revolutionaries, we communists, cannot afford to have friends."

"We have done things for the Revolution—both you and I, and many others—that would make our enemies' hair stand on end. For the Revolution, for Socialism, for the Comandante en Jefe, and for the Homeland, everything is valid. For everything else—friends, comrades, women, family, children, father, mother, etc.—there is no justification. You've been warned. I am officially informing you that the next time you take personal action for any reason without approval from higher authorities, you will simply be eliminated. The Revolution forgives no one. No one here is indispensable; we are all replaceable, and we'd rather award a posthumous medal to a martyr than give a second reprimand to a hero, if it comes to that."

After saying this, Arismendi fell silent for a few seconds. Rojas' face was ashen, paler than the white walls of the office. He couldn't find the words to respond; he could only stare at Arismendi's impassive face.

Arismendi stood up and said:

"This conversation is over. You may leave."

Rojas stood up, his legs barely able to support him, and with uncertain steps, he made his way to the office door. Before he could exit, he heard Commander Arismendi say to him:

"Remember this: men die, but the Party is immortal."

CHAPTER 28

Enrique, a nineteen-year-old who had been Yaser's neighbor and friend since elementary school, had been drafted into the Compulsory Military Service at the same time as Yaser. From a very young age, Enrique had been a *bitongo*, a term used to describe the children and relatives of Party leaders who lived a life of pleasure.

His father, who held a high position within the Communist Party in Havana, secured him a cushy spot serving at the Hemingway Marina, where the yachts of the Party and Government magnates, as well as diplomatic personnel in Havana, were docked. His mission was to "guard" these yachts and luxury boats, which allowed him to spend his days drinking beer on every boat he could find, sometimes enjoying Havana Club rum or even his favorite—Scotch whisky.

This was how Enrique lived, enjoying his privileges while the rest of the young men who had no one to "protect" them had to dig trenches for hours on end, day after day, march under the scorching sun, stand guard for eight hours straight in a sentry box, all so they could become men worthy of the Revolution, as they were made to believe.

One afternoon, while resting after lunch at a military base near Hemingway Marina, he saw his friend Yaser board a boat with two other soldiers and set out to sea. It struck him as odd to see Yaser there; he knew Yaser had been guarding a leader's house.

He continued to doze off, waiting to return to the marina for a cup of coffee. Instead, he decided to stay. He had a bad feeling seeing Yaser leave with those two soldiers who had a reputation for being first-class bastards. They always loudly expressed their disdain for the *bitonguitos* who, shielded by their families' power, lived like big shots while others sacrificed to the maximum.

Several hours later, tired of waiting, Enrique saw the boat return with the two soldiers, but Yaser wasn't with them. He thought about asking those two surly men about his friend but decided to keep quiet and ask around later.

The next morning, he woke up with a ravenous appetite, as usual. He went to the kitchen and asked the maid to prepare him a grilled ham and cheese sandwich, just the way he liked it. While he was eating breakfast, he overheard his father telling his mother about the news that had circulated: Yaser had died in a boating accident.

Enrique immediately went to the next room, where his father was having breakfast at the dining table. He asked his father if what he had heard was true.

"Why are you asking?" his father replied. "I know you're very close to Yaser, but the tone of your question is strange."

Enrique told his father everything he had seen the previous day and how uncomfortable the incident had made him feel. His father said:

"Are you sure about what you're saying? This is very serious."

"Yes, Dad, I even stayed there for a few hours. That's the place where they usually dock that boat."

"I'm going to call Yaser's father to find out what's really going on and get to the bottom of this."

Enrique didn't go to the marina that day. He called and said he was feeling unwell and waited until the afternoon to call his father, hoping he would know something concrete about Yaser's situation by then.

Around four o'clock, Enrique's father came home and discussed with his mother and him that the situation was murky, and if the suspicions of those close to Yaser were true, some heads would roll.

Enrique thought to himself: "If things like this happen among 'us'—referring to his father and Yaser's father—what must be happening to the people?"

He was somewhat disillusioned with the way the revolutionary government behaved and was sick of having to see and remain silent, the attitude that had been ingrained in him since childhood. "Do people not have their own thoughts and opinions that they can express?" He wondered if what they so proudly proclaimed about the "justice" of the Revolution was really true. He wanted to know for sure what was going on in the country, to have his own opinion and be able to express it as he should, but on the other hand, he thought about what his mother always told him: "You look better with your mouth shut."

What would come of all this? Would he finally understand, even a little, what that "Revolution" really was?

Time would tell.

CHAPTER 29

Inocencio didn't want me to help him move the boat for safety reasons. Despite his advanced age, he was very strong and accustomed to such tasks. He had spent many years dedicated to the noble work of fishing.

While he was handling the boat, I was checking the weapons and supplies, which would be the last things we would move.

As I was focused on this task, I suddenly heard a voice whispering through the closed backyard window:

"Inocencio, Inocencio, there are G-2 agents watching."

Hearing that chilled me to the bone. I rushed to the window, revolver in hand, and opened it to see who had spoken. But I saw no one. This alarmed me, and when Inocencio returned, I told him what I had heard. Alarmed, Inocencio said:

"Someone has ratted us out. We need to act quickly. You have to get everything out in an instant."

"But how, and through where?" I asked in terror.

"Come to my room quickly, help me lift the bed, and open a wooden hatch on the floor. Bring everything here and get in as fast as you can."

I did as he instructed, and after entering a hole about two meters high and one meter wide, Inocencio closed the hatch, and I heard the bed drop back into place. I gripped the rifle and revolver, ready for anything.

A few minutes later, I heard that unmistakable voice ordering the occupants of the house to come out. Inocencio took a few seconds to respond; I heard the following conversation:

"Are you Inocencio?"

"At your service," Inocencio responded, with a voice that impressed me with its steady tone. That old man was brave!

"Who else is in this house?"

"I live alone; there's no one here with me," Inocencio replied.

"We'll see about that," Gilberto said as he entered with the other officers, who had secured Inocencio by the arm.

I heard footsteps throughout the house as they searched every corner, checking closets, under beds—everything. Fortunately, they didn't notice the hatch where I was hiding.

After the fruitless search, they began interrogating Inocencio.

"Why did you take the boat to the beach?" Gilberto asked.

"I took my boat, which I had repaired, to go fishing. As far as I know, this hasn't been prohibited," Inocencio replied.

"Who has been staying with you these past few days?"

"I don't know who you're talking about. Since my son was imprisoned, I've been living alone."

"You're an elderly man, and I usually respect people like you, but if you're lying, I won't show any consideration. Do you understand?"

"I'm only telling the truth. Have you seen anyone in my house?" he replied.

"At least for today, don't go out fishing. That's an order. We'll see about tomorrow."

Inocencio accompanied the agents to the boat, where they spent a few minutes before returning to sit in the living room with the window open—a period that felt like an eternity to me.

After what seemed like forever, Inocencio came back to the room, knelt beside the bed, and whispered to me:

"Open it a bit so you can get some air; stay there until I tell you otherwise."

"Alright," I said, and I remained in that uncomfortable position, though now a bit more relaxed. Several hours passed this way. Inocencio closed the window, lay down on the bed, and almost at dawn, he lifted the hatch. I emerged from the hiding place, a bit stiff from the uncomfortable position, which reminded me of the day I left "the hole."

I explained to him that the bearded man was the officer who had made my life miserable, and for some reason, either supernatural or diabolical, he had crossed my path again.

All the plans we had carefully forged with so much care and love were falling apart. My life was in danger, as was Inocencio's, and this place was no longer safe. We needed to come up with another plan, but the main thing was to get out of there without being seen, which was going to be really difficult, if not impossible.

After dawn, Inocencio left the house and went to the boat. Nearby, a fisherman who was a member of the CDR was keeping watch. With great naturalness, Inocencio asked him what was going on:

"Why can't I take out my newly repaired boat for a test run?" Inocencio asked.

"Comrade, all I know is that I've been instructed to watch and not let you take it out. For the rest, you'll have to ask the G-2 officer."

"And where can I find him?" he asked.

"Go back home and wait; he'll come by later."

Inocencio returned and informed me of the conversation. I went back into the hiding place.

The hours passed, and in a state of maximum tension, I tried to make myself as comfortable as possible in that hole.

I heard my friend busying himself in the kitchen. He brought me a plate with some hot food. After eating, I handed it back to him.

Later in the afternoon, I heard a jeep pull up in front of the house and the sound of doors opening and closing.

The unmistakable, hateful voice of the bearded man asked Inocencio, this time more politely, to come in and have a word with him.

Inocencio, very naturally, invited him in and offered him coffee, which Gilberto and his assistant declined.

"Someone informed us that they saw you go fishing with someone else one of these nights, which is why we're keeping an eye on this house. Why did you put a mast and sail on the boat?"

"As you can see, comrade, I'm very old and need to rely on a sail to go fishing, which is the only thing that provides me with food. Rowing has become too heavy for me lately," he answered.

"It doesn't seem that way, since you moved the boat with ease."

"It's not strength, but skill, my friend. I've got years of experience."

"Either way, if you go out fishing, do it during the day. Night fishing is prohibited," Gilberto ordered.

"You can't even catch sardines during the day. You wouldn't know that because you're not a fisherman."

"Then eat sardines because if we see you going out at night, we'll shoot without warning, got it?"

He stood up, looking around as if trying to sense something that was alerting him, then got into the jeep and left, with Inocencio watching him as he drove away.

I came out of the hiding place and, in a low voice, apologized to Inocencio for causing him so much trouble.

He looked at me the way one looks at a son and replied:

"You haven't forced me into anything. I'm doing everything of my own free will, and I'm old enough to know what's right or wrong."

I was in a state of deep sadness and confusion. What would I do now? Would I manage to get out of there alive?

Once again, I had been lucky not to be discovered, but all my plans were ruined. I had no idea what was going to happen to me next.

CHAPTER 30

Saturnino Estanislao Rodríguez had been a fortunate man in life. After several years of fishing with a decrepit little boat, one fine day, he won twenty thousand pesos in the lottery. He had bought two sheets of tickets for five pesos and won the first prize. In an instant, he was overwhelmed with joy and made many plans. He considered buying a house or a brand-new car, but then he wondered if it wouldn't be better to buy a decent boat and secure his future with it. He decided on the latter and, after much searching, he bought a beautiful boat. It was built at the shipyards of La Cabaña and had everything he needed—a large refrigerator to freeze the fish, and a first-class, ultra-modern engine.

His real life began with that boat. He hired the son of a lifelong friend, a strong and determined thirteen-year-old boy, to be his assistant, and he started fishing and making money. Slowly, through hard work and sacrifice, he saved enough to build a ~~masonry~~ house with a large yard to plant fruit trees and a small vegetable garden that his children would tend to because he didn't want them to face the dangers he had to endure every day. He wanted his children to study at the university and become "somebody."

His assistant, Danielito, the son of his great friend Inocencio, became a first-rate boat captain. When Saturnino was unwell or sick, Danielito would go out with another hired fisherman and do the work, always with excellent results. He was an honest and hardworking man, just like his father.

Years passed, and Saturnino's life kept improving. He bought another boat, slightly smaller, and leased it to some friends. This way, his economic situation was thriving.

His house bordered Inocencio's at the back and faced the coast, so he decided to build a high concrete wall to protect his garden, where he had fruit trees that delighted him when he wasn't out at sea. He had mango, guava, ~~purple caimito~~, Indian coconut, avocado, red mamcy, Chinese oranges, and tangerines, as well as a vegetable garden that was the envy of many. His children and wife took care of it, growing everything from lettuce, tomatoes, eggplants, and peppers to watercress and even medicinal herbs that his wife knew how to use for different ailments. He left a door in the wall to communicate with Inocencio and so that Daniel, his son, could come over when needed.

Together, with his family, he lived a hardworking but happy life, because they lacked nothing and his children were all on the right track. Life was tough in those days, even more so with the problems caused by the heavy-handed government of Fulgencio Batista. One of his sons, the eldest, enrolled in the Army Officers' School and became a telegraphist lieutenant. He earned a good salary and was in love with his career.

One day, in the final months of 1958, he was sent to the Sierra Maestra as a telegraphist. While under the command of Cowley's troops, he was captured when Fidel triumphed.

He was unjustly accused of collaborating with Batista's regime and was sentenced to a year in the Príncipe prison, from which he emerged very disillusioned with the Revolution. He considered the sentence an injustice.

After he was released from the Príncipe prison, seeing that it had all been a deception and that Fidel's promises were all lies, he decided to leave for the United States.

It was a sadness for the whole family, but shortly after receiving news of how well he was doing in Miami, where he was working for a very powerful company with a very good salary, and the joy of having married a Cuban woman who had been in the city for some time and came from a very good family, they were comforted and saw the departure of their eldest son in a better light.

Around the same time that his eldest son left for the United States, the Government seized Saturnino's boats. For Fidel, having more than one little boat was like owning a fleet.

That destroyed him psychologically. Overnight, his small patrimony, which he had built with so much work, sweat, and tears, was gone.

He and his family couldn't accept it. His children left one by one for the North, following in their elder brother's footsteps. He wouldn't leave—one day, that madman who had taken power would have to go, and perhaps they would return his boats, and his life would return to how it was before.

The only thing that consoled him a little was that Daniel, his assistant, remained the captain of his favorite boat.

Daniel wasn't a communist, but he had supported the Revolution, perhaps because he didn't fully understand what it intended. He was doing the same thing he had done all those years—captaining his boat, although now it wasn't his true owner's boat but the Government's, which he regretted, but it wasn't his fault.

His father, whom he respected and loved very much, would say:

"Take care of my friend Saturnino's boat, because one day they'll have to return it to him."

It was the talk of old men because he knew there was no going back. But out of respect for his father and for the man who had been more than just his boss—a true friend—he accepted it with a smile so as not to disappoint them.

Time passed, and the revolutionary laws, designed to benefit the poor and the workers, weren't yielding the expected results. Every day, the situation became more critical. The fish they caught had to be handed over entirely to the Cooperative, and they could only keep a small amount for their own consumption. They were worse off than before because they didn't even have enough food. Moreover, everyone saw how the *mayimbes* were favored by the Cooperative's administrator. They left with their official cars filled with what they had worked so hard to obtain and were denied.

One day, some old friends of Saturnino's son came from Havana. They offered Daniel a thousand dollars to take them to Florida.

It was very risky, but with that money, he could start a new life in another place where he could have his own boat and become something more than just a government fisherman.

Unfortunately, he was caught, sentenced to ten years in prison, and his boat was given to another captain—an irresponsible man who was part of the Party. "That guy knows less about boats than my grandson," Saturnino had once told his friend Inocencio.

In 1979, Saturnino was diagnosed with cancer in his throat, for which he underwent surgery. He was left with a permanent hoarseness due to the radiotherapy sessions he had to undergo after the operation.

His friendship with Inocencio deepened. He saw the loneliness his poor friend was in and would visit him occasionally to talk.

One night, around eight o'clock, he went to Inocencio's house. He crossed the yard and heard him talking to someone. Saturnino wasn't a nosy person who meddled in others' lives, but since Inocencio was like a brother to him, he managed to overhear part of the conversation. A man named Homero had been sheltered by his friend because he was being persecuted by the Security. He couldn't hear the reasons clearly, but he knew his friend was helping someone who was against the Government.

His first reaction was to return home and talk to Inocencio the next day because he didn't want his friend to get into trouble with the law. After thinking it over, he decided to keep quiet and leave the decision to Inocencio, who was no youngster. If he asked for help, Saturnino would even assist him because he was his best friend and because he wanted to help someone being persecuted by those heartless and merciless communists.

One day, he was on the porch of his house and noticed strange activity at the house of the CDR President, the leader of the local Committee for the Defense of the Revolution. Some military personnel had come to visit him, and they returned several times over the following days.

Worried about this and suspecting that it might have something to do with his friend Inocencio, he began monitoring the movements of the CDR President. One night, he confirmed that they were watching Inocencio, who had taken his boat to the beach, apparently to go fishing. He had lent him his boat before because Inocencio said he was repairing his own. When Saturnino saw the Security people heading to his friend's house, he went through the back door and gave the alarm to someone there he didn't know but who was surely the person the G-2 was after.

That night, he anxiously waited to see what would happen, but apparently, there was no problem. He waited another day, and finally, he decided to have a frank conversation with Inocencio. He called him to his yard and said:

"You know you're like a brother to me. I'm not going to question what you're doing, but I'll tell you that the other night I gave a warning to someone who was at your house because the G-2 agents seemed to be after him."

"I knew the only person who could help me in this town was you, but I didn't want to cause you any trouble. We're both old now, and it doesn't matter much what happens to me. I want to help someone who seems like a good person to me, no matter the cost."

"You can count on my help from now on."

Inocencio told him my true story, which triggered an extraordinary sense of solidarity in Saturnino.

"The first thing we need to do is get your friend out of your house. He's in danger there."

"Do you have any idea how to do that?" Inocencio asked.

"We'll think about it together."

And we had a very fruitful conversation, through which I got to know that other wonderful person who had saved my life once and was willing to risk himself to help me.

Not everything was lost, I thought at the end of that conversation.

God always sent an angel to watch over me. I thanked Him in my prayers for placing so many good people in my path.

The coming days would be decisive in my life.

CHAPTER 31

Gilberto returned to La Palma that night, fuming with anger. Something had gone wrong in the entire operation, and he had a gut feeling that they had been outsmarted by that old fisherman.

He had investigated everything about the man's life and knew well that his son, a certain Daniel, had been arrested and tried for attempting to take a state-owned boat to the United States with a group of Havana residents, among whom was one of their informants, who facilitated the whole affair.

The CDR President was a highly trusted individual due to his past services, and the unverified information that he had seen someone going out to fish with the old man one night didn't sit well with him.

The way he had prepared the operation, nothing should have gone wrong. Therefore, something had gone awry and derailed the mission. His instincts were on edge, like when he embarked on a clandestine operation.

He arrived at dawn, entered his room, collapsed onto the bed fully dressed, and began to mull over recent events.

The image of Homero García, like a diabolical vision, appeared in his mind. Could it be that this had something to do with that man?

He needed to think more objectively; if he continued with this obsession, it would lead to his downfall. After much analysis, he finally fell asleep and, early in the morning, went to Lieutenant Salcedo to submit a report. He didn't want to risk getting into trouble with his superiors again, even though he didn't consider that "little lieutenant" his superior.

"Leave that investigation to the officer in Puerto Esperanza and focus on this order, which is very important," Lieutenant Salcedo said, handing him a memorandum requesting assistance with a case in the neighboring municipality of Cabañas.

Reluctantly, he went to fulfill the order. He was certain that something strange was happening in Puerto Esperanza, and something inside him told him that he, and no one else, should be conducting that investigation. But he didn't want to have any more problems. He would do what that incompetent lieutenant ordered, and that would be the end of it.

He spent several days on that mission. He was radiant with joy; with his shrewdness, he had uncovered a CIA espionage network that had been set up in La Cabaña with the arrest of several suspects. His superiors would see what he was capable of. They would value his intelligence, and he would once again be the respected officer he had always been.

Upon his return to La Palma, he was congratulated by Lieutenant Salcedo for his performance in the case, which boosted his ego. Salcedo now ordered him to go to the municipality of Alonso de Rojas to investigate an action by some counterrevolutionaries that required someone with experience.

Upon hearing the order, his first thought was that they wanted to keep him away from the unit, but when he read the report in his hands, he realized it wasn't an ordinary mission. As if in a vision, he immediately perceived that this had the mark of his rival, Homero.

He left without resting and without even having lunch, despite it being past two in the afternoon and having had only a cup of coffee with milk in his stomach. He went to the town of Alonso de Rojas, met with the officer in charge of Security, who was an old acquaintance from better times, and they went to the scene.

One of the rice storage silos had been destroyed, but it wasn't accidental because a poster had been left at the entrance of the company: "DOWN WITH INJUSTICE, LONG LIVE DEMOCRACY."

There was no need for further analysis; this was the work of his number one enemy. His nemesis had left his mark in the least expected place. But why in that area? That question hammered in his brain.

It felt like a trap. Should he fall into it like a defenseless rat?

He helped, or at least pretended to help, his comrade from the unit in Alonso de Rojas. He kept his suspicions to himself; they could brand him as crazy or obsessive, and he returned to La Palma, pondering the matter all the way. To him, there was no other explanation, but he wasn't going to tell his boss. He was going to devise his own plan, and when he had absolute conviction with evidence of what he had in mind, he would inform them. Then, he would have *carte blanche* on the matter. It would be his masterpiece. He would regain his former prestige. They would call him back to Headquarters in Pinar del Río.

Thoughts raced through his mind with an intensity he had never experienced before, and the plan brewing within him took shape with unusual clarity. His self-esteem, battered by recent events, slowly began to return.

If everything went according to plan, he might even reach headquarters in Havana. Everyone would recognize him for what he truly was: the master of Intelligence within State Security.

It was now or never.

CHAPTER 32

An old saying goes, "The Devil knows more because he is old than because he is the Devil." Those two seventy-year-old friends were endowed with natural intelligence and an extraordinary level of experience. After identifying ourselves and realizing that we had common goals, the three of us reached a unanimous agreement. I needed to do something with my personal touch as far away from that area as possible to divert the attention of that officer who was already becoming a burden to my friends.

Saturnino confessed to us that he had discreetly collaborated with some friends who belonged to an anti-government organization in the southern part of the province. They planned to carry out an operation at the rice silos in Alonso de Rojas, and he had helped them with supplies and a Colt .45 pistol that he had owned since before the Revolution, which had belonged to his son when he was in the military.

He was going to recommend me to one of them, someone he knew for sure could be trusted completely. He handed me a coded note that I couldn't decipher and the address where I could meet his friend. That very night, I left as discreetly as possible, crossing through Saturnino's yard to exit through the front of his house when he gave me the signal.

In addition to the .38 revolver, I took one of the Makarov pistols and two magazines of bullets. I boarded a truck belonging to a friend of Saturnino, who was traveling to Paso Real de San Diego. I stayed there and caught the last bus to Alonso de Rojas.

When I arrived in town, I went to the address Saturnino had given me and found an old house, likely from the early 1900s, located almost next to the local church.

It was close to two in the morning when I knocked on the back door with three spaced knocks, as Saturnino had instructed me. A male voice answered, asking who I was, and I replied:

"I've come to see the bodega mice," which was the password that opened the door to that place.

I was greeted by a man in his fifties, slightly balding, about 5.5 feet tall, with sun-darkened skin—probably a farmer.

"Come in quickly," he said as he saw me.

I entered a dimly lit room that seemed to be the dining room of the house, and after looking the man in the eye, I said:

"I've come on behalf of Saturnino to help with your objective."

"The attack plan has been thoroughly studied," he said after telling me to sit down and offering me a cup of coffee. "The important thing is to act quickly and get out of there immediately."

I agreed with him, and we went over what we needed to do.

He looked me up and down and found me a black shirt and pants that fit. After going over the plan several times, we set out together, dressed in dark clothing, around four in the morning. Wisely, he said:

"From now on is when the guards and militiamen get careless. It's also the time they take a nap because most of them have to work the next morning."

I was dealing with an expert in such matters.

Using two bicycles that he brought from somewhere I wasn't familiar with—I had to wait in a corner inside a doorway—we moved slowly but steadily, always staying as much as possible in the shadows of the houses until we took a road.

A few kilometers ahead, he ordered me to take a dirt path to the left, which led us to some almond trees. We left the bicycles leaning against the trunks.

We returned to the road, walked about eight hundred meters, and entered through a five-strand barbed wire fence, crossing a field that looked like a rice paddy between harvests.

We spotted some cylindrical structures several dozen meters tall, which were the silos where rice was processed, one of the main crops in that area.

Sticking close to the wall and holding our breath, we reached the entrance of the silos. With a key that my companion had, and which I didn't even ask where he got it from, we entered the building and headed to the area where the hoses that operated the silos were located.

After completing our primary task of halting the production of the silos, we set about putting up the posters—a seemingly innocuous mission, but as we all know, it was what most angered the Party and Government leaders.

Carefully, we reached the nearest silo. My mission companion took a poster that had been prepared in advance and a can of glue from a leather briefcase. As planned, while he chose the exact spot to place the poster, I stayed close to the darkest part of the silo and reached the back door of what was the company's management office.

I put up the poster I had made at my companion's house, which read: "DOWN WITH INJUSTICE. LONG LIVE DEMOCRACY," exactly like the one I had placed at the Herradura Junction months before, and returned to the silo.

My companion was waiting for me, ready to leave. We exited through the same way we had entered, retrieved the bicycles, and returned to the town in just fifteen minutes. We went to his house, where he took a motorcycle out of the garage. The engine was so quiet that it was barely audible, despite the bike being old. I got on with him, and we set off on the road to Consolación. Once in town, he dropped me off near the Terminal at one of the first stops on the Viñales road.

He shook my hand in friendship—a brief, fleeting friendship where only the necessary words were exchanged, and no questions were asked. Everything we had talked about related to the mission we had to accomplish. I watched my companion of those few hours ride off on his motorcycle and waited until a bus heading to Viñales picked me up. It was six in the morning, and at that hour, the bus had very few passengers. Before reaching the city of Viñales, I got off and walked to the exit for Puerto Esperanza. I hitched a ride until I reached the spot where I had left the weapons and watched the car disappear. I continued on foot and arrived at the house of a fisherman, who had been indicated to me as a safe place. I was not to speak with its inhabitants.

In that modest house, as if they had known me all my life, they offered me lunch. Afterward, I sat in the kitchen listening to the radio until nine o'clock at night—the time, according to the homeowner, that was best for me to make "my visit."

I took the least crowded streets and reached Saturnino's house. Entering through the side door that led to the yard, I crossed it and went to the back of Inocencio's house, where I saw the patio light was on. It was the signal that everything was in order. I knocked on the door in the pre-arranged manner.

My friend Inocencio let me in quickly and gave me a resounding hug when I told him the mission had been a success.

"They'll be looking for you in that area for several days, and we'll be able to move with more ease," Inocencio said.

"We'll see if they take the bait," I said with a smile.

"Now we'll see who's smarter, them or us," we both thought as if our brains were directly connected. And when we said that, we laughed for a long time.

That night, we met up with Saturnino, and I told him everything in great detail. We then set about planning our next mission: getting me out of there and putting me on a boat bound for La Yuma.

CHAPTER 33

Lieutenant Salcedo was surprised when Gilberto requested a day off. He had been in La Palma for less than a month, and during that time, he hadn't taken his regular rest period. He was always doing something and seemed only interested in work. Although it wasn't appropriate, even as his superior, to ask the reason for his request, Salcedo found it strange.

He knew from the reports he regularly received from all his subordinates that Gilberto didn't visit anyone, not even his mother, his only living relative. Since Gilberto had been sent to work with him, it was clear that he wasn't comfortable, and it didn't take an expert to notice that. Despite this, Gilberto tried to be efficient and demonstrate that he was diligent and took care of the missions assigned to him.

Since he had fallen out of favor—according to the reports, for acting on his own as if the Security Department were his—he was apparently trying to clean up the mess he had created. Salcedo knew that due to Gilberto's excessive self-confidence, innocent people had been blamed for crimes they hadn't committed. Gilberto wrote reports that had been disastrous for these individuals, and over time, his superiors realized that they were exaggerated and, in some cases, false. This was why everyone resented him—it was clear that everything he did was to stand out and elevate his prestige, aiming to climb the ranks within the Department.

It was widely known that Gilberto was introverted, unfriendly, and didn't socialize with anyone, not even his colleagues. Another striking detail was that he had no known women in his life—not friends, lovers, or girlfriends—and he wasn't even known to have relations with women who were generally recognized as easy to please, some in exchange for favors and others for small gifts.

This was why his request caught Salcedo's attention. Of course, he immediately granted it; he had no reason to deny it, though, as the saying goes, "just in case," he asked one of his best friends and collaborators to dress in civilian clothes and, with great caution, try to see what that "Machiavellian officer" was up to. It wasn't easy to have someone who wasn't even wanted by their superiors nearby, and Salcedo knew that this post wasn't just an ordinary Security unit—it was one of the places that the *Comandante en Jefe* was known to visit, even if only a few times a year, and he couldn't afford to have any of his members doing something that could cause problems in his work.

Salcedo had always acted with integrity and honesty, which was why he had been placed in that position, something he considered an honor, and he wasn't about to lose credibility because of an irresponsible or unscrupulous ambitious person. He knew of many similar cases that, in his personal opinion, tarnished the Revolution's good image, but he believed that anything done to protect it was valid, even if it was known to be wrong.

Vergara accepted Salcedo's request. He was the best officer Salcedo had ever known, both as a person and as a leader, and Vergara felt great pride in working for a Lieutenant who acknowledged his subordinates when they succeeded in their assigned missions. Leaders like that were rare. When given a task, even if it was an order, Vergara was determined to carry it out with the utmost pleasure.

It was an unusual request—to keep an eye on an officer from his own Department—but Vergara hadn't liked that Captain from the moment he arrived. First, because he was unsociable; second, because he gave off a bad vibe with those sunglasses he never took off; and third, because he had heard from other colleagues who knew him beforehand that Gilberto had had "problems" and that the department commander in Pinar del Río didn't have a good opinion of him.

There was something strange in the air; he had to carry out the assignment with the utmost discretion, as Salcedo had advised. Vergara dressed in civilian clothes and used his old 1952 Ford, which ran well despite its age, and waited for the Captain to leave in his Chevrolet so he could follow him.

He saw the Chevrolet take the road to Puerto Esperanza, enter the city, and go to the Security Unit. From there, Gilberto went to a street near the beach and entered a CDR (Committees for the Defense of the Revolution) office. He stayed there for about half an hour and then continued to the San Diego Junction, then on to Paso Real, went to Cubanacán, and from there headed to Alonso de Rojas.

In Alonso de Rojas, Gilberto took a road that led to the rice silos where an attack had taken place several days before. The damage to the hoses, which couldn't be replaced anytime soon, was still visible.

About an hour later, he left there and returned to Alonso de Rojas, stopping at a house with a sign that read "Municipal Directorate of the Committees for the Defense of the Revolution." He stayed there for over two hours before leaving again, this time taking the road to Consolación, continuing to the Herradura Junction, and using a dirt road to go deeper into the countryside.

Vergara, fearing discovery, went down a road about a hundred meters away, entered a wooded area to camouflage his car, and waited.

He waited for almost three hours until he finally saw Gilberto emerge, now heading back to the Herradura Junction. Gilberto went to the Police Headquarters, forcing Vergara to wait another hour. From there, the Captain drove to Puerto Esperanza and returned to the CDR office he had visited earlier. A few minutes later, he was back on the road to La Palma and went to the Unit, parking his car in the yard. Finally, he went straight to his room.

Vergara went to find his boss and reported in detail the route and places Gilberto had visited. His boss thanked him for the favor, asking him not to mention the request to anyone. This would be a secret between the two of them.

Salcedo analyzed what his colleague had reported. Just as he had suspected, that man was again engaging in activities on his own. He needed to inform the Commander and wait for orders on how to proceed.

The next day, Gilberto showed up looking for orders in a normal, routine manner. Playing dumb, Salcedo asked if he had enjoyed himself during his leave. Gilberto, a bit puzzled by the question, replied that he had gone to visit some friends in Pinar del Río and had lunch at his favorite restaurant.

"You like the food at Rumayor. It's excellent," Salcedo said in a friendly tone. "Gilberto, since you're the highest-ranking officer here and I have the monthly meeting with the Commander, I order you not to leave the Unit until I return," he said in a normal tone but with the severity of a command.

"Don't worry, comrade Lieutenant, I won't leave here until you order otherwise," Gilberto responded with a subordinate's attitude.

Salcedo went to the Commander's office, and as always, he was greeted with a hug, something that filled him with pride because his highest-ranking boss in the province treated him, not as a subordinate, but as a friend.

After enjoying a delicious coffee offered by the cheerful secretary and receiving orders for the missions he was to carry out, Salcedo asked the Commander for permission to discuss a somewhat personal problem, as he put it.

"Of course, man, any problem you have and that I can help with... I'll always be at your disposal," the Commander said warmly.

"You know, it's a bit of an awkward situation, but based on the friendship you've always shown me, I'll be honest with you."

He told the Commander everything he had done, even mentioning that it was unofficial because he had asked a friend, not a subordinate.

The Commander was deep in thought, and after a reflective pause, said:

"Salcedo, if it were anyone else telling me this, I'd take it differently, but coming from you, someone with unwavering honesty, and regarding someone like Gilberto, I appreciate what you did."

He added:

"Now this isn't just your concern. I want you to write a report about it and keep a close watch on that bastard. You must keep me informed of every step he takes. That's an order."

He praised Salcedo's work in La Palma, even mentioning that he was in line for a promotion, saying he wished he had dedicated, trustworthy men like Salcedo by his side and that they owed him a promotion.

He bid Salcedo farewell with another warm and sincere hug, asking him to leave as he had a very important meeting afterward.

"Don't forget to drop by one of these days with your wife; we can have lunch together and play some dominoes," he said as a farewell.

There was no doubt that Gilberto was getting himself into deep trouble; he might fool others, but not Salcedo. From the moment Salcedo first saw Gilberto, something made his stomach turn. He was going to watch him even when he was doing his business. There was no doubt about that.

A degenerate with delusions of superiority wasn't going to destroy his career and reputation. "Watch out, Captain Gilberto," Salcedo thought.

CHAPTER 34

The plan we had developed was intriguing and appealed to me from the very beginning. Inocencio and Saturnino were going to take a risk, but they told me I shouldn't feel guilty because, contrary to what I might think, they were excited about doing something meaningful with their lives.

"We old folks have to prove that we're still good for something and not just waiting patiently for death to come," Inocencio said.

"I'm not just old as hell; I've got a cancer that the doctors say is cured, but I know that once the crab's claws grab you, it doesn't let go," Saturnino said, half-joking, half-serious.

"We're ready to give our lives if necessary because we don't have much time left," Inocencio added, emphasizing, "Don't worry about this pair of old men; we don't have much left but a shave."

There were two proposals, and both were good. The first was to go in a boat with Saturnino to a small key between Cayo Inés de Soto and Puerto Esperanza, where I would wait until the next day when Inocencio would come during daylight with his better-equipped boat and leave it for me. Afterward, Saturnino would pick him up.

The second option was similar, except that I would leave from Puerto Esperanza and head to Pajarito Beach, passing through El Rosario, where Inocencio would pick me up and take me to a key they knew between Pajarito and Cayo Arenas, following the same plan as before.

Since both options were solid, we decided to choose one at the ideal moment for departure, which depended on the weather.

Both old sea wolves set to work analyzing the weather forecast for the next seven days. We needed a wide margin of time, even though the journey could be made in ideal conditions in just three days. We couldn't rely on everything going perfectly.

Two days later, we met in the afternoon and decided that night would be my departure. Saturnino's boat would carry the supplies—the tires, ropes, weapons, and everything that wouldn't hinder Inocencio's daytime journey.

Nervousness overwhelmed me, making my limbs tremble like the ground in an earthquake. I couldn't control it. I made a superhuman effort, telling myself that I couldn't falter at this decisive hour, and after a few minutes, I managed to calm down. I had a hearty and abundant dinner and prepared to wait until eleven o'clock, the agreed-upon time to leave.

Everything was organized. I placed all the materials in two empty brown sugar sacks. Saturnino told me he would go first, and if he didn't return within five minutes, I should leave. That's what I did, and with Inocencio's help, who was keeping watch in all directions, I made my way to the beach where Saturnino's boat was. I boarded, and we set off, with me practically lying at the bottom of the boat while my friend rowed. You had to see how easily that man, despite his age and health problems, rowed and moved the boat through the calm waters of the beach. It was years of experience.

When we lost sight of the coast, I stood up and asked him to let me help, but he replied that I would have to row a lot starting the next day. We continued for about two hours until we finally reached a small key, about fifty meters in diameter, made up almost entirely of mangroves.

"When the tide rises, it shrinks by twenty-five percent," Saturnino warned me. "So I recommend you stay in the center of the key and don't let anyone see you. If you hear any noise from a plane, hide as best as you can so they don't know you're here." He warned me that if Inocencio didn't encounter any problems, he would be on the key by sunset and that I shouldn't waste the provisions as I might need them in the future.

He gave me a hug, the kind only given to beloved children, and wished me luck. I memorized the names of his children and the address of one of them and promised that I would visit him and tell him what his father had done for me. I watched him row away with such natural ease that I couldn't help but feel envious until he disappeared.

I entered the mangrove thicket, situated myself in the center as best as I could to avoid being seen by anyone, and settled down to sleep until dawn. During the day, I needed to be extremely cautious and keep my eyes wide open.

At sunrise, I woke up, eaten alive by mosquitoes, which I hadn't even felt biting me. I took out a can of food from the previous day that could spoil and made it my breakfast, filling my belly to sustain me for the entire day. From that moment on, I would only drink water, but in small amounts, as Inocencio and Saturnino had taught me.

The day seemed endless. I measured the sun's ascent in the morning millimeter by millimeter and its descent in the afternoon, which was even more excruciating.

My thoughts flowed, sometimes optimistic, sometimes pessimistic. I thought they had detected the departure the night before and that they had caught Inocencio... In this way, the day dragged on, slow and crushing, until around five in the afternoon, when I saw a boat with sails approaching the key from the predicted direction. I recognized Inocencio's boat and his figure, and a deep joy completely overtook me. Things were going smoothly, I thought, as I watched the boat approach the beach.

Now, the final stage remained, which was risky because, despite having received instructions from experienced people, theory and practice are never the same.

This would be my trial by fire. But I was determined to go through with it. The risks didn't matter; the decision and courage to carry it out were ingrained in every pore of my skin.

I ran to meet my friend Inocencio with a smile on my face, something I hadn't done in a long time. Such was my happiness.

CHAPTER 35

G ilberto was certain that the incident in Alonso de Rojas was the work of Homero; he just had to prove it, and he intended to do so on his own, without interference from anyone. Salcedo had placed a watchman on him, preventing him from taking any initiatives.

He requested a day off; ever since he had been stationed there, he hadn't taken a single moment for himself—it had all been work. He felt he was entitled to it. Salcedo apparently didn't give much importance to his request, though the way he looked at Gilberto felt a bit unsettling. Gilberto knew that scrutinizing gaze wanted to uncover something; he suspected Salcedo would report to the Commander, which could result in unpleasant consequences for him. Let Salcedo think what he wanted—Gilberto had to conduct his own investigation, and it wasn't a crime to do so.

He went to Puerto Esperanza to see if there was any new information regarding the incident with the old fisherman. He spoke with the Security officer, who informed him that nothing unusual had been observed. Then he spoke with the president of the nearby CDR, who said he was keeping watch day and night but hadn't detected anything abnormal since then. The old man, Inocencio, only went out during the day, as ordered, and infrequently at that.

From there, Gilberto went to Alonso de Rojas and spoke with a trusted acquaintance from the regional CDR. They concluded that someone from outside must have helped to put up the posters.

He then visited the silos and interviewed the administrator, the night guards, and other workers there who were considered trustworthy according to the Secretary of the Party's core group. The opinions were contradictory—some in the unit said that anyone unfamiliar with the area and the company couldn't have reached the location and selected the spot with such precision. They believed it might have been someone from outside, but the act itself seemed to have been carried out by locals.

Gilberto reviewed the photos of the poster from the Herradura Junction and the ones placed on the administration's door. He confirmed that not only did they say the same thing, but they also had the same handwriting and distinctive features. There was no doubt—it was Homero's work.

From there, he returned to Puerto Esperanza. He had to stay alert; he wasn't going to be fooled again. That stunt in the south to draw attention to the area was clearly an attempt to confuse the investigation. Homero wasn't going to fool him—not this time. Perhaps someone else, but not him.

The stratagem unfolded clearly in his mind. Homero had orchestrated a nearly signed act in the south, diverting attention to that region and its surroundings while planning to escape through the north. Gilberto was convinced that Homero wanted to leave Cuba.

What purpose did he have in staying there without his family? Gilberto knew these romantic types who couldn't live without the people they loved. Love—what was that word? He had instinctively thought of it but didn't really understand its meaning. He hadn't felt it for his mother, the person he valued most. Besides, he had no reason to love anyone; his parents had made him defective. He hadn't found a woman worth loving in his entire life. He had no siblings (not even that had his parents given him), no children—so who was he supposed to feel that sentiment for, which everyone claimed was the most beautiful and profound in the world?

Therefore, Homero must be planning his escape to reunite with his wife and that little boy with the dumb face. But Homero hadn't counted on the fact that to deceive Gilberto, he had to be more skilled than he was.

He reconnected with the CDR member, who acted like a rabid dog whenever counter-revolutionary *gusanos* were mentioned. The man hated them as much as Gilberto hated Homero.

He returned to La Palma, knowing he shouldn't stay away for too long so as not to arouse the lieutenant's suspicions. He was tired, so he went straight to his room and took a cold shower to refresh his mind; he continued to think about everything he was planning to catch his mortal enemy.

He had breakfast early and reported to the boss, who requested that Gilberto stay in charge of the Unit because he had to attend the monthly meeting at the Provincial Headquarters. This filled Gilberto with joy because it felt like recognition of his work. Finally, he was being given his due.

The only thing he didn't like was the boss's comment about how good the food was at Rumayor. But it was true—Rumayor was one of the few places where you could savor a good Creole meal. Gilberto decided not to dwell on his boss's remark.

Being in charge of the unit, he could now take his time digging through the lieutenant's files, to which he hadn't had access since his arrival.

He sat in Salcedo's cushy swivel chair, acknowledging the man's good taste—the bastard even had a well-organized and beautiful office. There were portraits of the *Comandante en Jefe*, Raúl, Che, Camilo, landscapes of the Viñales Valley, Soroa, and some family photos. In one, Salcedo appeared with his wife, seemingly newlyweds. In another, he was with his two children, all smiling and looking happy. Gilberto felt that familiar anguish squeezing his chest when he saw photos of united, happy families. Would he ever have something like that in his office, perhaps in the central offices of the Department, or who knows, in the Ministry of the Interior?

One thing that had caught his attention was that not even they could enter the house that the *Comandante* had on the outskirts of town. Those were some distrustful people. The *Comandante*'s personal security didn't trust anyone, not even their own mothers. They would crack down on anyone without distinction. Gilberto recalled a time when Fidel was visiting, and the Minister of Sugar tried to discuss a matter with him without permission. The *Comandante*'s security officers grabbed him by the neck, put him in a car, and told him to get lost as quickly as possible. What a tough bunch! Not even a fly could enter without the *Comandante*'s permission.

He had even thought about what he would say if he ever met the *Comandante en Jefe*—he would ask to be transferred to Havana, telling him that he had been with Che's troops and highlighting his capability and intelligence. But after thinking it over, he decided it wasn't wise to face those guys because they didn't care if you were a G-2 officer, a Minister, or a Central Committee member. The *Comandante* only allowed those he wanted and found useful to approach him.

That evening, Salcedo returned, looking worried. Gilberto thought maybe he had been scolded at the Provincial Headquarters. The lieutenant told him he could go rest after asking a few questions about the day's events, and Gilberto retired. He was tired from doing nothing. Martí once said, "Nothing tires more than rest." Gilberto agreed with the *Apóstol* because it had been weeks since he had the opportunity to arrest someone or interrogate a suspect. If it weren't for that pain-in-the-neck Homero, he would have been terribly bored. He wanted action, but he was sure that soon he would have it and would achieve his objectives. He was as certain of that as he was of his own name—Gilberto.

CHAPTER 36

Saturnino returned to Puerto Esperanza quite exhausted. It had been a long time since he had rowed so much, and the activity had worn him out. He left the boat moored on the beach and went straight to his house. Upon entering, he noticed that Inocencio was in the yard, waiting for news. He reassured him and then went to sleep.

The next day, he woke up with aching bones and muscles. After breakfast, he went to see Inocencio, who was already up. He recounted everything in detail, including the exact spot where I would recognize him.

Inocencio had an early lunch, and at three in the afternoon, when the sun was less intense, he naturally headed to his boat. He rowed out about a hundred meters before hoisting the sails and, with a sustained push, sailed away from the coast toward that key where he had often spent nights waiting for a school of fish to appear. His concern was that other fishermen frequented those keys to rest or wait for good weather. But I knew he would arrive from a specific direction, and I would only reveal myself when I recognized his boat.

Both Saturnino and I had been very careful not to pass near the Coast Guard posts or places where people known as professional informers lived. Those types kept an eye on everyone, including themselves, either for free or perhaps not entirely free, as their despicable actions earned them prestige as revolutionary combatants, which could favor them in obtaining positions within the cooperatives or the seafood factory in the city.

When he was halfway there, Inocencio had a hunch. He looked back and saw that another boat was following him from a distance. It could have been another fisherman in the area, but just in case, he changed course and approached the coast again to ensure he wasn't being followed.

Indeed, he could see that the other boat was following him, and not wanting to reveal anything, he went to a spot where he usually fished, lowered the sails, anchored his boat, and pretended to fish.

Shortly after, he saw the other boat approaching and did his best to appear focused on his task. The other boat did the same, engaging in a simulated contest to see who would tire first.

After more than half an hour, Inocencio raised the anchor and maneuvered closer to see who was bothering him, realizing that he was being followed by Fortunato, the president of the CDR in his block—a notorious informer who spent his life spying on everyone and who harbored a grudge against him because of Daniel.

Now he had to come up with a big plan because this character was dangerous, and any misstep could ruin the entire plan we had worked so hard on and put both my life and his at risk.

He passed close to Fortunato and, smiling, said:

"*Compay*, I'm having no luck today—not even a tadpole has bitten."

Fortunato, obliged to say something sensible, replied that he was in the same situation and thought it was time to head back home. Saying this, he raised the anchor and, thinking that Inocencio was going to return, turned to follow him.

That's when Inocencio played a trick on him. Almost cutting him off, he made a sharp turn and, passing on the opposite side, said as if to himself, "I'm heading to Cayo Arenas because I found a nice school of yellowtails there a few days ago." He inflated the sails to the maximum, and taking advantage of a favorable gust of wind, sped away swiftly, leaving the bastard Fortunato unsure of what to do. Surely, seeing that Inocencio would realize he was being pursued too closely, he decided to return to inform the Captain of the fisherman's intentions so they could go after him at Cayo Arenas, which was closer to La Palma than to Puerto Esperanza. Fortunato knew that, despite his old age, Inocencio had a temper that could turn him into a fierce opponent when angered.

He had to endear himself to the G-2 ~~people~~, but risking getting stabbed and left for the sharks wasn't in his plans. He wasn't brave enough to do something crazy.

Noticing Fortunato's retreat, Inocencio changed course as quickly as his boat allowed, steering toward the small key where I was waiting for him.

He needed to signal me to leave urgently because after they scouted the vicinity of Cayo Arenas and didn't see him, and he didn't return to Puerto Esperanza, the situation would become difficult to control as he wouldn't have an explanation for his boat's disappearance.

After sailing without slowing down, he finally spotted the key he was looking for. He entered the area we had agreed upon and saw me emerge onto the beach to greet him with a smile on my face.

Without much preamble, he told me what had happened and his suspicions that he was being watched and followed by Fortunato.

He helped me bring the supplies from the center of the key, and after arranging everything so it would be easy for me to access, he urged me to set sail as soon as possible.

I was visibly worried about Inocencio. I knew that when they detained him, they would mistreat him.

Inocencio, in an authoritative tone, said:

"You're going with the boat as planned, and don't say another word because time is gold. Forget about me—I know how to handle myself." He pushed me onto the boat and helped me set off, not without reminding me of the essential instructions and wishing me good luck.

I steered the boat in the exact direction, and as I waved goodbye, while he raised his hand from the beach, I felt a deep sense of pride for the bravery of those two fishermen who had helped me with unwavering solidarity and honesty.

For a long time, I kept thinking about them. I couldn't concentrate on navigating, so with a mental effort, I told myself that if I continued like this, I wouldn't get far because, combined with my inexperience, I was also failing to focus on what I needed to do.

I thought about my family, about Dolores and Vladimir, who were waiting for me. I thought about what would happen if I made a mistake and ended up back on the shores of Cuba, and I mentally reviewed everything Inocencio and Saturnino had taught me.

It was time to apply the theory. I put my trust in God and the Virgin of Charity of Cobre, protector of sailors; I prayed an "Our Father" and a "Hail Mary" and dedicated myself fully to the difficult task ahead of me. I knew from the start that, once again, Almighty God would help me.

CHAPTER 37

Fortunato was keeping a close watch on Inocencio and Saturnino, day and night. He was determined to earn praise from the G-2 comrades and possibly get their help in achieving his long-desired promotion within the Cooperative. He had always wanted the position of administrator, but it was always denied to him, as he was considered unfit for the role.

He was sure that something suspicious was happening in his neighborhood, and to prove that he was an expert CDR member, he monitored every move the old men made.

One night, as he passed by Saturnino's house, he overheard a conversation involving three people in the yard. There was no doubt in his mind that those scoundrels were plotting something. He refrained from calling the G-2 officer because he didn't have concrete evidence to back up his suspicions.

It was past eleven o'clock at night when he noticed suspicious activity at Saturnino's house. He waited to see what would happen but saw nothing in front. He decided to take a walk around to see if he could detect anything and then saw Saturnino's boat leaving. "There's no way that old man, who can barely move, has suddenly decided to go fishing at this hour," he thought.

It had been a long time since Saturnino had taken his boat out, and this seemed fishy to Fortunato.

He tried to find a boat to follow him, but Saturnino had disappeared into the night. Frustrated, he returned to see what Inocencio was up to. He noticed the light in the living room was on, but he couldn't discern if anyone was there.

That night, Fortunato decided he wouldn't sleep until Saturnino returned. If he didn't see him by dawn, he would call the Captain early in the morning. He would personally inform him over the phone.

In the early hours of the morning, he confirmed that Saturnino had returned. Saturnino left the boat moored on the shore and went inside his house. It was possible that the old man had gone out for one of his last fishing trips. Fortunato couldn't see if he was carrying any fish in his hands.

He lay down in bed but could barely sleep, causing his wife to reprimand him for disturbing her. Half-asleep and with a slurred voice, she warned:

"Tomorrow, you're going to have to explain why you were sneaking around all night."

When he woke up, he went to the beach to check Saturnino's boat and found nothing unusual. However, he noticed that there was no fish, no bait remnants, or anything to suggest a fishing trip had taken place.

Inocencio's boat was also there, but he hadn't gone fishing for days. Fortunato realized he needed to keep an eye on both of them—they were definitely up to something, and it couldn't be anything good. Later, he would call Captain Gilberto and inform him of everything that had happened since the previous night, but he wanted to gather more information before doing so. He dedicated himself to watching both houses. He wasn't going to work that day and would ask the Captain to excuse his absence.

The revolutionaries might see him as a hero, although others had always considered him a snitch. But Fortunato didn't like that word—he wasn't a snitch; he was a faithful guardian of the Revolution's ideas and principles. He believed that, eventually, he would hold an important position because not everyone was willing to make sacrifices for the cause.

He barely ate lunch, asking his wife to serve him on the porch so he could keep an eye on Saturnino's house. However, he couldn't see Inocencio's house from there ~~as it was situated behind Saturnino's~~.

So, he left and positioned himself on a bench near the beach where he could watch both houses. He was certain that they were conspirators, likely involved with the CIA, given the G-2's intense interest in them.

In the afternoon, he saw Inocencio heading towards the beach in the direction of his boat. Fortunato hid behind a wall and observed as Inocencio sailed out to sea. He quickly rushed to his own boat and began maneuvering to catch up to Inocencio's, which, after recent repairs, was light as a feather.

He spotted Inocencio in the distance and, without getting too close to avoid being recognized, followed the old sea wolf until he could see that Inocencio was approaching the coast. He had to get closer to see clearly if Inocencio was going ashore, picking someone up, or just fishing. He realized that Inocencio was fishing when he saw him holding a fishing line and making maneuvers.

Fortunato anchored his boat and pretended to fish as well. After some time, he noticed that Inocencio was raising his anchor and heading in the opposite direction. Fortunato resumed his pursuit, not wanting to lose sight of him. There were many keys in that area, and he could easily lose track of Inocencio.

He was only a few meters away when he saw that the old man suddenly made a sharp turn, passing almost directly in front of him. As they crossed paths, Fortunato heard Inocencio say that he hadn't had any luck that afternoon and was going to try another spot. Fortunato couldn't let him get away, so he discreetly turned his boat around to follow him. The old man was a master with the sail and the rudder. Inocencio made another sharp turn, passed by Fortunato's side, and continued in the direction he had initially been heading. Fortunato was left confused—it was too late to turn around and follow him because Inocencio would surely notice. The old man was known to be a grump, and everyone feared him when he got angry because he could become ferocious. It was dangerous for someone to confront him in such a secluded place. If Fortunato pushed his luck, Inocencio might throw him to the sharks, and no one would ever hear from him again. It was better to head back. He would inform the Captain as soon as he got back and see what orders he would receive.

Fortunato knew there was something hidden, as fishermen say, "in that cave, there are crabs." When a crab is in danger, it hides in a cave, and no one can catch it.

He reached the beach and went straight to the Security post, asking the soldier on guard to call Captain Gilberto of the G-2 in La Palma. He had urgent information to give.

A short while later, he informed Gilberto of all the strange movements he had detected and then went home to wait for the Captain, as ordered.

Now Fortunato was working directly with a G-2 officer. He was going to be the envy of all his comrades. Perhaps they would even choose him as the Municipal President of the CDR.

Once Gilberto was informed of everything, he tried to wrap up what he was doing as quickly as possible. Without much thought, he returned to the Unit and concocted a flimsy excuse to get permission from Salcedo to go to Puerto Esperanza to take care of a personal matter, as he told him.

Gilberto was conducting an inspection at a store where an illegal sale had been reported. It was a ridiculous order from his boss to investigate something that fell under the jurisdiction of the police, not State Security. They were being paid to address security issues, not the black market. But what choice did he have? He had to be obedient and couldn't complain much. He realized that no one at the unit liked him. Everyone was fond of Lieutenant Salcedo. Who had ever heard of subordinates having such affection for their superiors? A boss was supposed to give orders, command, be feared, and be respected—not adored by their subordinates. The only ones who should be adored were the *Comandante en Jefe* and the Minister of the Revolutionary Armed Forces, ~~General of the Army~~ Raúl Castro.

He couldn't stand such softness. That was why the inept Chief of Police would always call Salcedo whenever there was a problem, and as usual, Salcedo would agree to carry out ridiculous missions that had nothing to do with his obligations.

He received a radio message about a phone call from Puerto Esperanza from a CDR president.

The Lieutenant authorized his trip to Puerto Esperanza, and Gilberto used his Chevrolet instead of the official jeep to avoid taking the driver, who was an ass-kisser of the boss.

He drove as fast as that old clunker would go. He lamented the car's deplorable condition and dreamed of the brand-new, factory-fresh car that would surely be assigned to him in the not-too-distant future when he captured Homero and that gang of counter-revolutionaries—surely CIA agents. And if they weren't, he would fabricate some evidence to make it seem that way—he was a master at that. He would be decorated, praised, and promoted because no one had helped him; he had personally handled everything, and all the glory would be his.

He arrived at Fortunato's house, who had become an important ally in his mission, and listened attentively to what his informant had to say, asking the smallest details to form a concrete idea of everything.

There was no doubt—something significant was brewing, perhaps related to Homero's escape. It was clear that all the maneuvers of those two old men, who were not fond of the Revolution, along with his intuition that Homero was behind it all, would lead to victory.

"Did you say Inocencio mentioned Cayo Arenas?" he asked again. "We need to divide our forces. You must have friends among the fishermen who know the entire *cayería* (group of small islands) well. I order you to gather some of them and start searching every key in the area, no matter how small, looking for any signs. Needless to say, you should go armed; and if you see the guy I described to you before, Homero García, don't hesitate for a moment—arrest him in the name of State Security. You're authorized to do so."

"All I ask is that you don't inform the local Security comrades; this is a mission I'm personally assigned to," he said with an authoritative tone, not as a request. "Meanwhile, I'll go to Pajarito Beach and personally inspect Cayo Arenas and its surroundings."

He got into his car and floored the gas pedal. He drove like a madman through the streets and soon after down the road to Pajarito.

He arrived half an hour later and went to the Administrator of the small fishing cooperative on that small beach. He ordered the Administrator to prepare the fastest boat they had, gather some experienced fishermen who were well-versed in the area, and ensure they were proven revolutionaries. When the Administrator tried to make excuses, Gilberto scolded him for obstructing national security operations and threatened to report him to his superiors if he didn't follow orders quickly and with absolute discretion.

The poor man had to run off to find a motorboat that was ready to go out to work. He feared State Security—those people didn't trust anyone. But he was also concerned because the fuel quota assigned for the month was running out, and he hadn't been able to meet productivity goals, which would have serious consequences.

He spoke with two of the fishermen he trusted most and explained that this was a G-2 mission, so they couldn't refuse.

He brought the boat with the two fishermen, and Gilberto ordered the Administrator to go along as well.

"Captain, I have a ton of things to take care of here, and I'll lose today's catch if I don't go get ice," the Administrator tried to excuse himself from participating in that half-crazy adventure.

"I don't care if everything rots. I don't give a damn," Gilberto said angrily at the objection to his order.

Did those idiots think they were going to thwart his plans? If they didn't move quickly, he swore by his mother, he would start shooting.

He finally managed to set off in the boat, which wasn't very fast, something he complained about to the Cooperative Administrator.

"It's the best and fastest we have. We're a small Cooperative with limited resources, comrade Captain," said the poor man.

"Then push it to the maximum speed, straight to Cayo Arenas, and every time we pass by a small key, pull in to check it out."

He wasn't a man accustomed to the sea. As soon as he got on and felt the waves tossing the boat and the endless rocking, he started feeling unwell. His skin turned cold as ice, his head spun nonstop, and he was overcome with an overwhelming urge to vomit, eventually collapsing on the floor of the boat. He felt terrible nausea and ended up vomiting.

He had to overcome all this—how was he going to lead men on a mission if he couldn't even accompany them on a boat? He made a superhuman effort and managed to sit up. He saw the fishermen exchanging discreet, mocking glances and thought that those ignorant fools owed him respect, and if they didn't show it, they would regret it. He wasn't in the mood for games, and if he was going through this, it was because he wasn't used to it.

Every time they passed a small key, he asked the fishermen to get closer. He personally, with a pistol in hand, inspected it. In some, it wasn't even necessary to get off the boat—they could be checked from the vessel. After a journey that was pure torture due to his miserable condition, they finally reached Cayo Arenas.

"Captain, this key is big; it will take a long time to search it," one of the fishermen said.

"We'll split up and search," Gilberto retorted.

"Forgive us, but we're not armed, and if this man you mentioned is very dangerous and armed. If he find him, we'll be in big trouble."

"I've never seen such cowards as you," Gilberto said. "We'll go together," he continued.

Those words didn't sit well with the fishermen. They were honest, simple people, but not cowards. They simply weren't going to risk their lives for anyone.

They got off the boat, leaving one man to guard it, and the rest went with Gilberto. They searched every inch of that seemingly endless key. The search took a long time. The fishermen, exhausted and resentful of the way that officer had treated them, asked to return.

"Comrade Captain, if I were hiding, I wouldn't do it on such a big key where so many people come," said one of the fishermen.

"Where would you do it?" Gilberto asked curtly.

"There are many small keys between Puerto Esperanza and Cayo Inés de Soto that would be ideal. Only fishermen go there when they're tired or seeking shelter from bad weather."

They returned to Pajarito. When they arrived, Gilberto got off the boat without even a thank you. In a foul mood, and got into his car to head to Puerto Esperanza. The fishermen's reasoning made a lot of sense. If he were on those keys, Fortunato would have already found him.

When he reached Puerto Esperanza, he went straight to the CDR. Fortunato's wife gave him a message from her husband, saying they would meet at the Cooperative's office.

He arrived and came face to face with Fortunato, several fishermen, Inocencio, and Saturnino.

Fortunato, trying to look important, reported as if delivering a military briefing:

"Comrade Captain, we found the two suspicious individuals in Saturnino's boat," and he pointed to Saturnino. "They were coming from the vicinity of Cayo Inés de Soto. We interrogated them, but we haven't been able to get any information yet. Inocencio's boat is nowhere to be found."

Gilberto realized they had made an important breakthrough. He would interrogate them and get them to talk one way or another. He went to the Administrator's office and asked for the suspects to be brought in, insisting that he be left alone with them. He didn't want any witnesses.

"You know that helping counterrevolutionaries is a crime. It's called complicity. Tell me what you know about Homero García, and I promise you won't be punished due to your advanced age," he said in his usual interrogative style.

"We don't know anything about the person you're mentioning," Inocencio said.

"I don't know anyone by that name either," Saturnino added.

"I'm not going to beat around the bush; I don't have much time. You know the consequences of standing up to the Revolution. Your children have already paid for their mistakes," he said, glaring at both of them, and added, "Not only you, but also your family can be punished. Even your son, who is serving a sentence," he referred to Inocencio, "could be harmed if I file a negative report, saying he's complicit in your activities with that filthy worm."

"You people are worthless," Inocencio said angrily. "You send innocent people to jail and then threaten poor old folks like us who haven't done anything wrong."

Gilberto restrained himself from slapping that insolent old man.

"I'm not kicking you because of your age and because this isn't the ideal place. Otherwise, you'd be swallowing those words."

"We know that you people don't respect the elderly," Saturnino said.

"You're the ones who don't respect yourselves by helping people who, in complicity with the CIA and the Yankees, want to harm the progress of the Revolution."

"We don't know anything about the CIA or the Yankees. That's just something you made up to harm us for free," Inocencio confronted Gilberto with these words.

Gilberto grabbed him by the shirt and lifted him from his chair, ready to give that renegade a beating for his disrespect. He held back. He had to act more intelligently. He needed to maintain control and not go overboard.

He left the office and asked Fortunato if they had found anything suspicious.

"Well, Captain, I don't know if it's important, but on one of the keys, we saw something that looks suspicious. There are traces of what seems like someone having spent some time there."

"Damn, why didn't you tell me earlier? I've been wasting time interrogating these two stubborn old men, and Homero might be far away by now."

He took the two fishermen to the State Security Unit and ordered them to be kept in custody until he returned. The officer in charge asked what the charges were. Gilberto, annoyed and in a foul mood that he couldn't shake for days, said:

"Write down whatever you want but keep them here until I get back. OK?"

"They're two old men, and they're well-liked by the community," the officer said.

"They're accomplices in acts against the Revolution, and they'll be treated as such until proven otherwise, which I doubt because I have enough evidence to incriminate them. When I return, I'll do all the paperwork."

"Then I'll wait for your return to file the official report."

Gilberto left in a rage. Those damn bureaucrats were the ones who most slowed down the victorious march of the Revolution. When would they learn that such nonsense made them a hindrance?

He returned to the Cooperative and now headed with Fortunato and his friends to the Coast Guard Unit.

He spoke with the Unit Chief and said with an air of superiority that he was on a highly dangerous mission in pursuit of a notorious CIA agent and needed their support to capture him; he had reliable information that the agent was fleeing to the United States in a boat carrying strategically valuable documents.

The Unit Chief said he needed to request permission from the Central Coast Guard Command to mobilize an armed boat.

Gilberto insisted that the more time they wasted, the fewer chances they had of capturing him.

The Unit Chief left for a few minutes and said they had granted his request, but the responsibility for the operation was theirs.

Gilberto was irritated by the officer's attitude but didn't argue—he just wanted to get going.

They went to the dock, boarded a large, well-equipped boat with anti-aircraft guns, and set off, taking the fishermen who were familiar with the area and knew the key where Homero had supposedly been hiding.

They arrived at the key, inspected it, and indeed saw signs that someone had been there. Gilberto's instincts hadn't deceived him. Homero had been there.

He gave the description of Inocencio's boat to the Coast Guard sailors, and they set off north in pursuit of his mortal enemy.

It was now or never.

Salcedo was quickly informed about Gilberto's strange behavior right after he received the phone call from Puerto Esperanza. The lieutenant decided it was best to authorize Gilberto's request to leave, and as soon as he did, he called the Commander to bring him up to speed.

The Commander's reaction was immediate and forceful.

"I'm going to personally take care of this matter," the Commander told Salcedo. "It's not to undermine your authority, but after all, he's an officer of higher rank than you."

"I understand, Commander. It's a relief for me because I'm dealing with the issue of infiltrators around Las Cadenas... where most of my forces are concentrated."

"I agree with you, Salcedo. Focus on that mission, and I'll handle Gilberto. But keep me informed about that fool's actions," the conversation ended abruptly.

The Commander then called the Puerto Esperanza Unit and requested updates on Gilberto. The officer in charge of the Unit informed him that Gilberto had been making inquiries in the area and had later left. As far as they knew, he was pursuing a CIA agent supposedly being sheltered by two local fishermen.

The Security Office in Puerto Esperanza had already been contacted by the Commander himself to report on Captain Gilberto's activities, without revealing the reasons behind the request. They deduced that the Captain's actions were not well regarded by the Commander. But since Gilberto was an officer of high rank in the province until recently and had now been placed under the command of a Lieutenant in La Palma. They found themselves in an ambiguous situation. What should they do? Cooperate with the Captain or not? What was imperative, however, was to inform the Commander personally, as ordered, of all the Captain's steps.

When Gilberto brought in the two fishermen to be detained, they called Lieutenant Salcedo, who, in turn, informed the Commander.

The order they received was not to imprison the old men but to keep them in their homes under close watch and strict surveillance.

Inocencio and Saturnino were released, but not without being warned that they were forbidden to leave their homes.

An officer went to the Cooperative to learn all the details of Gilberto's activities and the fishermen who were helping him. Upon receiving the information that the Captain had left on a Coast Guard boat in search of a certain Homero García, they reported everything to the Commander.

Meanwhile, Salcedo, who was fully engaged in dealing with an infiltration in his territory—where a fast inflatable boat had been found and someone had seen three unknown individuals around the area heading into the woods—couldn't keep up with Gilberto's actions. However, the reports he received left him astounded.

From the moment he saw Gilberto arrive, Salcedo knew that this man was going to cause him trouble. They had assigned him someone of a higher rank to command, who was also being punished for taking actions on his own initiative without consulting his superiors. He also knew that this typically resulted in expulsion from the Corps, but for reasons unknown to him, that hadn't happened. He would have to bear this heavy burden, and no one could predict the consequences it would bring.

CHAPTER 40

The Commander asked his secretary to make a series of phone calls, including one to the Minister of the Interior. The secretary immediately began attending to his requests. The first call was to Lieutenant Salcedo at the La Palma Unit.

The Commander agreed with the Lieutenant that it was better for him to handle the case of the infiltrators but recommended that he keep him informed about Gilberto. He couldn't remove Gilberto from the case because, at that moment, he was still a subordinate and didn't want to damage his morale.

He ordered the Puerto Esperanza unit to keep him informed of the Captain's activities and to refrain from taking any action without consulting him directly.

When he spoke with the Minister, he briefed him on everything that was happening. In a previous report, the Minister himself had advised giving Gilberto a chance, but any slip-up should be reported immediately.

The Minister first ordered him to personally investigate the situation; second, to abort any mission that could compromise the image of the Ministry of the Interior, especially at a time when the Human Rights meeting at the United Nations was approaching. They had to be very cautious about the already tarnished international image due to the abuses they were committing against the population, particularly in the case of the dentist Homero García, who, according to all evidence, had been wrongfully judged and convicted. Captain Gilberto played a leading role in the conviction. Third, the Minister instructed him to prepare a detailed report on the case so that, if necessary, the Institution could clear its name by expelling that individual from the ranks of the Ministry to use him as a scapegoat for all the unjust acts that could be attributed to the Organization.

The Commander reclined in his leather chair and regretted being so lenient with Gilberto. There was no doubt that the man had serious psychological issues. Maybe he was outright insane.

He could have handled the situation more intelligently. After all, the Captain wasn't from the Pinar del Río province, and that could have been an excuse to "return" him to his own. It would have spared him the problems that were now troubling him.

But it wasn't time for regrets; he was going to personally take care of the matter. He ordered his operations jeep and was giving instructions to his secretary when he received an urgent message.

He picked up the high-security phone and received an order that required immediate compliance. He had to go to the Cubanacán area because the *Comandante en Jefe* had decided to go on a hunting trip with an important international political figure, and he had to personally oversee the *Jefe*'s security preparations.

~~What a terrible time for the~~ *~~Comandante en Jefe~~* ~~to decide to go hunting!~~ At that moment, he had to drop everything and take care of that. There was no excuse or pretext. He left instructions with his secretary to keep him informed about the Gilberto case and rushed to the Cubanacán farm. The boss is the boss, and orders are not to be questioned but followed.

He spent the entire day occupied with Fidel's visit; late at night, he returned to his office and saw the messages his secretary had left. He didn't like the latest developments regarding Gilberto at all, but he was utterly exhausted. He hadn't slept for over twenty hours, and the stress of the *Comandante en Jefe*'s visits always left him completely drained. He decided to sleep for a few hours and head to Puerto Esperanza in the morning to personally resolve the situation. He ordered one of his officers to call ~~Puerto Esperanza~~ and release the two fishermen that Gilberto had detained. Because of that impertinent fool, the Human Rights Commission could harm him if they found out that two old men, one of whom had cancer, were being held without convincing evidence.

He woke up with a headache so severe that it made it impossible for him to work efficiently. He knew that day wouldn't be pleasant.

He arrived at his office and hadn't even sat down when his secretary asked for permission to speak and informed him of something that made his hair stand on end. Gilberto had taken off in a Coast Guard boat to chase after that man, Homero.

But what was happening in his province? Had everyone suddenly gone mad, or had that wretch turned his territory upside down?

He urgently called the Coast Guard and learned about the incident with Gilberto and the lies he had concocted to take the armed boat.

Was it possible that such things were happening? He couldn't believe it!

He rushed to Puerto Esperanza in his jeep, and as soon as he arrived, he picked up an officer and went directly to the fishermen's house.

He was courteous and apologized for the rough treatment they had received from Captain Gilberto. He tried to see if he could get any information from the fishermen without pressuring them, but it was impossible. He quickly realized he was dealing with people who held honesty in high regard.

He left for the Cooperative and learned something that hadn't been reported to him, which worsened his headache like never before. During the fishing trip led by Fortunato, they had damaged two boats and injured a fisherman they mistook for the person the G-2 Captain was looking for, according to the Administrator. The fisherman had filed an official complaint with the police after being attacked at sea while resting on a small key. He had been shot at; fortunately, he hadn't been hit by a bullet, but while trying to hide, he had fractured his foot. The poor man would be out of work for at least three months, and as an independent worker, his family would suffer greatly. His large family depended on what he brought home to sustain them.

He was informed that the fishermen were on the Coast Guard boat with the Captain and immediately requested communication with the boat and, through the Unit Chief, ordered them to return to the base immediately.

His head almost exploded when they replied that they were being threatened by Captain Gilberto, who was armed with a rifle and demanding they continue the search. They didn't want to engage in a confrontation with Gilberto, who had the support of two armed fishermen—it would be a bloodbath, and they were trying to negotiate with him.

He was so overwhelmed by his headache and in such a foul mood that he had to apologize to the Coast Guard Base Chief for getting upset and blaming him for allowing Gilberto to take the boat.

He radioed his secretary, asking her to inform the Minister of everything that had happened and waited for a response. He went to the Unit and asked for a bed to rest for a while—his head felt like it was about to explode. He took two more tablets his neurologist had prescribed for his migraine.

Minutes later, the Minister's response arrived. He was ordered to request a helicopter, find Gilberto, and bring him back under arrest to Pinar del Río. He would face a court-martial. Such behavior could not be tolerated; according to the secretary, those were the Minister's exact words.

He requested a helicopter, and while waiting, he fell asleep for a few minutes, ~~seemingly~~ as a result of the medication~~'s effects~~.

CHAPTER 41

As I moved away from the key and saw Inocencio's figure shrink until it disappeared from view, I couldn't have imagined what awaited me on that journey.

I focused on everything they had taught me. Now was the time to put theory into practice. I thought: "If I learned to do so many complicated things in my career, how could I not learn this?" But it wasn't the same as pulling a tooth or doing a filling—this was venturing into a sea where even the most experienced fishermen, who had dedicated their entire lives to that profession, had perished fighting against its dangers.

The sea is beautiful and beneficial to humanity because it provides food, serves as a means of transport, and has many other uses. But it is also treacherous. When you least expect it, it places unforeseen dangers in your path. From terrible sharks and other dangerous fish to bad weather, heat that dehydrates and burns your skin, hunger, thirst, and that absurd feeling of being surrounded by water but unable to drink it. There were treacherous winds, immense waves, ocean currents, and many other things that made it loved and revered but also feared by all.

There are scholars of the sea—oceanologists—there are scholars of the weather—meteorologists—and many other "ologists," but there's a University called the "UNIVERSITY OF LIFE" that doesn't teach theoretical classes. You only learn there through practice. Years and years of sailing from one place to another, sometimes in fragile vessels that don't have the minimum safety, day and night, in the early hours of the morning; hours and more hours rowing, poling, sailing, motoring in all the different ways you can use to venture and explore the sea. Those who spend their entire lives in that university acquire knowledge that commands respect. That was the case with my friends Inocencio and Saturnino.

I was relying on the learning I had received from my teachers. It was really a very short time of classes, and my basic knowledge was nil, but I was gambling with the most precious thing a human being has—life—and that makes even the most foolish person learn.

A gentle, pleasant wind propelled my boat. The sea was calm, with discreet waves that allowed it to move swiftly and majestically. That's how the first six hours passed. I had stored the watch in a nylon bag to keep it from getting wet. Every time I checked it to confirm the time, my thoughts flew to the farm at Entronque de Herradura, where the remains of my father's great friend and later my own dear friend, Don Torcuato, lay buried. I thought that if I survived this adventure and was lucky enough to return to my homeland, the first thing I would do would be to ask for a Christian burial in a place worthy of that great man.

With mathematical regularity, I consulted the compass and the position of the stars. I analyzed the ocean currents, the speed, and the strength of the wind, all as they had shown me. That night there was a full moon, and the sea looked as if it were daylight. It was cool, and I was greatly encouraged to see that I wasn't practically tired at all. Before dawn, the wind began to decrease in strength. There came a time when my boat came to a complete stop. As I was strong and willing, I put on a pair of leather gloves and began rowing slowly and steadily, just as they had taught me. "You mustn't fight the oars and the sea; you have to make both elements work together," Inocencio used to say. In this way, I made little progress, but I didn't get stranded waiting for the wind.

The repetitive task of rowing over and over made my thoughts return to my youth. Those were wonderful days at the institute in Pinar del Río. That's where I met the woman who would later become my beloved wife, Dolores. I remembered our first encounters, the first furtive glances, the first smiles, the stammered words we exchanged, the wonderful feeling when our skin touched, the first kisses that I practically stole because she, pure and chaste as she was raised, didn't have the malice of girls her age; the poems I wrote for her almost every week, especially on Mondays because I spent the weekends writing them with passion; the visits to her house on Tuesdays and Thursdays because we had to follow the rules of proper living that were very traditional in her family; the years of waiting until we both graduated from university, and finally the happy day came when our hearts were united forever at the altar.

These and many other thoughts raced through my mind as I slowly rowed across the calm and tranquil sea.

At ten in the morning, the breeze began to blow again, softly at first, but as time passed, its intensity increased, as did the size of the waves that made my boat sway in a way that left me a bit dizzy. Hunger and thirst began to gnaw at me, but faithful to what I had learned, I only took small sips of water. That precious liquid had to be used sparingly. Every hour, I ate a couple of crackers and some of the sweets Saturnino's wife had prepared with great care, even though she didn't know me or had ever seen me. As a basic precaution and to avoid implicating her in such a delicate matter, I didn't want to make myself visible to anyone.

In the evening, I grew nervous at the approach of a relatively large ship. From the moment I spotted it, I realized it was coming from the opposite direction, heading straight toward me. I tried to make a discreet maneuver to avoid the encounter without straying from my route, but it was impossible—minutes later, it was almost on top of me, about five hundred feet away, and I didn't know how to control the situation. If that iron giant came crashing down on me, there wouldn't even be a piece of Homero left for the sharks. When I saw the ship was just a hundred and fifty feet away, I realized it was starting to turn to avoid me. Apparently, they had spotted me because as they passed by, less than eighty feet away, they gave two warning honks. I could almost see the people on the deck—some of them seemed to be looking at me with astonished and incredulous faces.

With the same speed at which it had approached, the ship moved away, leaving a trail of foam for more than a kilometer and causing a wave over two meters high that gently lifted and lowered my boat.

Would that passenger ship notify the Coast Guard of my presence? Both the Americans and the Cubans were to be feared. Sometimes the American warships would send you back to the country. If they were Cuban, they might kill you and throw you to the sharks. I thought it was better to be killed than sent back to Cuba.

The sun set on the horizon, and I prepared to spend my second night at sea. At nine o'clock, sleep began to overtake me. I positioned myself so that I couldn't move from there, tied the rudder to my arm, fastening it to my body in such a way that the course wouldn't change. I knew that at any moment, I would inevitably fall into the arms of Morpheus. Before that, I opened a can of sausages and ate them with a piece of bread that was already quite stale, took a few sips of water, and remained in that position for a long time—several hours.

When I opened my eyes, it was still dark. I checked my watch, and it was 4:20 a.m. Fatigue had made me sleep as if I were in a bed with a foam mattress. I untied myself and moved because I was somewhat stiff from the forced position of so many hours. I took a few sips of water and tried to orient myself by the stars. I realized I was slightly off course, so I corrected it with my limited knowledge toward a direction that seemed correct.

Hours passed, the sun passed its zenith once again, and the afternoon began to fall. It was five o'clock, and I was completely bored. The sun's rays had wreaked havoc on my skin, leaving it red and sore. My whole body ached, and the wind had completely died down. I started rowing, now with less strength because everything hurt. I spent more than two hours rowing, and there came a time when I couldn't continue and had to stop. I had no more energy left. I looked out at the sea, hoping the wind would start up again, and saw a fin of a fish that at first seemed to be a shark. It was just for an instant, then it disappeared. I became very worried. I thought: "Oh my God, sharks at a time like this when I can't even move." I looked up at the sky and asked the Lord for help.

While I was trying to see if the shark would reappear, my body suddenly shuddered. Again, a boat, now not as big as the previous one but moving very quickly, appeared. It was dark, seemed military, and was coming from behind me. "Oh my God, could it be a Cuban Coast Guard?" I asked myself.

It couldn't be—I tried to reason—because I must be too far from the Cuban coast for their Navy ship to be in these waters.

"Could it be that without realizing it, I'm heading back to Cuba? I can't believe it. All my effort and sacrifice, all that my friends and I have endured, in vain?" First, I had to confirm that it was military and second, that it was Cuban, and while I was deep in these thoughts, I saw the shark's fin again, quickly passing by my side.

I began rowing instinctively and frantically. Whatever the case, my survival instinct was giving orders, and I was following them.

When the boat was a hundred meters away, I could see it was a warship because it had towers and spikes that looked like cannons or machine guns. Shortly after, I realized it was Cuban!

"What horrible thing have I done in my life to deserve this punishment?" I thought, looking up at the sky, trying to see God. But in that tragic, terrifying, uncertain moment... I had a fixed idea. I wouldn't let myself be caught alive. Thank God there was a shark, possibly hungry and used to human flesh. Who knows how many Cubans like me, who couldn't bear to live any longer in that country ruled by the tyrant, had served as food for that fierce animal.

At less than twenty meters away, unable to see clearly due to my physical exhaustion and the glare in my eyes from the continuous exposure to the sun's rays, I thought I saw a familiar figure on the deck. I could make out an olive-green uniform, a black beard, and dark glasses reflecting the sun's almost perpendicular rays on the sea at that hour. Was it an obsession, or was I seeing ghosts? That couldn't be anyone other than the evil Gilberto! I couldn't believe it! Was I dreaming or seeing visions?!

The boat kept getting closer, and at that moment, I heard a noise coming from the sky. It was the sound of a plane. I looked up and saw a small plane with two occupants signaling to me, but I couldn't understand what they wanted to say. Since they were pointing to the opposite side of the Cuban Coast Guard, I looked in that direction and saw another boat approaching, which also seemed military. My God, another Cuban Coast Guard. One wasn't enough, I thought, now in a state of panic.

Suddenly, I remembered my weapons. Of course, in all that confusion and with my exhaustion, I had forgotten about the weapons. I stood up from where I was and went to get them, but at that moment, I heard gunfire coming from the boat that was now almost fifteen meters away from me. I saw Gilberto more clearly now, shooting at me with a rifle. Instinctively, I dropped to the floor of the boat, put on a life jacket Saturnino had given me, and without a second thought, I jumped into the water. I was going to take cover behind the boat, thinking that if the shark that had been circling me for some time now saw me, it would surely attack. That would end my suffering. At least I would serve some purpose—shark food. That was better than being captured and taken back to Cuba. Those sharks surely weren't as evil as the bearded Mephistopheles who followed me wherever I went.

CHAPTER 42

Gilberto had learned much at the Higher War School of the Ministry of the Interior (~~Minint~~). He had also gained a lot during the three-month course he spent in Minsk alongside guerrillas from Colombia, El Salvador, Nicaragua, and countries in the Middle East, each specializing in their own fields.

He was pleased because, despite the short duration of the course—only three months—he had learned a lot. Those Soviet officers were fierce. They knew everything imaginable and much more about the art of making enemies talk.

Additionally, he had formed a friendship—if one could call it that—with an officer from an Arab country. He never reveal which one, but practiced fundamentalism, a doctrine within extremist Islam to the point that its members felt pleasure and joy in offering their lives for their cause. His Arab friend was taking a course on explosives and mines, and the only confession Gilberto managed to extract from him was that the knowledge would be of great use to him and his comrades in the future when they faced imperialist and Zionist enemies. This Arab reminded him of his friend Hans, who had instilled in him ideas he now knew were Nazi. The fervor that both men had was extraordinary.

"One day, I will be a hero," Ahmed, the name the Arab went by, would say.

Gilberto admitted that he didn't share the idea of being a hero, much less giving up his life, which was the most precious thing he had. But without a doubt, the man was interesting, which was why they had struck up that kind of friendship.

Whenever they met in class, he admired the overwhelming interest that man had in learning everything the Soviet instructors taught.

One thing he didn't quite understand was that Ahmed didn't feel attachment or respect for all Arabs like him. He said that only those who thought like him deserved respect. Not everyone was like them, dedicating their lives to their principles. There were many in his people and other Arab nations who lived peacefully with imperialist and Zionist enemies. He was not like them. He was pure. He was superior.

Gilberto felt the same way—not all his comrades were like him. Even within Minint itself, there were those who held religious beliefs and occasionally spoke of God. What was this belief in God or religions when Lenin said that religions were the opium of the people?

There were those who said that Americans weren't bad, that it was the leaders who didn't know how to guide their people. How could it be allowed for a Minint member, who was the safeguard of the Revolution and socialism, to say that there were good Americans? Not him; he was like Hitler. He thought the same as his idol. It was necessary to eliminate races, and Americans were of a special race. Those democrats with their freedoms were destroying the world. What was this freedom and democracy where people did whatever they wanted? It wasn't possible; that was incorrect. You couldn't live in a country where the laws were so lenient.

It was necessary to govern with an iron hand. The masses had to be taught the rigidity of principles, the purity of socialist ideas, and why not? They should learn from Hitler. Now that was a ruler with an iron hand! He didn't allow such displays of licentiousness. Stalin was also an idol to him. He was a firm, secure ruler who didn't tolerate weakness among his people. He imposed his will and patriotic fervor, and that was how it should be; anyone who stood in the way of socialism had to perish. Stalin and Hitler were his idols.

That was why he also felt a certain admiration for Ahmed. It was clear that Ahmed was going to have a future. The hatred he felt for the imperialists was something Gilberto greatly appreciated. One day he asked him:

"Ahmed, why do you say that one day you'll be a hero?"

"Because one day I will give my life for my cause, but with my life, many of the lives of the 'imperialist dogs' will go as well," Ahmed answered with a mix of hatred for his enemies and pride in himself.

Surely, that three-month course taught him a lot. He learned not only the arts of military intelligence but also to harbor even more hatred for imperialists, absurd democrats who boasted about their freedoms, and everyone who opposed the ideas and rigid principles of socialism.

The only thing Gilberto had never managed to learn was how to swim. He had an overwhelming fear of the sea, rivers, anything with water, even pools.

It seemed that he had some childhood trauma that imposed this fear, sometimes irrational, of water that prevented him from learning something so necessary. His instructor would tell him that not knowing how to swim was too dangerous for a Security agent, who would sometimes find themselves in extremely dangerous situations. But there was no way he could lose that terror of water. "One day, this is going to cause me problems," he thought.

On his way back to Cuba, he spent a day in Moscow, where he took the opportunity to visit Red Square, and especially the mausoleums of Lenin and Stalin. There, admiring his idols, he wondered why Hitler didn't have a mausoleum too; even if his remains weren't there, at least a memorial to the one who had bravely fought to lead his people to victory over the impure. True, the Soviet Union had been opposed to Hitler, but he was absolutely sure that if Hitler had won the war, he would have made a pact with the Soviet rulers. Stalin wasn't so foolish as to disregard a German victory over the imperialist English and Yankees. At least that's what his disturbed mind thought.

When the bus took him to Sheremetyevo Airport 2, he felt that his life was going to enter a new phase from then on. What he had learned was going to be very useful to him in the future. He would go far—he predicted it himself.

But he had indeed learned a lot in that course. His teachers were excellent; they had the mathematical precision of a clock. They were efficient and didn't show any signs of weakness. They were true teachers whose teachings he was going to carry forward in his professional life.

"That was a real school," he thought.

CHAPTER 43

While the Commander slept, he was plagued by a recurring nightmare. In it, he vividly saw the report that his secretary had placed on his desk, a memory that filled him with dissatisfaction. Despite the many atrocities he had committed in his life as a member of State Security—sometimes even killing or ordering the torture of CIA agents to extract information—he had never consciously condemned an innocent person.

The report detailed the arrest in Havana of a counterrevolutionary named Juan Pérez González, a member of the Pro-Human Rights Committee, who was distributing proclamations from abroad urging the population not to respect the laws established in the name of the Pro-Human Rights Movement of Cuba and the Christian Movement for Peace.

These proclamations had arrived in Cuba from the United States by air and were dropped by parachute in the region along the Viñales road weeks earlier. The report specified that an employee of the El Rosario farm had used a green olive jeep belonging to the farm's management one Sunday morning, accompanied by another individual. Both were dressed in the MTT uniform, and after stealing the vehicle without authorization, they retrieved a box from a parachute near the reservoir located at kilometer five and a half on the Pinar-Viñales road. They then took the box to a location near Viñales where they transferred it to a private car. This car carried the box to Havana. Inside the box were proclamations from the United States, which read:

PEOPLE OF CUBA

THE CHRISTIAN MOVEMENT FOR PEACE AND THE PRO-HUMAN RIGHTS COMMITTEE OF CUBA URGE YOU TO PEACEFULLY, IN ACCORDANCE WITH CHRISTIAN LAW, APPROACH THE AUTHORITIES OF THE COUNTRY TO REQUEST A REFERENDUM SO THAT ALL THE PEOPLE OF CUBA CAN DECIDE THEIR POLITICAL FUTURE. THIS REFERENDUM, TO BE OBSERVED BY THE UNITED NATIONS, WOULD DEMONSTRATE TO THE WORLD WHETHER THE

PEOPLE OF CUBA WISH TO CONTINUE UNDER A SOCIALIST REGIME OR A MULTIPARTY DEMOCRACY. WHATEVER DECISION THE PEOPLE MAKE WILL BE SUPPORTED BY CUBAN INSTITUTIONS ABROAD. THIS REFERENDUM WOULD PREVENT BLOODSHED AND THE IMPOSITION OF ONE TYPE OF GOVERNMENT OR ANOTHER ON THE PEOPLE.

WE WANT PEACE FOR THE PEOPLE.

SIGNED: CUBAN PRO-HUMAN RIGHTS COMMITTEE CHRISTIAN MOVEMENT FOR PEACE

The aforementioned Juan Pérez González had confessed everything without much pressure and had been judged and sentenced to four years in prison for his activities.

The report concluded the investigation into the box that had been dropped in the territory on Sunday, March 6, 1979.

When his aide woke him because the helicopter he had requested was waiting, the Commander recalled that event with a mix of guilt for not intervening in the unjust sentence handed down to Homero García and anger because Captain Gilberto's actions—first in condemning Homero and then hunting him like an animal—were causing more problems than if the Americans had invaded his province.

He, too, was guilty because, like Pontius Pilate, he had washed his hands of the matter when his actions should have been more honorable. He had also contributed to the imprisonment and injustice committed against Homero. Now he was paying the consequences.

He boarded the helicopter, and they set off in search of the Coast Guard boat that Gilberto—completely unhinged—was steering toward what could become a disaster.

During the flight, they informed him that a small plane, apparently from the counterrevolutionary organization Brothers to the Rescue, was flying over the area and that the Coast Guard had detected an unknown vessel on the radar, seemingly military and possibly American.

Things were taking a turn he didn't like one bit. A clash between Coast Guards over a fugitive was the last thing he had expected to happen in his life.

They were nearing the scene when he received a radio communication informing him that Captain Gilberto was firing at a boat containing a presumed "rafter," and despite attempts to stop him, they had been unsuccessful because the Captain was threatening them with a rifle every time they asked him to cease.

"Do whatever it takes to stop that madman," the Commander ordered over the radio.

CHAPTER 44

The captain of the Coast Guard boat wasn't very enthusiastic about the mission that the State Security officer had imposed on him. After all, he wasn't from State Security; he was with the Border Guard Forces. He had his own methods and discipline. He also didn't like the way orders were given to him as if he were a subordinate. But since he had been ordered to assist in that mission, albeit somewhat reluctantly, he set out in search of the enemy that had been assigned to him.

Gilberto had ordered him to head to the key and then go north, but what was this about giving orders to an experienced sailor by someone who, just by listening to him, you could tell knew nothing about navigation? But despite his lack of navigation knowledge, Ensign Nicolás, the name of the Coast Guard captain, realized that this man had a knack for detecting, especially the counterrevolutionary they were pursuing. It was remarkable. Therefore, he ordered the crew to follow that same route, and shortly after passing the key, they headed north.

The Coast Guard boat sped through the sea at a breathtaking speed, which, luckily, was calm, providing tremendous visibility. For this reason, when Gilberto asked Ensign Nicolás how long it would take to catch up with Homero, he felt great joy upon hearing that if they were on the right path, they would spot him in just a few hours. Moreover, the boat's radar would detect him much sooner.

Two hours passed, and when they hadn't detected anything, Gilberto began to hurl absurd curses at the captain:

"Why haven't we made contact, not even on the radar?" he asked in an irritated tone.

"This boat has radars, not a magnet that attracts enemy boats," the captain replied sarcastically, as Gilberto had worn him down with his insinuations and demands.

"I want to catch that scoundrel now," Gilberto said. His face, almost impenetrable due to his thick black beard and those dark glasses that left no room to scrutinize, could be guessed to be livid with rage.

A sailor approached the captain and informed him that they had detected a boat on the radar. Upon hearing this, Gilberto rushed to the bridge and began scanning the horizon with binoculars.

"It's him, it's him; I'm sure it's him," he repeated incessantly.

The captain and the sailors couldn't understand what this man was feeling. It must have been a very serious personal issue...

The second officer of the boat, who was very close to Ensign Nicolás and who also disliked the abnormal attitude of this Security Captain, said jokingly:

"Captain, could it be that this Homero cuckolded our little captain?"

"Well, if it's not that, it must be something similar because I've never seen anyone so obsessed with an idea and with so much hatred," Nicolás replied.

Minutes later, the silhouette of a boat appeared on the horizon, growing closer as the Coast Guard boat approached. There was no doubt—it was Homero; he could see him with the binoculars. Gilberto felt an immense sense of triumph. He asked Fortunato for the AK rifle, and without listening to what Ensign Nicolás was saying, he began firing bursts of bullets at the boat in rage.

"You can't do that. It's against international regulations," Nicolás said.

"Forget about international regulations or anything like that. My rules are to finish this guy off as quickly as possible."

"Please, if you don't calm down, I'll have to take the rifle away from you."

"Try it if you want. If you get in my way, I'll put a bullet in your head," Gilberto said, consumed by uncontrollable fury.

Fortunato and his companions were scared—this wasn't normal. Two officers against each other. But they had come with Gilberto, and it was him they were going to support. So they stood by his side to protect him.

Nicolás and the crew were alarmed. This wasn't normal. They had never been in a situation like this. But they thought that with a little patience, they could stop that madman since a fight on the boat wouldn't benefit anyone.

Gilberto fired again at the boat, where he could now see Homero's face. He wanted to destroy him, to turn him into a sieve. On the third burst, he saw Homero fall into the water.

Hysterical, he screamed, "I got him! I got him!"

Then he saw Homero resurface on the other side of the boat, and with even more rage, he fired again. He changed the magazine again and again, but the damn man wouldn't die. It must have been because the boat was moving at a slower speed, and the waves were tossing the vessel so much that he couldn't hit his target.

He ordered the boat to stop. The captain complied and devised a plan with his sailors to immobilize Gilberto, disarm him and his friends, and detain the suspect in the boat, who at that moment was more sympathetic to the crew than those three absurd characters. He might be a counterrevolutionary, but they were a pack of crazy fools, and they were starting to get angry with them.

At that moment, the captain was informed that a plane, apparently from the counterrevolutionary organization Brothers to the Rescue, was flying over them and possibly filming them machine-gunning a boat in the open sea.

"Captain, stop this madness. Don't you see that if they're filming us, we'll have an international incident that will affect both us and our government?" Nicolás shouted.

"I don't care if they're filming or whatever. I'll finish off that son of a bitch even if Coppola himself is filming us."

While Gilberto continued firing, a boat from the north appeared, something that surprised everyone.

"Captain, an American torpedo boat is to starboard," the second officer informed.

"Gilberto, stop this now. We're facing an American torpedo boat better armed than us, and we'll have to face it if you continue," the captain said.

"Even if it's an aircraft carrier, I don't give a damn. I'll finish Homero even if I have to take on the entire American Navy."

The torpedo boat radioed that they were not to attack the boat, a sailor reported.

Gilberto continued firing uncontrollably at Homero's boat; the torpedo boat was approaching, and bullets were almost whistling across its deck. Then, the torpedo boat fired some warning shots into the air with anti-aircraft guns, putting the entire Coast Guard crew on high alert.

Captain Nicolás, realizing the gravity of the situation, signaled two sailors to try to restrain Gilberto and take the rifle away from him when he was distracted.

Gilberto's friends, seeing the American torpedo boat, were scared and moved away from the captain, who was struggling with the sailors.

In one of Gilberto's maneuvers to free himself from the two sailors, he jumped over them and stood on the boat's edge; suddenly, he lost his balance and fell into the sea.

"Help! I can't swim; please help me!" Gilberto shouted from the water, horrified and trying to stay afloat.

Captain Nicolás and the crew looked at each other and finally heard the exclamation:

"Man overboard!"

With slow, almost deliberate movements, they went to get a life preserver to throw to Gilberto. They tied a rope to the life preserver and went to the edge to try to save him.

CHAPTER 45

I was terrified. Bullets whizzed around me, and some struck the boat, which was beginning to take on water through the holes. The Coast Guard boat was approaching and was less than twenty-five meters away. I felt the engines stop and could hear a discussion among the men on board. I clearly saw Gilberto, sometimes aiming at me and firing, and other times pointing his weapon at the rest of the crew. Beside Gilberto, and apparently terrified, were two fishermen, judging by their attire.

Every time he fired, I had to dive into the sea, swallowing mouthfuls of salt water. My physical condition was pitiful. I had almost no strength left.

At that moment, I heard another burst of gunfire, this time from a heavy, anti-aircraft weapon on the opposite side. It was the boat that was about fifty meters away, firing warning shots into the air.

I was being attacked from both sides by both vessels. I was in the water, half-dead from fear and fatigue, unarmed, being attacked by two boats, and with a plane circling above me. It was enough to drive anyone crazy...

I felt the bullets hitting my boat again. I submerged myself again, purely by instinct. If I hadn't been hit by now, it was because Gilberto was a terrible shot. Less than fifteen meters away, armed with an AK-47—a weapon I was familiar with from my military training, known for its extraordinary accuracy—and he still hadn't hit me, or at least I didn't feel any bullet wounds on my body. He was either a very poor marksman, or the hand of God was protecting me.

After one of my dives, as I surfaced to breathe, I saw the shark's fin again. My vision was completely blurred, but I saw that fin cutting through the water towards me at an astonishing speed.

Again, I felt a burst of bullets, and my life jacket was hit by one of them, causing it to deflate. I dove instinctively, and when I tried to surface, I couldn't make it. I didn't have the strength. I began to sink into those transparent waters. I still managed, despite my desperation, to pinch my nose with my fingers, but it was a futile effort—I kept sinking deeper and deeper.

My mind flashed with the speed of lightning to images of my loved ones, my parents, my wife, my son, and so many friends who had helped me, apparently in vain... Suddenly, I felt myself being lifted by a soft body that, almost with maternal tenderness, was pushing me to the surface. I couldn't clearly distinguish what was pushing me upward. When I managed to breathe in air mixed with water, I felt as if I had risen from heaven back to earth. It was as if I had died and been revived.

That fish or marine animal that had lifted me from the depths of the sea submerged and reappeared again. It was a dolphin, no doubt about it, and it looked at me as if to say: "I'm here to help you."

I had seen something about the intelligence of dolphins in movies, but I never imagined they could go as far as to save people. I approached it, held onto its fin with both hands, and mounted its smooth and silky back. The fish began to swim at a gentle pace, as if it could sense that I was physically very weak; it was heading towards the boat that had appeared last.

The agility and skill of these marine animals are impressive. From time to time, it emitted a sound, like a message of encouragement, and with the amazement caused by all these events happening in what felt like years, I felt comforted. It was something supernatural.

Again, I heard shots from the Coast Guard where Gilberto was. I managed to look back and, with great difficulty, saw that a hand-to-hand struggle was taking place between Gilberto, who was holding the rifle with the barrel pointing up, and two sailors from the Coast Guard.

I turned my gaze forward and could clearly see the boat towards which the divine animal was taking me. On one side were several sailors holding life preservers tied with ropes; they were shouting in English for me to come closer.

The dolphin, as if it understood human language, placed me almost directly beneath where the sailors were. I felt two life preservers fall on me, and I managed to grab one. I put it under my arms and began to feel myself being lifted. For a moment, I looked back at the Cuban Coast Guard and saw Gilberto fall into the sea, sinking, only to resurface moments later.

I saw that the sailors were about to retrieve a life preserver, but for some reason, it seemed to me they weren't in much of a hurry when I finally saw two of them leaning over with the devices in their hands. Gilberto was sinking, desperately waving one of his hands. Finally, I didn't see him emerge from the waters again. It seemed that the time for judgment had come.

I felt exhausted. I heard a voice saying, "Give me your hand," or something like that. I raised my arm and was lifted to the deck of the boat. The last thing my eyes captured was that dolphin, that guardian angel God had sent me at the most difficult moment of my life, standing on its tail, perpendicular to the sea, whistling beautifully, with an expression that looked like a smile.

It was signaling to me about my near future. FREEDOM.

CHAPTER 46

Commander Pineda was informed of what had happened on the torpedo boat with Captain Gilberto. An official report, meticulously altered according to the interests of the Provincial Command of Pinar del Río, was waiting on his desk for his approval and signature. The secretary had spent hours typing it and was ready to leave; it was already eight o'clock, and she was very tired from the day's hustle and bustle.

Pineda stopped her just as she was about to leave and asked her to stay a little longer because he wanted to go over the report and make some changes. He wanted the text to be impeccable, to ensure that the problems caused by Gilberto's scandal were clearly addressed and wouldn't trouble him anymore.

Just as he was making corrections, he received a call from his immediate superior.

"Hello, good evening, Chief. How's your health?"

Due to his long-standing relationship with his boss, he spoke with a degree of familiarity and affection, as their wives were close friends who visited each other frequently.

"Hello, Pineda. I'm fine, thank you. I'm calling because this case involving that fool Gilberto has escalated, and the higher-ups in the Party want to know all the details personally, not in writing, from A to Z. Do you understand?"

"I understand, Chief. What should I do then?"

"Come here as soon as possible. We'll meet in the parking lot of my house at seven in the morning to go see the Minister together."

"Is this matter that serious?"

"More serious than you can imagine, so you can understand the urgency."

"OK, see you at seven in the morning."

This gave Pineda a bad feeling. The Minister himself wanted to know everything about the case of Homero García. What would he say? The truth? It was too complicated. He could already foresee himself getting tangled up with the Minister, who was an uncompromising man who expected to hear the truth that suited him. That truth was often far from the actual one. If something didn't sit well with him, there would be a blow-up, and things would get very difficult. You had to be a mind reader to know exactly what he wanted to hear.

He dismissed the secretary after finishing the revisions to the official report, asking her to retype it and leave it on his desk before two in the morning since he would be taking it to Havana.

The poor woman was devastated by the request, but being accustomed to such servitude, she took the report to her desk and began typing it again.

Pineda lay down on his bed and asked his driver to wake him at two in the morning so he could leave for Havana as quickly as possible. He wanted to arrive before seven so his boss wouldn't have to wait for him; his boss was very punctual and demanding about it.

The few hours he tried to sleep were restless, filled with nightmares. He thought about Gilberto and his blunders, the repercussions they had had for him and the entire command, and the impending meeting with the Minister that kept gnawing at his mind. He knew that the Minister didn't tolerate nonsense, and any slip-up on his part could cost him dearly... and on top of that, there was the matter of his foolish wife and the young recruit, which was still on his mind, torturing him—not so much because his wife had cheated on him, but because of what had happened to the young man. Now that he was worried about the Minister's intentions, he feared they might bring up what he had done in coordination with Rojas. He knew well, as did everyone else, that if you were inefficient in your role and deviated from the guidelines of the Revolution, it didn't matter if you had fought in the Sierra or in the underground, or if you had given your life for the Commander-in-Chief or the Minister of the FAR (Revolutionary Armed Forces); if they deemed you unnecessary or inefficient, they would deal with you quickly. And there were only two ways to resolve it: either they stripped you of your rank and position, putting you under house arrest until the bosses remembered you, or they simply executed you, depending on the severity of the situation.

After picking up his boss, they headed to the Minister's office, where he was working early in the morning. They were ushered into his office, and after the usual formalities, the Minister told Pineda to explain everything about the case.

Commander Pineda began with the arrest of Homero, the subsequent events following his escape, Gilberto's pursuit, and finally, Homero's rescue by the Bahamian Coast Guard.

He explained, without much detail, that Gilberto had made a mistake because Homero had nothing to do with the parachute drop and that the real culprit had already been tried. An inner voice told him to be as accurate as possible with the events, leaving no details out, even though the Minister was urging him to speak only about the essentials.

When he finished, he waited for the Minister's reaction and glanced sideways at his boss, who hadn't uttered a single word.

"Very well," said the Minister. "Now, Pineda, what you said here today is not what you're going to report officially, OK? Is that clear?"

"Understood, Comrade Minister," Pineda replied in a martial tone.

"Then," the Minister emphasized, "here's what actually happened in broad strokes. You'll embellish it and send it to me for review before the copies are distributed.

"That Homero García was a counterrevolutionary assassin who had carried out several attacks, and for that reason, he was imprisoned and tried. As a CIA agent, he was aided by that organization to escape with the intent of continuing to carry out those attacks. Captain Gilberto, I don't remember his last name, shrewdly and at great personal risk, tried to eliminate that CIA agent, but unfortunately, the agent managed to escape after being rescued unconscious in the high seas by the Bahamian navy. Captain Gilberto gave his life for the Homeland and the Revolution. For this reason, we propose that Captain Gilberto be posthumously awarded for his bravery in fulfilling his duty and for the services rendered to the Revolution and the Communist Party of Cuba. In this way, the matter is resolved, and as always, the Revolution has emerged victorious once again by neutralizing a powerful enemy agent of the People's interests. That's all. You may leave." He abruptly ended the meeting.

The two officers left the Ministry without saying a word. They were confirmed communists who had earned their ranks heroically in the Sierra Maestra and who had committed atrocities in the name of the Revolution, but they were speechless, confused, and overwhelmed. That action was more than they could have expected. It exceeded all their expectations.

They didn't speak a single word on the way back. His boss asked to be dropped off at his office, and Pineda decided to stop by his house to check on his children, whom he hadn't seen in who knew how long.

He arrived at lunchtime and found everyone seated at the table. His wife greeted him with a "How are you?" His two sons greeted him with a "You're here, Dad?" And his daughter, who was already eighteen years old, looked at him, got up from the table, and, claiming she had important classes at the University, left without asking her father how he was—something he would have liked.

"Have you had lunch?" Darli asked, disinterested.

"I had lunch at the Minister's dining room," he lied.

His two sons got up and left the dining room without saying goodbye to their parents, heading to their rooms and blasting rock music, which irritated him.

He looked at Darli for a moment, who remained impassive at the table. He went to the fridge, opened a soda, took two sips, and was about to leave when she said she wanted to tell him something important before he left. He ignored her, got into his jeep, and brusquely ordered his driver, "To Pinar, fast and far away," a phrase that conveyed his irritation, his insult, and how absurd his life had seemed lately.

Something had failed in his family. His wife had betrayed him, his children didn't love or respect him, the example of selflessness and sacrifice he had tried to instill in them hadn't had the desired effect. It wasn't enough to provide them with material things—food, clothes, a good education, cars—everything that the rest of the population lacked except for the leaders who had everything they wanted. None of that mattered to them. He had even heard his wife say once that their children had ideological deviations. He had tasked her with doing everything possible to correct that, to talk to them about the sacrifices they had made so they could have this life, so they wouldn't suffer the deprivations they had experienced in their own childhood and youth. But apparently, she only thought about how to cheat on him with the first man who came along. His children probably knew what had happened, and he regretted not telling them as normal parents do. But he justified himself by saying that due to his intense work (he justified himself uselessly), he hadn't acted as a good father should. He knew he wasn't a present father, and his absence in their daily lives had brought about these fatal consequences.

Unfortunately, he was entirely to blame, but he didn't want to fully admit it. Sometimes, he even forgot their names. "Life's tough," he thought, but what could he do? The tasks of the Revolution didn't wait for anyone, and he had been given this task, and he would fulfill it even if it meant sacrificing his entire life.

Everything seemed absurd to him—the behavior of his wife, his children, his boss, his subordinates, his Minister, and sometimes even the attitude of the Commander-in-Chief himself left him in a state of inner dissatisfaction that tormented him.

He couldn't commit the crime of doubting the Revolution. He represented the safeguard of the most profound interests of socialism. He had to rid his mind of all the doubts that terrified him.

It was the problems with that damned Homero, that son of a bitch Gilberto, the care he had to take in expressing his opinions and writing reports. Everything conspired to cloud his mind, even though he knew he had enough courage and political conviction to set aside those worries and continue his march, always leading, always in favor of the most profound and pure principles of the Revolution.

At home, Darli couldn't hold back her tears. She had long wanted to tell her husband that their children wanted to leave the country, that they had no faith in the Revolution, that they despised the life they were living, and that others, including their classmates and even relatives, criticized them, calling them "daddy's kids," "government leeches," etc., which was offensive and filled their lives with sadness.

If they managed to leave, it would be the hardest blow he could receive as a father and as a leader of the Revolution.

It might even cost him his position, his rank, and even the Communist Party card he held as the most sacred thing in his life.

Ironies of fate.

CHAPTER 47

I was attended to by officers of the Bahamian Navy, not the United States as I had initially thought. They gave me blankets for the cold, a hot tea that I greatly appreciated, and subjected me to an interrogation in English, of which I understood nothing.

"No 'inglich,'" I told the ones asking those questions.

They brought in an officer who spoke a little Spanish and understood some of it. He asked me a string of questions to which I had little to respond. It became clear that these officers had no real grasp of what life was like in Cuba under the Castro-communist regime. They seemed oblivious to the political and economic realities on the island and the suffering of Cuban citizens.

They left me alone in a cabin for a while and then interrogated me again. They insisted on knowing why I was being shot at. They asked if I was smuggling drugs, if I had them in the boat, and a lot of nonsense that naturally irritated me because I knew nothing about drugs and had never in my life experienced anything related to them.

I had been rescued by them, so I owed them my gratitude and shouldn't have been irritated by their questions, but the truth was that they were driving me crazy. Finally, they left me alone. I lay down on a bunk and managed to sleep despite my physical exhaustion.

Some time later—I couldn't say how long—they woke me up because we had arrived at my destination and it was time to disembark.

After giving me dry, clean clothes that looked like a prison uniform, they handcuffed me, took me ashore, and put me directly into a van that had "POLICE" written in red letters.

More than two hours later, they brought me to a building that was obviously a prison. They handed me over to some guards, who took me to an office where there were other officers who interrogated me again, this time in Spanish, fortunately.

I recounted everything again, but deep down, I was convinced it was all in vain. They didn't believe a word I said. After finishing that final round of questioning from everyone present, they gave me a small nylon bag with a bar of bath soap, a bar of laundry soap, a toothbrush, and a small tube of toothpaste. They took me to a barracks where there were more than fifty people, all wearing the same uniform, and pointed to a cot for me. I sat down, still not knowing where I was, what I was doing there, or why I was imprisoned.

Exhaustion defeated me, and I fell into a long, lethargic sleep on that cot.

Irregular and confusing dreams paraded through my mind. I saw my family, my house, and the malevolent figure of Gilberto: "hawk eyes"; and like in a blurry movie, episode by episode, I relived everything that had happened to me from the very first day.

When I woke up and found myself in that barracks, the only thing that came to mind was a popular Cuban saying: "Out of the frying pan and into the fire."

CHAPTER 48

I threw myself, sweaty, onto the cot and looked around the place. The faces of those present were anything but friendly. They were faces of people who mostly looked like criminals. There were Black, white, mulatto, and even Chinese people. They all looked at me with suspicion and hostility.

It was six in the evening, according to my watch, which I kept carefully as it was a gift from my friend, but I didn't know there was a one-hour difference, so it was actually seven. At the same time, at the guards' command, everyone lined up at the door of the barracks, spoon in hand, because they were serving dinner.

I realized then that I hadn't been given any utensils, so when it was my turn, I asked the guard for something to eat with. He pointed to my hands and indicated that I should eat with my hands if I wanted to. I was being treated like an animal. What an outrage! Where was I? For God's sake! I sat down wherever I could find a spot and began to eat what they called food. Hard, slightly rancid bread, greasy bacon, a slice of almost rotten tomato, and for dessert, a sweet that I never figured out what it was, just sugary.

After eating, everyone took their plastic plates to a window where, after rinsing them under a stream of water, they tossed them through an opening.

I did the same as the others, and while I was brushing my teeth, a white man with receding hair, a thick black mustache, a sullen look, and a somewhat hoarse voice, who clearly seemed to be Cuban like me based on his way of speaking, approached me and said:

"Who are you? Obviously Cuban. I'm just warning you to be careful, sleep with one eye closed and the other wide open, and don't trust anyone. My name is Pedro, but everyone calls me Ovas because I'm from a little town in Pinar del Río called that."

"I'm from Pinar too, with great pride," I responded as an introduction. "My name is Homero; I'm a dentist, and you can consider me your friend from now on."

"You're off to a bad start if you think there are friends here right from the get-go."

"I don't know, but you seem like a good person, plus you're from Pinar del Río, and all of us from Pinar are top-notch, right?" I said.

"Not all of us," he said, "but anyway, I like you. OK, friends," he offered a thick, calloused, strong hand like those given by sincere people.

I offered mine, and in its contact, I felt he was a good person, honest. It was that kind of handshake given with sincerity. It couldn't be wrong.

I spoke with him for a long time in a low voice so that the others wouldn't overhear. I quickly realized that this Ovas guy was respected by almost everyone there. They looked at him with deference, which gave me a good feeling. If I became his friend, I would be respected too. He explained so many necessary things for surviving there that when compared to Cuban prisons, the difference was minimal.

The day ended, and after the lights went out, as Ovas had advised me, I slept halfway, constantly startled, on alert.

At dawn, they woke us up; we lined up again and received a pot of something that looked like powdered milk with a sweet and chocolatey taste.

I had barely finished when they told me I had a visitor. Ovas, who was beside me, said it was probably the immigration representative, that I shouldn't worry since they spoke Spanish, but not to get my hopes up because it was a routine visit, and they usually resolved little or nothing.

In a room a bit more pleasant than the previous ones, I was very politely greeted by a tall, olive-skinned man with a mustache who introduced himself as Mister Jonás in perfect Spanish.

After asking the same questions as the Bahamian officers, I explained the events without much detail because it seemed Mister Jonás wasn't very interested in what I was saying. He confessed that the chances of going to the United States to reunite with my family were very slim and that it was very likely I would be deported to Cuba, which caused me immense panic.

"Mister Jonás, if they deport me to Cuba, I'm sure they'll execute me," I said, unable to hide my terror.

Mister Jonás looked at me with indifference, spoke a few unimportant words, and told me, without much enthusiasm, that he would do his best to help me. With that, he left, and I was taken back to the barracks.

I felt disappointed, terrified, confused. I had gone through all of this only to be sent back to Cuba.

When Ovas approached me and noticed the state the interview had left me in, he put an arm around my shoulder and said consolingly:

"Don't worry, my friend, they're not going to send you back to Cuba, or I'm not Ovas."

But what could he do to prevent it if that man, who seemed to be an important figure, couldn't?

"Calm down, buddy," said Ovas in a friendly tone. "I'm going to explain something to you, and afterward, you'll tell me if you have enough guts to do it. If you do, we'll get out of here to Yuma."

I began to feel a tingling in my armpits, like I often did when danger was approaching.

"What are we going to do?" I asked firmly. "Count me in for whatever it is; I'm not a coward, as you'll see."

"I'll explain it in detail after we get a visit from our friends in Miami."

"People from Miami are coming?" I asked, excited.

"Not only are they coming, but they're bringing us decent food, clothes that we desperately need for when we get out of here, and they'll connect us with our families in Miami," he emphasized with joy.

"What great news, buddy!" I exclaimed with enthusiasm.

"But remember, everything is absolutely secret. You need to be as discreet as possible so everything can come together," he cautioned.

It was like seeing a very bright light at the end of the tunnel.

I lay back on the cot, and praying to the Lord, I asked for strength to carry out this task, which only He, with His divine power, could give me.

Without knowing for sure what the challenges of our next adventure would be, I fell asleep, dreaming of beautiful things.

CHAPTER 49

Commander Pineda received a call from the Ministry, summoning him to an urgent meeting.

"Again with Gilberto's mess," he thought as he hung up the phone. "Is this fool going to make my life impossible again?"

He called his driver and swiftly headed to Havana. Lately, he had faced many setbacks and wasn't going to make the Minister wait a minute longer.

He arrived in Havana and went straight to the Minister's office. As soon as Pineda arrived, the secretary ushered him into the meeting room, where several chiefs were already gathered, including his immediate superior, who didn't even greet him. After so many years of fighting together, this man, who had once called himself a friend and brother, didn't even acknowledge him. What could have happened? It seemed serious.

He sat where he was directed, and within moments, the Minister appeared. His face clearly showed that something very bad had happened. He took a deep breath and, looking at Pineda with eyes that seemed demonic, said:

"First of all, how long has it been since you've seen your children, Pineda?"

"Well, Comrade Minister, I don't recall exactly, but it's been almost a week since I last saw them. You know I've had problems with my wife, and I've lost track of things at home."

"Let's see what you think of this recording of a phone call between your wife and your children," the Minister said, pressing the button on the recorder in front of him:

"Mom, it's me, José Miguel. We're in New Jersey, safe and sound, well-treated, and in high spirits." [...] "My dear children! What great joy it brings me to know that you're well and that your dreams have come true." [...] "We'll come to get you as soon as we can. Don't worry." [...] "We'll talk more about that later. For now, the important thing is that you're safe and happy."

As Pineda listened to the recording, there was no doubt in his mind that it was a conversation between Darli and their three children. Cold sweat drenched his uniform. Was this real, or was he dreaming? It was real, no doubt. With each word spoken by his children, it felt like a hammer was striking his brain. When the conversation ended, a heavy silence filled the room. After this tormenting silence, the Minister spoke again.

"Tell me, Pineda, what do you have to say about this conversation? What arguments can you make after hearing this?"

"I... I... I don't know how this could have happened. You know, Comrade Minister, that I've been a faithful and diligent servant of my revolutionary duty, of my tasks leading Security. Perhaps I neglected my family a bit, didn't give them the attention they needed, but this... this... I didn't expect this. I'm telling you as sincerely as possible—I didn't expect this."

"If a government official can't instill the principles of socialism, the values of the Revolution, in his own children, what can we expect from his subordinates, from the people he leads? From the people who expect strength and radical principles from their leaders? From the people who want their leaders to speak with firmness?"

"I understand..." Pineda stammered.

"Let me speak; I haven't given you the floor," the Minister shouted irritably. "Look, to be honest, without harboring any resentment, without wanting to tarnish your revolutionary career, your crimes aren't counterrevolutionary at all. You can't be accused of something you didn't do. But the fact that there are ideological deviations within your family, and when I say family, I'm not referring to nephews, brothers, etc.—we're talking about YOUR CHILDREN, the fruit of your being, and these are not just anyone—they are your true FAMILY... You will retain your rank, but as of this moment, you are relieved of your duties as Provincial Chief of the State Security Department of Pinar del Río Province. You will be reassigned to administrative tasks at the DTI offices in Aldabó. Both I and those present here, who consider you a revolutionary, want you to remain aligned with the unalterable principles of this great Revolution. Do you have anything to say?" the Minister demanded. "Since there's nothing more to discuss, this meeting is concluded," he finished with bitterness and disappointment.

Pineda left the meeting with great difficulty. He could barely muster the strength in his legs to walk. His former comrades didn't speak to him; instead, they turned their backs on him without even looking at him.

When he reached the Ministry parking lot to find his jeep, he was informed that the driver, following superior orders, had left for Pinar del Río. They pointed out an old, unattractive Ford from the 1950s that had been assigned to him.

The orders were clear. He was to report to the Aldabó offices immediately. He got into that old wreck, which felt like a dishonor considering his immaculate, except for a few minor errors, revolutionary life as a communist.

He entered the offices, reported to the director, and was assigned a desk piled with papers, with the order to handle them as if he were just another secretary.

He sat there, trying to process everything. He went outside to the yard and sat on a faded, unstable bench. He reviewed what his life had been like up until now.

He saw himself as a young man in the Sierra, fighting under the command of Camilo Cienfuegos, that invincible man of the Rebel Army whom he so admired. He recalled when he first met Darli before Sinforosa, who had filled their sack with sweet potatoes and yucca; the years when he was promoted from one position to another, always climbing in rank and military grade; when he was assigned his first home, modest but comfortable; when he was appointed Chief of the G-2 in Pinar del Río and given the house they now lived in—a two-story mansion with a pool and garage for four cars, which he had practically never enjoyed because the work was too much, and he had to forget about the pleasures of daily life. The grim memory of the day Captain Gilberto told him about the case of Homero García also came back. Why hadn't he gotten fully involved in the case, leaving that incompetent Gilberto to do as he pleased? He would have reacted rationally. If that guy was innocent of what he was accused of, with a little shaking up and letting him go back to his blessed home, he would have avoided all that mess that cost him dearly. So dearly that it could even cost him his life. Yes, his life, because what was the point of living if he had lost everything, even the moral integrity he had always prided himself on?

It was too much, too much for him—too many incidents, countless mistakes. At that moment, although he had never believed in God or any religion except when he was a child and his parents took him to church, he looked up at the sky and saw a beautiful, solitary white cloud shaped like a throne, in which he seemed to distinguish a figure with a white beard, wearing a robe that covered his entire body, who said to him with incredible sweetness: "Come, my son, I forgive you."

He mechanically drew his pistol from its holster, and saying, "Forgive me," he pulled the trigger.

A shot echoed in that small park, and Pineda's lifeless body fell gently in front of the bench.

CHAPTER 50

I woke up the next day feeling a bit more upbeat and cheerful. We received a visit from an organization of Cuban exiles that provided extraordinary help to those of us who found ourselves in that prison.

The visitor was an elderly woman with gray hair, clearly friendly and talkative.

"Don't worry, Homero," she said with a reassuring smile on her lips. "Everything is prepared to transport you to the United States as soon as you manage to get out."

"Listen," I said, concerned, "you speak as if it's very easy to escape from this prison."

"Don't worry about the details; everything has been planned," she said as she bade farewell.

I ate those delicacies that Migdalia—that was her name—brought with genuine pleasure. I tried on the clothes she provided, although I couldn't wear them there. I stored them in a transparent nylon bag that was left under the cot mattress.

Ovas was waiting for me in the barracks with a very good demeanor.

"Look," he said, pointing to a Miami newspaper, *El Nuevo Herald*.

I saw a front-page news story about the weather, and at the moment, I didn't understand what it had to do with our escape.

"The hurricane, a category 2 storm with winds over 100 kilometers per hour, will strike the Bahamas in the early hours of tomorrow. Precautionary measures are being taken by the authorities, as although it won't make landfall, the hurricane-force winds and heavy rain will be felt throughout the islands."

"And is a hurricane going to get us out of here?" I asked foolishly.

"Not the hurricane itself, but we're going to use it for our escape," Ovas explained, then began to detail what we were going to do.

It was just a matter of waiting for that damn hurricane to finally arrive. Never in my life had I been so eager for a natural disaster like this to come. But it was the salvation of the group that, according to Ovas, was going to participate in the escape.

At dawn, the gusts were already battering the prison forcefully. The windows were closed, but since almost all of them were defective or poorly nailed down, the wind began to enter with such force that it produced a ghostly noise. It whistled so loudly that it was terrifying to hear, especially knowing that hundreds of people were locked up in that barracks.

Ovas came to see me and signaled for me to follow him to the bathrooms. When we arrived, he climbed onto the shoulders of one of the others there, took hold of an iron bar on the window that had previously been sawed through, and with little effort, detached it. With that bar, he applied pressure to the remaining two, bending them enough to create an opening of just over twenty-seven inches—just enough to slide through with some difficulty.

They tied several sheets together, making a rope, which they secured at one end to one of the bars and let the other end drop outside. The wind intensified, and the electricity had been cut off to prevent accidents. The day turned dark due to the presence of the atmospheric phenomenon, which was terrifying just to hear. The gusts of rain poured in through the window with force.

"We'll go one by one, starting with the thinnest to test the strength of the sheets," Ovas said.

With that, a mulatto man about forty-five years old named Roberto slid down without much effort, despite the wind and rain, and after a few seconds, we felt a few tugs—signals that he had reached the ground without difficulty.

Ovas signaled for me to go next, and I did, finding Roberto crouched down, watching the guardhouse, which, due to the hurricane, was deserted at that moment.

When the last of the six of us participating in the escape had descended, Ovas pointed the way with his right hand and invited us to follow him with his left.

We reached the wire fence that was usually electrified, though not at that moment due to the power outage. With pliers he pulled from his pocket, Ovas cut the lower wires, and we began to crawl under the upper ones.

There wasn't a soul around; it was impossible to believe we were doing this under such extraordinary circumstances. Only desperate madmen could attempt it. The authorities would only realize the escape after the hurricane had passed, so we had limited time to reach the place planned by Ovas, who was the only one with that information.

"I trust no one," he had told me, and indeed, only he knew what had to be done. He pulled out a sort of map of the streets we had to traverse. Walking was difficult because of the wind and rain, but with great effort, we managed to advance several blocks. We knew that as soon as they realized the escape, they would come after us like hungry wolves. At one of the corners, there was a bar that, like all the buildings and houses, was shut tight. There wasn't a soul in the vicinity. Ovas reached the door and knocked hard four times, spaced out. From inside, a voice was heard saying a phrase that no one but Ovas understood.

It was a password, to which Ovas responded as arranged. They opened the door, through which we could barely squeeze due to the beastly force of the wind.

An old mulatto man over seventy years old received us, and when the last of us had entered, he asked for help closing the door again.

He spoke very poor Spanish, and we could barely understand him. Without much ceremony, Ovas asked him to get straight to the point, fearing the police forces would soon pursue us.

The old man explained the route we should follow from there, gave us a bottle of rum, some candles, matches, a nylon bag with crackers, another with a block of ham, and a gallon of water. He wished us luck, helped open the door to let us out, and saw us off.

We stepped outside. The gusts of wind and rain were so strong that at times they reached speeds of a hundred kilometers per hour, making it impossible to walk. With superhuman effort, holding hands to avoid getting lost or being swept away by the force of the wind, we reached an iron gate that led into the garden of a house. We followed Ovas, who led us to a small masonry house. With a key that the old man from the bar had given Ovas, we entered the house. From a distance, we could barely make out a Victorian-style mansion.

CHAPTER 51

I t had only been five days since Pineda's death. Darli was inconsolable and furious because, as punishment for the incident with Yaser, she wasn't allowed to attend the funeral. She received a phone call informing her to gather all her most important personal belongings because she would be assigned a new home. The reason given was that the current house was too large for just one person, with no further explanation.

At first, she was filled with anger, clearly thinking it was a punishment against her. But after calming down and thinking more clearly, she realized that the house was full of memories, most of them unpleasant. It would be better to change her surroundings, and this realization soothed her.

As she was packing her clothes into cardboard boxes, she came across the small safe that was in the closet. The safe had belonged to the family who had lived there before them—the original owners, whose property the government had seized. They had left for the United States when their businesses and properties were taken from them.

She remembered that on two or three occasions, her husband had opened the safe; she had seen him do it and remembered the combination. Out of simple curiosity, she opened the safe and found several documents in folders related to her husband's work, which didn't interest her. But at the bottom, wrapped in newspaper, she found two small packages that turned out to be bundles of cash. One was Cuban money—several months' worth of Pineda's salary, which he almost never withdrew from his envelopes because all his expenses were covered by the Ministry of the Interior, and he practically didn't buy anything unless absolutely necessary. When she counted it, it totaled 9,874 pesos. Opening the other package, she was surprised to see American dollars. There were handwritten notes by Pineda that said things like: "drug shipment intercepted at Cape San Antonio" and another that read: "counterrevolutionary group from Consolación del Sur. Paid by the CIA."

Darli wasn't very intelligent or educated, but she wasn't stupid. She knew that these American dollars had been secretly kept by Pineda. With how introverted and distrustful he had been, she was sure no one but him—and now her—knew of their existence.

She hid both packages deep within one of the boxes of clothing, alongside her lingerie, thinking that no matter how degenerate they were, they wouldn't dare search through her intimate clothing. She thought it might come in handy in the future, and she was right because her future wouldn't be very pleasant as long as she lived in Cuba under that regime.

The next day, several soldiers from the Mandatory Military Service and two officers from the Ministry of the Interior arrived. Without much conversation and with little regard, they began loading her belongings—only personal items and a few inexpensive decorations. When she asked the officers if she could take some of the bedroom, living room, or dining room furniture, they simply told her no.

They scrutinized the few boxes they loaded and occasionally searched them without asking permission. Darli was nervous, fearing they might find the money, but thankfully, they didn't.

Recently, she had begun to believe in God again, as she had when she was in the Sierra with her deeply religious family.

This had strengthened her spirit, and without realizing it, she had felt an internal relief that kept her calm. She hadn't experienced this in a long time. It was a peace that helped her endure the tribulations she had faced over recent times.

They took her in a jeep, leaving the Miramar neighborhood, passing through the Línea tunnel, taking Paseo street, and after crossing the Plaza de la Revolución, they headed straight for Vía Blanca and then entered the Santos Suárez neighborhood. They arrived at Gómez Street and stopped at a building that looked like it had been neglected for many years. They unloaded her belongings from the truck, opened the front door, and handed her the key. They didn't say goodbye to her. They got back into their jeep and left, leaving her standing at the door, not knowing what to do.

She entered the small living room, which had only a two-seater sofa and an armchair, both very simple in appearance. She moved to the next room, the bedroom, which had an iron bed with a hard, uncomfortable mattress, a dresser, and a small two-door wardrobe. She continued to the dining room, which was just three meters by three meters; and finally, the tiny kitchen and bathroom, where only two people could barely fit. There was a small cement-paved patio with a fifty-five-gallon water tank and a cement wall dividing her apartment from the neighbor's.

What a difference from the mansion she had lived in until now! How generous the "Revolution" was when it suited them, and how sadistic and evil when it didn't! She was beginning to see the reality. When she was the wife of Commander Pineda, Chief of the G-2 in the province of Pinar del Río, she had lived like a bourgeois. Now that she was the ex-wife of the late Pineda, who was no longer held in high regard due to his "mistakes," she was just a simple Cuban citizen without privileges, without ostentation. ~~so to speak~~—just another "common citizen" like everyone else.

She spent several days organizing and getting used to her new situation. At times, she would reflect on what she was doing and wonder why there were citizens who weren't with the Revolution. She had thought they were arrogant, ambitious, ill-intentioned people who needed to be fought, just as her ex-husband had done. It wasn't right for them to oppose the system—they should have been like them, exemplary Revolutionaries. Now she was beginning to realize that she had been the one who was wrong. She had lived in a fantasy world, a giant soap bubble that was now bursting in her mind.

Fortunately, she thought, they had left her a modest pension that would allow her to scrape by. Additionally, she had the money she had taken from the safe and some pesos she had always saved for some of her purchases.

Tired from all the hustle and bustle and deep in thought, she went to visit a neighbor who was the president of the Committee for the Defense of the Revolution (CDR). She introduced herself as the widow of a Commander and asked for permission to make a phone call.

One of her few friends, who was also disgraced for divorcing her high-ranking husband, agreed to inform two others in a similar situation so they could meet at the Floridita to have a few drinks and talk about their new lives as "divorcées."

When they met outside the restaurant, they greeted each other warmly, requested a table, and set out to forget their troubles.

Fortunately, one of them had become more than friends with one of the restaurant's captains during her days of opulence, and he was working that day, facilitating their entry.

They ordered drinks and some snacks: appetizers of ham, cheese, and seasoned olives.

They spent hours talking, drinking, and eating like four friends who had no problems in their lives. Eventually, the conversation shifted to their personal issues. Each shared their current situation, how badly things had gone for them lately, the difficulties they had never known before—the long lines for the bodega, for the clothing store, hours and hours in the sun that burned their once silky skin, having to walk everywhere because only one of them had managed to keep her Lada after the marriage… and all the hardships of their new real lives.

Darli cautiously asked how much it would cost to buy a car that wasn't in bad condition at that time. She knew that the only cars available for purchase were those from before 1959, and many of those were in terrible shape, so she inquired about cars that weren't too "run-down."

The most knowledgeable among them seemed to be María José, who had many connections with the Minister of Transport and had worked as the assistant administrator at one of the government car workshops in Havana. She had contacts with the mechanics who kept her informed about these matters.

"Are we talking Cuban pesos or American dollars?" María José asked Darli.

And Darli, being very cautious, said in Cuban pesos.

"My dear, with Cuban pesos, you can only buy a junker. Plus, you'd need a ton of pesos," she said with a laugh.

Rosa Helena, who was the most serious of the group and someone Darli often confided in, especially about things that seemed problematic back then, and for whom she had always felt sympathy, said:

"Darli, don't be afraid to tell us you have dollars because all of us have them in one way or another. We don't go around shouting it from the rooftops, but among us, there's no need to be afraid or hide it."

"OK, let's talk dollars. How much could a reasonably reliable car cost?" Darli asked.

"A reliable car, as you say, that also has official paperwork so no one can question it, could be between five thousand and nine thousand dollars," María José said. "Plus, we have the right people who will never say they bought it in dollars," she emphasized.

"Great. Let's say between five and six thousand dollars," Darli said openly.

The four of them agreed to help Darli, and after a few more drinks, they said their goodbyes, concluding a few spiritually comforting hours that they all desperately needed.

Since Darli had moved to the new neighborhood, a cousin of one of her neighbors, with whom she had developed a mutual fondness, had told her he was a mechanic. She mentioned that she might be buying a car that a friend was selling and that she would appreciate it if he could check it out when she got it. He gladly offered to do the service for free, of course, as he said very seriously because he wasn't a money-grubbing person, and what he earned at the workshop where he worked was enough to support himself.

A few days later, she was notified about the car purchase. She went to her friend María José's house to see it. It was a 1957 Chevrolet, two-door, red and white, that appeared to be in very good condition—at least it looked nice, as she told her friend. The price was reasonable at $4,800. They completed the necessary paperwork for the transfer of ownership. The seller and she agreed that it was a gift from an old friend, and Darli drove off in her pretty car to show it to Pepe, her neighbor's cousin, to get his opinion.

Pepe tested the car, thoroughly inspected it for rust or any damaged parts, but finding no defects, he approved it and told her she had made a great purchase. As a discreet person, he didn't ask about the price or anything, and she was grateful for that.

They agreed to go have a few drinks at the Habana Riviera, where there was a very good show, and Pepe had access due to his friendship with the hotel manager since he was the mechanic who serviced the manager's car.

They had a wonderful night, and in the end, Pepe was offered a room at the hotel. That's where Darli's romance began—one like she had never experienced in her life. She found her soulmate, a serious, formal, loving man, an expert in love and in bed—the ideal man. From that day on, she would be the happiest woman alive.

But there was one situation she had never even considered. Pepe confessed to her that he was a dissident of the government, that he had been imprisoned for two years at the Combinado del Este prison for his opposing views—where most of those who oppose the Castro-communist Revolution are held.

At first, she reacted with fear due to her previous mindset and confessed her fear to Pepe. Pepe explained that he hadn't done anything he needed to repent for, that he was a conscientious objector who only expressed his ideas without doing anything illegal.

After much thought and deep analysis of the incongruity of the situation, Darli decided to follow her heart. She set aside her old life and her animosity toward those who thought differently from the government. She thought of her children, who also weren't supporters of the Revolution, and decided to start a new life, to fully open the doors of her heart to the man that Providence had placed in her path, and to forget all the bad things she had been taught.

She would be herself and nothing but herself, despite everything. She would be free in thought as she had always dreamed. She would finally be HAPPY.

CHAPTER 52

It was seven in the evening in the city of Miami. The Pérez family was seated at the table in their modest Hialeah apartment, finishing their dinner. Agustín Pérez Delgado had once been one of the best gynecology specialists in Cuba, a university professor who worked at the Maternity Hospital on Línea Street. However, upon arriving in the United States at over fifty-five years old, with limited knowledge of English and numerous relatives in Cuba to support financially, it had been difficult for him to revalidate his Doctor of Medicine degree to practice the profession he loved most.

By the whims of fate, which are never written in stone, he had to dedicate himself to finding daily bread for his family in Miami and for his relatives in Cuba by doing countless jobs, none of which were related to his professional background.

It was truly a pity that a brain with so many solid and firm skills, with so many years of experience in medical practice and teaching, had to work in those various jobs which, while not degrading, caused him much sadness—especially because he realized that his capabilities were being wasted.

The phone rang, and no one wanted to answer it. It was annoying to get calls at such an inconvenient hour. Perhaps, like many times before, it was just another pesky telemarketer, relentless with their intrusions at all hours.

Due to the persistence of the ringing, Agustín glanced at his mother-in-law, Rosalía, and asked her to check the number on the display of the phone. She said it wasn't anyone she knew. Agustín was about to tell her not to answer, but then, driven by a particular instinct, he decided to get up, and after reading the number, he picked up the receiver and answered in a somewhat disinterested tone:

"Hello?"

On the other end of the line, a pleasant, courteous female voice apologized for calling at such an hour:

"Is this Dr. Agustín Pérez? Are you the one I'm speaking with?"

"Yes, that's me. What can I do for you?"

"This is Migdalia Granda. I'm with an exile organization that assists people of Cuban origin who are detained in the Bahamas."

These words gave him a strange feeling.

"Your phone number was given to me by your friend from Cuba, Dr. Homero García, a dentist from Pinar del Río."

"Homero... Ah yes, Homerito. Tell me, what's going on with my friend?"

"Well, Homero is imprisoned in a Bahamian jail. He left Cuba on a boat and was picked up by the Bahamian navy. Since you were always good friends, and he doesn't know the address or phone number of his uncle, where his wife and son are staying, because they recently moved, he asked me to call you to see if you might know."

"What a shame! I don't have it either. I was just talking to my wife the other day, saying we needed to get in touch with them."

"Well, sorry to bother you. Please, if you do find out, let them know that Homero is imprisoned in the Bahamas and inform me," said Migdalia.

"Don't worry, it's no bother at all. If I find out anything, I'll immediately let you know at this number."

"Thank you. Good night."

Agustín was tired, but his friend Homero was in a difficult situation, and his family needed to know. Without a second thought, he finished his dessert, went to the bathroom, and then left in his car, heading straight to the house where Dolores had previously lived.

He arrived at 70th Avenue and 7th Street SW and searched for the house where Dolores had lived. He knocked on the door, and a plump woman with short hair answered, eyeing him suspiciously and asking who he was and what he wanted.

He explained why he was there and anxiously asked if she knew where Dolores had moved.

She responded that she didn't but that a friend from work did know. She invited him in and called her friend on the phone. The friend provided Dolores's new address, and Agustín quickly set out to find her. He got a bit lost because she now lived in a gated condominium neighborhood, where once inside, it was easy to get disoriented. He hadn't encountered a guard or anyone who could give him directions until, wandering from street to street, he finally found the house he was looking for.

Vladimir, Homero's son, who he knew very well because he had delivered him, came out to greet him.

"Mom, Dr. Agustín is here," Vladimir called to his mother.

Dolores, who was in the kitchen, immediately ran to embrace her great friend, with whom she had deep ties of friendship.

After a warm greeting, the doctor told her about Homero.

"Homero imprisoned again?" said Dolores, anguished.

"Yes, but at least this time it's not in Cuba."

"What should I do?" she asked anxiously.

Agustín explained that she needed to call Migdalia, who had spoken with Homero in the Bahamian jail. She would explain some important details.

Agustín apologized for having to leave so quickly—he had to work early in the morning—and asked Dolores to keep him informed of any updates.

Dolores rushed to the phone and called Migdalia, who told her in great detail about the interview with Homero. She asked for Dolores's address because there were some personal matters she needed to discuss.

Thirty minutes later, Migdalia's car pulled up in front of Dolores's house. After the customary greetings, Migdalia entered the house, sat down, and detailed what she had agreed upon with Homero, the plans they had, and the urgent need to bring him to Miami.

To that end, they had contacted a boatman who was involved in smuggling in those areas, and for a modest sum, he would bring them all from the Bahamas.

Migdalia assured her that there was no need to worry because the organization she belonged to would cover the costs, and later, when Homero started working, he could repay them little by little.

Dolores couldn't think clearly. All of this was overwhelming, giving her goosebumps. Once again, Homero, the love of her life, was in trouble. "How much longer?" she silently asked, looking up at the sky as if asking the Lord with deep anguish. "My God," she thought, "grant me this request. Bring my husband back safe and sound. I ask you with all my heart."

Migdalia observed her in that moment of distress and respected the silence. She could sense what was going through the mind of that good woman, but she couldn't imagine the incredible odyssey that Homero had endured up to that point.

CHAPTER 53

We spent the night locked inside that small house, which we assumed was meant for the mansion's gardening tools, though we barely slept due to the deafening noise of the hurricane.

When the first rays of the sun appeared, we felt the calm that comes after every storm and decided to discreetly open the door of the little house.

Ovas, who knew whom to contact, stepped out, using the half-toppled bushes—downed by the storm—as cover to reach the back of the mansion. He knocked on what seemed to be the servants' quarters.

He contacted the cleaning lady, a trusted person of the mansion's owner, who had been waiting anxiously, fearing we hadn't made it through the fierce weather. She told him to wait in the little house for a visitor she was expecting.

Sure enough, about half an hour later, the maid named Maritza arrived with a distinguished-looking woman who appeared to be the mansion's owner.

She introduced herself as Doris Urquiza y Zubizarreta, a Cuban resident of the Bahamas who had emigrated from Cuba in the 1960s after Fidel and his crew had stripped her family of their assets. They had owned a sugar mill, two rum factories, and another for animal feed. They had barely managed to move part of their wealth, combined with what they had in Bahamian banks, which allowed them to reorganize and return to the businesses that communism had confiscated in Cuba. The Bahamas had become their new home and their resurgence in the business world.

Mrs. Urquiza explained that they were in contact with some boatmen who, among other things, transported people "irregularly"—she avoided saying "illegally"—who would take us to Miami. She also mentioned that the people who had contacted her had been in touch with our families and kept them informed of events. All that remained was for us to leave without difficulty, with God's favor. We were to remain calm and stay out of sight during the day; they would get us out at night.

The day passed slowly and unbearably hot, but we all understood that if we were discovered, we would be in serious trouble.

Around three in the afternoon, we heard a Bahamian police vehicle pull up in front of the gate. We carefully peeked out and remained on high alert, fearing the worst. Would we be sent back to prison?

The maid who had received us went to the gate to attend to the officers. They conversed for a few minutes before leaving. Shortly after, Migdalia came to explain that the officers had asked if they had seen any strange people lurking around the mansion.

Migdalia had told them that the lady of the house was busy with her affairs and couldn't attend to them at the moment, but they were unaware of any irregularities on the property. She assured them that the lady enjoyed great prestige and was highly regarded and respected in government circles. She emphasized to us the need for caution and not to be seen.

Later, Migdalia brought us a hearty and delicious dinner. We ate until we were full, and when night fell, she returned with Mrs. Urquiza; they brought us water, light snacks, and special flashlights that we were to use to signal the boatmen.

We went to the agreed-upon location on the coast and waited for the exact time. At eleven o'clock sharp, a boat arrived with a very quiet engine, and after signaling with the flashlight that emitted a violet light, we boarded. The boat was about twenty-five feet long, and two white men, roughly in their forties, quietly indicated where each of us should sit.

We moved along the coast at a slow pace; it was still littered with seaweed and debris left by the hurricane. After we were about a kilometer out, the boat sped up to its maximum speed. In the darkness of the night, we noticed some dark bundles on the floor of the boat, leaving us little room to stretch our legs.

The crew didn't say a word. For two hours, the boat glided smoothly and quickly, but then the weather started to worsen—the wind picked up, and the waves began tossing the boat like a walnut shell.

Suddenly, we saw some lights in the distance. When we asked the crew, they confirmed that they were the lights of Miami.

But then, to our great alarm, we heard sirens and saw red and blue lights approaching us. It was the United States Coast Guard. It didn't take a genius to figure that out.

The man who seemed to be in command of the boat spoke to the other in English, which we didn't understand. They stopped the boat and, with a brusque gesture, signaled for us to jump into the sea. We hesitated, but when they drew automatic pistols, they pushed us into the water without a second thought, telling us to swim or we'd drown.

Ovas told them we only had two life jackets, but without even acknowledging us, they sped off in the opposite direction of the Coast Guard, whose crew, in pursuit, didn't notice us in the water.

Two of our group didn't swim well, so we gave them the life jackets. The rest of us swam toward the lights that indicated our freedom and, most importantly, our salvation.

The sea grew rougher as we struggled, stroke by stroke. A feeling of dread weighed on my chest—first, because there was always some obstacle in my life, and second, because I was worried about my companions, especially those who couldn't swim well. I was a well-trained swimmer, and even I was finding it hard to make progress. At times, I had to float for a few minutes to gather strength and fill my lungs with air.

Stroke by stroke, I saw the lights of Miami getting closer. Just as my strength finally gave out and I began to sink, I felt something solid beneath my feet and realized I had reached the shore.

CHAPTER 54

At that moment, I realized I had reached solid ground. In front of me, I could faintly see a beach with white sand stretching for a few meters, and beyond that, a wall or seawall about a meter high. I walked to the beach with great effort and collapsed on the warm sand, completely exhausted. I took deep breaths to fill my lungs with oxygen and rested for a few minutes. After feeling somewhat better, I walked over to the wall and climbed it, seeing that on the other side was a street or road with headlights of a car approaching in the distance.

I stood firmly by the roadside and signaled for the car to stop, but it passed by without slowing down.

For a moment, I didn't know what to do or which direction to take—whether to go right or left. It didn't matter; there were lights from buildings in both directions. I started walking by instinct, and after a few minutes, I saw another car approaching, this time from the front. I signaled again, and this time the car slowed down, passed by me, and then stopped, signaling for me to approach.

"Thank God there are still good people in this world," I thought. The driver asked from a distance what I was doing there at such an hour. I replied:

"I'm a Cuban exile, and I just arrived. Please help me; I'm lost."

"Come on, my friend, get in the car. I'll take you wherever you want to go," said the driver with a friendly smile.

"My name is Gustavo; I'm Cuban just like you, and I'm at your service. Where are we heading?"

"I don't know," I said, disoriented. "All I know is that my family lives in Miami."

"My friend, Miami is very big. There are several million people here, most of them Cuban. You need to give me an exact address so I can help you."

"I'm not sure because my wife and son, who live with my uncle, recently moved, and I don't remember their address. I lost the paper where I had written it down."

"Do you have a phone to contact them?"

"I only have the phone number of a friend's family who was in my group, but we got separated in the middle of the sea."

I suddenly remembered the rest of the group. What had happened to them? Had they made it to the shore like I did?

I gave him the phone number I had memorized, and the man walked over to a nearby payphone and called the number I gave him.

I overheard someone giving him an address, which he repeated to me twice so I could memorize it, and we set off in that direction.

We arrived at a two-story house, luxurious on the outside to say the least. The neighborhood where we were was called Cocoplum or something like that, and according to the driver, it was a wealthy area.

At the door of the house were several people, among whom I recognized my friend Ovas, who came running to meet me and gave me a big hug. He said, excitedly:

"We're in the Yuma, buddy! Didn't I tell you we would make it?"

We began laughing heartily, slapping each other on the back in joy at finally being reunited and free.

I thanked the man who had driven me there and cared for me through thick and thin. Once he left, I realized I only knew his name, Gustavo.

That's how it was—some people with bad tempers and ill will would mistreat or kill you if they could, while others, like guardian angels, would lend you a hand without even thinking about rewards. That's life. That was the world I lived in.

CHAPTER 55

The Ovas family, from what I could gather, was doing very well financially. They welcomed me warmly, despite the short time Ovas had been with them. He had briefly recounted the events we had lived through in recent days. They had been informed by the people who contacted them from the Bahamas prison and were waiting for us near the place where the boatmen were supposed to drop us off.

They offered me clean, new clothes—very nice ones, too—and after a comforting warm shower, I dressed and ate a Cuban sandwich that completely satisfied my hunger.

There, both Ovas and I briefly recounted the adventures we had lived through in recent times.

Anselmo, Ovas's cousin, told me that what I had been through was worthy of a novel—necessary so that everyone could know about the barbarity imposed on the Cuban people by the Castros and their cronies, especially on someone like me, who, through no fault of my own, had been on the brink of death, mistreated, and humiliated to the extreme. He couldn't understand how I hadn't gone mad from all the abuse.

They suggested I spend the rest of the early morning resting and offered to help me find my family's address as quickly as possible.

After a hearty breakfast, fully awake and refreshed, I remembered my friend Dr. Agustín's phone number, and they quickly connected me to his house.

Unfortunately, neither Agustín nor his wife María were at home; they had already left for work early in the morning. His mother-in-law answered, saying that Agustín had already contacted my family. She provided their address and phone number, and I quickly called Dolores. After repeatedly trying without success, I realized Dolores must be at work at that hour, and Vladimir at school, so I asked Ovas's cousin to take me to the address I had to wait for their return.

"Are you going to wait outside the house all day?" Anselmo asked me. "It's more prudent to wait for the answering machine to prompt you to leave a message, and when they call you back, you can return right away. If they see someone unfamiliar standing outside a house for a long time here, they call the police, thinking it's one of the many criminals that abound here."

I took Anselmo's advice; after all, I had no idea how daily life worked in Miami.

Using Anselmo's cellphone, which I was already learning to use, I called and waited for the answering machine to kick in. I left a message with the phone number and address where I was staying.

"I'm sorry, Anselmo. It's just that I desperately wanted to see the house where my two loved ones live," I said anxiously.

"Then let's take you to see the house so you can leave a note on the door and on the phone's answering machine; that way, you'll feel better."

"You don't know how grateful I am for all your care and trouble," I said, feeling emotional.

"It's no trouble at all. We're here to help and support each other—that's why we're from Pinar del Río," Anselmo exclaimed jokingly.

We rode in his brand-new, zero-mile BMW, as they say here. What a beautiful car! I never thought I'd get into a car like that—I used to think my 1957 Studebaker was the most beautiful car in the world. Just thinking about it rusting at the bottom of the sea, becoming a home for the fish that abound in those waters, filled me with nostalgia. But I was lucky that those G-2 villains and the gang of communist bastards weren't enjoying it at that moment.

We arrived at the house (at least it would be my house from now on), "my house." As Anselmo explained, it was a "townhouse" or something like that—a house connected to others of the same style and form. I found it very beautiful on the outside.

That was going to be, in the near future, my "love nest." There I would live day by day with my beloved Dolores and my dear son Vladimir. How would they be? Fat? Thin? With joyful faces or suffering expressions? These were questions that my subconscious repeated over and over.

At the insistence of my new friends, we took a reconnaissance tour of Miami, partly to help me get to know the city and partly to distract me so I wouldn't dwell too much on the wait.

They took me to "Downtown," the heart of the city, to "La Sagüesera," Little Havana, where most of the Cubans lived, and to Miami Beach—a very beautiful place. But in my mind, there was only room for my beautiful family. Their names were etched in gold in my heart.

We had lunch at a famous Cuban restaurant called La Carreta, with food just like it used to be before the communist dictatorship in Cuba.

We returned home. Time passed, and my friends tried to distract me, but I was absorbed in a single thought—my family.

It was five fifteen in the afternoon. My anxiety was reaching its limit—I was restless, uneasy, upset... and then, suddenly, the phone rang. I picked up the receiver before the first ring even finished and answered:

"Hello, hello, hello? Is that you, Dolores?" I asked with uncontrollable anxiety.

"It's me, my love," answered that voice that sounded like crystal bells to me. I couldn't say anything more. A lump formed in my throat, preventing me from uttering a word.

On the other end of the line, there was also silence. We were both experiencing the same psychological trance.

Finally, after a monumental effort, I began to speak with affection, with uncontrollable love, to the one who was my reason for being. I asked her to put Vladimir on the phone, my voice filled with anguish.

"Daddy, daddy, come quickly—I'm waiting for you," Vladimir said with his sweet, articulated, and endearing voice.

"I'm coming, my dear little one," I said with great difficulty.

CHAPTER 56

Dolores was desperate to reunite with me, and I was equally eager to see her, so I said:

"Let's not talk any longer; I'm coming over immediately."

"Okay, we'll be waiting for you with open arms, my love."

The reunion was wonderful, even more emotional than I had ever dreamed. Both Dolores and Vladimir were telling me so many things at once that I was overwhelmed.

Dolores shared her story, which was incredibly beautiful, recounting the solidarity and affection she encountered from everyone since she arrived in Miami. She described reuniting with her elderly uncles and cousins who lived a bit far from Miami but had moved there to help her with anything she needed. They lived in Palm Beach and had taken Dolores in for some time at their home.

Dolores mentioned her quick reunion with Rosita, a friend and fellow student from the Faculty, who introduced her to her father, the owner of several businesses, including one of the best restaurants in Miami. There, they immediately found her a job, first "under the table," as they say in Cuba, and then legally.

She recounted how things gradually improved, thanks to God's almighty help at every moment.

Rosita managed all the administration of the restaurant and two other businesses her father owned. She was pregnant with her third child and had only a few months left before giving birth.

Rosita taught Dolores everything from start to finish, as if she were her sister. She introduced her to the world of capitalist administration, which was entirely different from the socialist one they were used to in Cuba. When Rosita went to give birth, she left Dolores in charge of the business with her father's consent, who was also a wonderful person.

At first, Dolores felt like she was taking on the weight of the world, but over time, she realized that she could handle it—and much more.

The salary, which started at seven dollars an hour during her learning phase, soon increased—first to ten, and more recently, with her new responsibilities, it had reached twenty dollars an hour. She never thought she would earn such a substantial salary. When she got her driver's license, my uncle gifted her a car that was mechanically sound, but which Cubans jokingly referred to as a "transportation."

It was a 1978 Oldsmobile, which for her meant a luxury car. She began doing the grocery shopping, going to work, and taking short trips.

When Rosita gave birth, unfortunately, she couldn't return to work. Besides her two previous children, the newborn had a heart malformation that required all her care until, over time, he could be operated on. Thus, Dolores officially became the administrator of Papá Goriot, the name of the restaurant owned by Rosita's father, Leonel. He was a very enterprising man, serious in character but affable and sincere, who had great confidence in Dolores.

When Rosita realized she wouldn't be able to work for a while, she bought a family van. Then she offered Dolores her new car—a beautiful, economical Toyota that she had purchased with a good down payment, leaving modest monthly payments that Dolores could easily manage. Rosita's cousin was the manager of the dealership and readily agreed to let Dolores take over the remaining two years of payments.

"But why would I need two cars?" Dolores had asked.

"Very simple—Homero will be here soon, and you can give him the Oldsmobile," Rosita replied.

Then Dolores took me to the garage where she had her car stored, covered with a tarp to protect it from dust. She uncovered it, and I saw her four-door gold-colored automatic car.

"Goodness!" I exclaimed, astonished and perplexed. At that moment, I thought, "I've arrived in the United States, and right off the bat, I have a house, a car, and of course, the other 'C'—care—which is important too."

She told me that Leonel, given the short time she had been in Miami, had served as her cosigner, and with a small down payment, she had bought that lovely house. It wasn't luxurious, but it had everything necessary for a family to live comfortably. When I started working, we would pay the monthly installments together.

I was sure that not many people had been as lucky as we were, and I saw the past as a nightmare. The past would remain in the past; from now on, my life would be happy and honorable. I wouldn't have to hide to express any opinion. No one would persecute me for having different opinions from others, not even the government. I would finally live in a democratic country and try to forget the suffering that the communist government had caused me.

I needed to forget that horror movie that I didn't want to see again, nor did I want anyone else to see it.

From now on, I would live a new life, the kind that everyone in this world aspires to, the kind I wished for my fellow countrymen who were still struggling in misery because of the Castro-communist dictatorship.

I wanted to forget all the bad things. I wanted to erase from my mind and heart the incredible odyssey of Homero García.

END

AUTHOR'S BIOGRAPHY

Jesús Uriarte was born in San Juan y Martínez, a province of Pinar del Río, Cuba. The son of a grocer and a housewife, he grew up in a middle-class home. He completed his high school education at the Instituto de Pinar del Río and graduated with a degree in Dentistry from the University of Havana. He later specialized in Maxillofacial Surgery and became a professor of this specialty in the Department of Stomatology in Pinar del Río, affiliated with the University of Havana.

While working at the Miguel Enrique Hospital in Havana, he was hired by the UNDP (United Nations Development Program) to train doctors in his specialty in the Republic of Mozambique. After completing his contract, he clandestinely traveled via South Africa to Portugal, Madrid, and finally arrived in Brazil, where he worked as a dental surgeon for nine years.

His professional life was always crowned with success, but in 2002, due to the rise of President Lula da Silva to power in Brazil, he was dismissed from his position as a commissioner for the Prefeitura of Criciúma, Santa Catarina, for political reasons. This led him to travel to the United States, where, due to his advanced age, language barrier, and limited financial resources, he decided not to continue his professional career. Instead, he devoted himself to the noble task of assisting Cuban rafters arriving in the Florida Keys on precarious boats, hired for this purpose by the USCCB (United States Conference of Catholic Bishops). Through this humanitarian work, he was able to witness the hardships faced by Cuban citizens yearning for freedom.

He is now retired and lives in the city of Hialeah, Miami-Dade, Florida. There, he dedicates his time to writing novels, some of which he began twenty years ago and remain unpublished. He hopes that their publication can serve as a testimony to a painful era that neither Cuba nor any other country deserves.

About the Publisher

Read more at uriartepublishing.com.